"Unless I Miss My Guess, You're the Kind of Woman Who Loves to Flirt With Danger."

"You're wrong," she denied, aware only of the raw masculinity of his strong features and the power of the hand which held her bound to him.

"Prove it." Before she could protest further, his head lowered and his lips touched hers softly. She gasped and his mouth pressed against hers, hard and demanding, claiming her lips in a kiss that warmed her body and promised to find her spirit. The heat of desire in his body flowed into hers and she yearned for more.

LISA JACKSON
was raised in Molalla, Oregon and now lives with her husband, Mark, and her two sons in a suburb of Portland. Lisa and her sister, Natalie Bishop, who is also a Silhouette author, live within earshot of each other and do all their work in Natalie's basement.

Dear Reader:

Romance readers have been enthusiastic about Silhouette Special Editions for years. And that's not by accident: Special Editions were the first of their kind and continue to feature realistic stories with heightened romantic tension.

The longer stories, sophisticated style, greater sensual detail and variety that made Special Editions popular are the same elements that will make you want to read book after book.

We hope that you enjoy this Special Edition today, and will enjoy many more.

The Editors at Silhouette Books

LISA JACKSON
Pirate's Gold

Silhouette Special Edition
Published by Silhouette Books New York
America's Publisher of Contemporary Romance

To John and Ermie

SILHOUETTE BOOKS

Copyright © 1985 by Susan Crose
Cover artwork copyright © 1985 George Jones

Distributed by Pocket Books

All rights reserved, including the right to reproduce
this book or portions thereof in any form whatsoever.
For information address Silhouette Books

ISBN: 0-373-09004-8

First Silhouette Books printing January, 1985

10 9 8 7 6 5 4 3 2 1

All of the characters in this book are fictitious. Any resem-
blance to actual persons, living or dead, is purely coincidental.

Map by Ray Lundgren

SILHOUETTE, SILHOUETTE SPECIAL EDITION and
colophon are registered trademarks

America's Publisher of Contemporary Romance

Printed in the U.S.A.

BC91

Books by Lisa Jackson

Silhouette Intimate Moments

Dark Side of the Moon #39
Gypsy Wind #79

Silhouette Special Edition

A Twist of Fate #118
The Shadow of Time #180
Tears of Pride #194
Pirate's Gold #215

Pirate's Gold

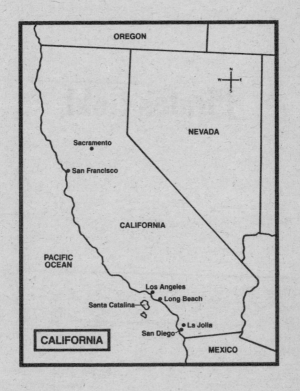

Chapter One

*R*evenge.

Just the sound of the word appealed to him. It hadn't always been so. Once Kyle Sterling had considered it a pointless waste of time and effort. But that seemed a lifetime ago, long before the accident, and now he savored the bittersweet flavor of revenge.

The antique clock on the hand-hewn mantel ticked off the endless seconds of the long afternoon. With each sweep of the second hand, Kyle vowed to get even with his ex-wife for the needless pain she had unwittingly inflicted upon his child. He sat at his desk and stared at the phone, as if by watching the black instrument he could make it ring. It didn't.

Impatiently he strode across the airy room. At the bar he paused and then poured himself a stiff shot of bourbon. One hand rubbed his neck to loosen the tension in his shoulder muscles as he paced restlessly before the wide bay window and the view of the serene Pacific Ocean. He frowned into his glass and absently swirled the amber liquid. Deep lines of worry surrounded his piercing gray eyes when he examined his life. He didn't like what he saw. For thirty-seven years he had been kidding himself, caught in the reckless struggle for success.

The last ten years had taught him much: the shallow value of wealth, the folly of quick friendships and the brutal reality that a man had to stand alone, trust his own instincts and survey the rest of the world as the enemy. Kyle's thin lips twisted into a grim line of self-contempt that hardened the rugged angles of his famous features. Some people might call his ideology paranoid, or at the very least jaded. Kyle Sterling saw it as the simple truth, taught him by the mistress of deceit, his ex-wife, Rose Sterling. Or Sterling Rose, as she preferred to be known. Because of Rose, Kyle had learned a seething passion for revenge.

He seriously doubted that he would be foolish enough to trust a woman again, and he found that he really didn't give a damn one way or the other. The less he had to do with the opposite sex, the better. This whole wretched week had only reinforced his opinions, and he realized that his daughter was the only thing that really mattered to him.

He drained his drink, set the empty glass on the window ledge and loosened his tie. Though he expected a visitor later in the day, he didn't care that he looked as dog-tired as he felt. Ryan Woods was coming over later in the day to talk about business. Kyle had long awaited Ryan's report. He should have been anticipating the afternoon with relish, but he wasn't. No matter how he tried, Kyle couldn't take his mind off his child and his fear for her.

After contemplating another drink, Kyle rejected the idea and drummed his fingers restlessly on the polished surface of the cool window frame. His stormy gray gaze moved over the craggy cliffs on which his Spanish-style manor stood. He had to squint against the ever lowering sun. In the distance, brightly colored sailboats skimmed elegantly on the horizon, breaking the expanse of aquamarine sky and sea.

"Ring, damn you!" he muttered through clenched teeth as he glanced malevolently at the phone. Beads of sweat collected on the back of his neck, and his nerves were stretched to the breaking point. Yesterday's visit to the hospital and the gut-wrenching scene with his daughter still haunted him.

He remembered Holly's strained face, flushed and wet with hot tears. Her dark eyes were filled with anger, and her voice echoed down the hospital hallways when she screamed at him. "Go away. I hate you, Daddy . . . I don't want you here. I don't. Just go away and leave me alone, like you always have. I don't need you anymore!" The white bed sheet had been twisted in her fingers, and the nurses had had to subdue her. The last picture in his mind was of Holly holding her face in her hands and sobbing hysterically, her slim shoulders shaking from the ordeal. She looked young and pale in the sterile white room. At the doctor's request, Kyle had left the hospital, but Holly's words had continued to reverberate dully in his mind.

He raked his fingers through his coarse hair and glanced once again at the clock. How long could the operation take? Two hours? Four? It had been nearly five hours and still he had no idea as to her condition. All of his wealth couldn't buy him peace of mind or assure him that his daughter would ever be the same as she had been before the accident that had nearly taken her life six months ago. Holly had recovered, though slowly, and this last operation, a delicate one, was designed to repair her damaged uterus. Her life was no longer in jeopardy, but the center of her womanhood was.

Kyle considered calling the hospital again, but pushed the thought out of his mind. It had been less than an hour since his last call, when he had been politely but firmly told that Miss Sterling was still in surgery. Wasn't a father allowed any rights? Or had he given them up ten years ago when he and Rose were divorced?

The twinge of doubt he felt when he thought about Holly and the agony she had suffered at her mother's hand forced him to turn away from the window. He crossed the room, grabbed the opened bottle of bourbon and, despite his earlier abstention, splashed another drink into his glass. It was gone in one swallow.

Once again he tried to blame Rose for his daughter's hatred of him, but a nagging thought that he was partially at fault refused to leave. Even the pain that Holly was enduring, wasn't it in some indirect manner his fault? Though two parents were divorced, didn't a father have some responsibility to protect his child?

His thin patience snapped and he found that he couldn't wait another minute in the den. The appointment with Ryan Woods was still a couple of hours away and the damn phone refused to ring. Kyle felt as if the brushed plaster walls were closing in on him. He could feel a muscle working in the corner of his jaw as he stalked down the tiled corridor toward the far end of the rambling hacienda.

His voice interrupted the stillness as he approached the kitchen. "Lydia?"

The elderly Mexican woman he employed was hard-of-hearing and didn't respond to his initial greeting. He entered the immense room filled with hanging brass pots and trailing vines. Lydia was working industriously on the countertop. The soft Mexican ballad she was humming was familiar to him; he remembered it from his childhood. She was kneading dough for home-baked bread. It was her usual Friday afternoon ritual, the same routine Kyle had witnessed for many of his thirty-seven years. "Lydia?"

The plump woman turned around to face him as she wiped the flour from her hands on her worn apron. A slow, warm smile spread over her round features. "I thought you were in the den."

He returned her grin with an uneasy imitation. "I was, but I couldn't stand it any longer." She nodded as if she understood him perfectly. "I'm going out for a while."

"But you haven't heard from the hospital?"

The corners of Kyle's mouth turned downward. "No."

"Are you going there?"

Kyle hesitated, but shook his head. "I don't think so. Ryan Woods will be here shortly."

The older woman didn't budge. "But certainly you can change your plans. Mr. Woods will understand; he has a family of his own. What is business when you have a daughter in the hospital?"

"Rose is there," Kyle responded, hoping to satisfy the kindly old woman.

Lydia's dark eyes snapped. "Hmph!" She repinned her graying hair before making a quick sign of the cross over her ample bosom. "That woman is no mother," she muttered under her breath. *"You* should be with Miss Holly!"

"Apparently the divorce courts didn't think so, nor does Dr. Seivers."

Lydia turned her attention back to the dough and attacked it with a vengeance. "What does he know about families?" She continued to talk to herself in Spanish, and Kyle suspected that Rose was getting the verbal abuse she deserved.

"Holly doesn't want to see me."

"That woman, that Rose, she poisoned Miss Holly's mind against you!" Lydia waved her hands frantically in the air, dusting the room with white flour. "Miss Holly, she's too young to know what to think!" This time the stream of Spanish was too rapid for Kyle to understand at all.

The telephone shrilled and Lydia's voice quieted as Kyle reached for the receiver. Lydia watched his movements with worried brown eyes. She had cared for Holly as an infant and loved her still. Rose had never approved of Lydia, even though the Mexican woman had helped raise Kyle. Though Lydia had suffered the insult of being pushed aside once the divorce was final, she had never stopped caring for Kyle Sterling's only child.

Kyle's greeting was an impatient hello.

"Mr. Sterling? This is Dr. Seivers." The voice on the other end of the line sounded weary.

"How is my daughter?"

"She's fine. Came through the operation like a trooper. She's down in Recovery now."

Despite the optimistic words, Kyle detected a hint of hesitancy. "Then you were able to correct the problem?"

There was a slight pause. "That remains to be seen. I'll have to be honest with you, Mr. Sterling. Right now I'd give Holly a fifty-fifty chance of a full recovery. . . . You have to understand that her uterus was badly scarred from the accident. Though her fallopian tubes weren't damaged, the uterine wall was ruptured. It will take time to determine the success of the surgery."

"What happens if the operation doesn't work?"

"There's no reason to borrow trouble, Mr. Sterling."

"It's a simple question, Doctor."

There was an audible sigh as Dr. Seivers decided how much he could tell Holly's father. "We'll have to see," he replied evasively. "But if she doesn't heal properly and continues to hemorrhage, I'll probably advise additional surgery."

Kyle's hand clenched around the receiver until his knuckles whitened. "What kind of surgery?"

Dr. Seiver's response was patient but grim. "I would most likely recommend a hysterectomy."

The weight of the doctor's words settled on Kyle's shoulders like lead. His tone was emotionless, but his face was stern. "Dr. Seivers, my daughter is only fifteen."

"And lucky to be alive. Six months ago, she was fighting for her life. Today she's nearly recovered."

"But she's a child . . ."

"You asked me a hypothetical question—I answered. I'm only giving you my professional opinion. With any luck at all, we won't be faced with the possibility of another operation. Holly's very strong. A fighter. She's had to be for the last six months. There's a good chance that she'll be fine."

Kyle wasn't reassured. "I'd like to see her."

Once again there was a weighty pause in the conversation. "I think you might wait a few days, Mr. Sterling. It will be several hours before she's out of the recovery room and after that I'll keep her sedated. Any emotional outbursts or trauma at this time couldn't help her condition."

"She's my daughter, damn it!"

"And she's my patient. I saw her reaction to you yesterday. Are you willing to risk the chances of her recovery?"

"Of course not!"

"Then take my advice and give Holly some time to get well before she faces the emotional strain of seeing you again. Her mother is with her at the moment."

Kyle withheld the hot remark forming on his tongue. He had no choice but to listen to Dr. Seivers. He was the

best gynecologist in California, perhaps the western
United States. Ben Seivers was calling the shots. "All
right, Doctor. I trust that you'll keep me informed of
Holly's condition. If there's any change, you'll call?"

"Of course."

"Thank you."

Kyle replaced the receiver slowly into the cradle.
Lydia's warm brown eyes widened and her round face had
paled. "Miss Holly?"

"She's going to be fine. The doctor assured me that she
came through the operation with flying colors." Kyle was
grateful that his voice sounded more convincing than he
felt.

Lydia studied the strain on Kyle's face above his
cheekbones. She knew him as well as anyone and couldn't
be put off easily. "But you are still worried about her."

His face softened. "Yes." There was no reason to lie to
Lydia. "The doctor thinks her chances for a full recovery
are very good, but at this point, he can't be certain."

"*Dios,*" Lydia whispered to herself.

"I'm going out for a while—just to walk around and
clear my head. If Ryan gets here, show him into the den
and fix him a drink, okay?"

Lydia nodded quickly. She was fingering the cross
suspended from her neck and quietly praying for Kyle's
child. When Kyle closed the door behind him, she began
working the bread dough feverishly. It wasn't fair. Miss
Holly's pain and suffering, all because *that woman* got
drunk and lost control of the wheel. *"Dios."*

The ocean always had a way of calming him. Whenever
the problems in L.A. became too much for him, he would
drive down the coast to the old Spanish house overlooking
the sea. On the uncrowded beach, with the endless miles
of the Pacific stretching before him, Kyle Sterling always

found a way to work out his problems. Today was an exception. No amount of walking against the salty breeze could quiet the voice of anger within him whenever he thought about Holly and the fact that Rose had nearly killed her. He grabbed a fistful of sand and tried to hurl it out to sea. The dusty granules spread in the wind and filtered back onto the beach.

He climbed the wooden stairs along the cliff and tried to turn his mind away from his child and back to the record company. Over the last few months he had grown careless as his concern for his daughter had overridden his interest in his business. For the first time in his life, he found it difficult to concentrate on record sales. For once, something was much more important than any business problem; and yet, he couldn't ignore the fact that things weren't going well for him businesswise. For several years record sales had been slumping and Sterling Recording Company had posted losses rather than earnings until recently. Just when things had appeared bleakest, the introduction of videotapes on cable television had boosted sales. Now the problem was the cost of producing quality video images. For the past couple of years Sterling Recording Company had used free-lance artists and production companies for the video recordings, but the trend was toward in-house work. There would be more control if the videotapes were produced by Sterling Records and thereby several problems would be controlled: cost, quality and pirating, a phenomenon that had only recently come to light.

Right now, Kyle had no interest in his business, but he realized that he couldn't let his company crumble along with his personal life.

When he reached the top of the sea-weathered stairs, Kyle took one last searching look at the sea. Not finding an answer to his worries, he retreated into the house and noticed through the foyer window that Ryan Woods's car was parked near the garage. Kyle hurried to the den and forced a severe smile as he opened the door. "Sorry I'm late," he apologized as he entered the room. Ryan was seated in a high-backed chair near the desk.

"No problem." Ryan was a man of about thirty; slim, with receding black hair and a keen mind. He stood and accepted Kyle's handshake, noticing Kyle's uneasy smile. It was the same restless smile that had accompanied large deepset brooding gray eyes and graced the jackets of several country albums ten years earlier. Kyle Sterling's music hadn't been hurt by the fact that the man was ruggedly handsome. Ryan Woods doubted that the platinum albums adorning the walls of the den would be there today if Kyle Sterling hadn't been so damnably earthy and sensual. Sterling's voice had been classified as mediocre and his ballads were too complex for most of his audience, but Kyle Sterling was a shrewd man who had used his striking looks to his advantage. He had turned his songs into money that he had invested in an ailing recording company. Within five years, Sterling Records had become one of the most prominent recording companies in the country.

Kyle poured himself a drink, offered Ryan another and took a seat near his guest. His eyes seemed haunted. Something was eating at Kyle Sterling and Ryan suspected that it was more than the pressures of running the company. He kept his suspicions to himself. If Kyle wanted to talk about his personal problems, the man would have to initiate the conversation himself. If not, so be it. Ryan Woods hadn't earned his reputation as a crackerjack troubleshooter by sticking his nose where it didn't belong . . . unless he was paid for it.

Kyle took an experimental sip of his drink, rested his head on the back of the chair and came straight to the point. "I assume that you've come here with some sort of proposal."

Woods inclined his balding head and nodded. "Finally."

"Good! I owe you for this one, Ryan. I just haven't had the time to put all the information together. This is a major decision."

"That's what you pay me for."

Kyle mutely agreed. "Let me guess what you found out: You think I should handle all the videos at the studio—produce them at Sterling Records."

Ryan shifted uneasily in the chair. He was seated near a large bay window and noticed that dusk was beginning to paint the sky in uneven streaks of magenta and carmine. The warm Pacific sun had settled behind the calm sea and only a few dark sailboats were silhouetted against the horizon. Outside, the view was spectacular. Inside, the wealth of Kyle Sterling surrounded him. It was evident in the thick weave of the imported carpet, the immaculate shine on the tiled floor, the expensive grain of the modern furniture and the original surreal paintings on the thick plaster walls. But with all his fortune, still Kyle Sterling seemed . . . disenchanted.

Ryan snapped open his briefcase after finishing his drink and declining another. He pulled out a sheaf of neatly typed papers and handed them to Sterling. "You're not going to like what I found," he warned.

"Let me be the judge of that. The way we've been handling production of videos has been a thorn in my side for the last two years. We need more control." He studied the pages thoughtfully. Ryan Woods had done his homework and proved in dollars and cents exactly why in-house production was imperative.

He leaned back in his chair and pushed the reports onto his desk. "All right, you've convinced me. We'll hire a crew, the best we can find, and give them a suite of offices on the third floor.'' He noticed the look of hesitancy in Ryan's eyes. ''Is there a problem with that?''

Ryan shook his head. ''Not really. I suppose it will make things easier—for everyone.''

''What are you getting at?''

Ryan reluctantly handed Kyle one final report. ''You asked me to check into the pirating problem we had a few months ago . . .''

''You're not telling me that it still exists?'' Kyle asked, astounded. Had he neglected his business that badly?

''See for yourself.'' Ryan nodded toward the report.

Kyle's dark eyes scanned the black print and his frown deepened into a scowl of anger. His gaze was even when it was raised to meet the pale blue eyes of Ryan Woods. ''You're certain of all this?'' Kyle asked, skeptically running his fingers over the pages.

''I'd stake my reputation on it.''

''You just have.'' Kyle rubbed his thumb over the edges of his straight white teeth and his eyes narrowed in thought. ''Damn!'' he cursed, mainly at himself.

''What is it?'' Woods inquired. He'd known Kyle for eight years and had seen the dangerous look of anger in the recording company's executive more than once in the past.

''It's just hard to swallow, that's all. We've been dealing with Festival Productions for over three years. Everything we've gotten from them has been the best— top quality recordings.'' He shook his head as if trying to dislodge a wayward thought. ''Why would Maren McClure try and rob me blind?''

''She only owns the company. It doesn't necessarily mean that she's involved. Anyway, the problem will be solved once you stop dealing with Festival, and as far as I can tell only three of the tapes have been copied and sold on the black market.''

Lydia knocked on the door, refreshed the drinks and provided a tray of sandwiches before announcing that she was leaving for the weekend. Kyle managed a quick smile for her and then turned his attention back to the problem at hand.

"All right, Ryan, so you think we should just ignore the problem and maybe it will just go away?"

Ryan smiled and set his partially eaten sandwich aside. "Unfortunately, it's not going to be that simple."

"That much I already know."

"Then you realize that you have some long-term contracts with Festival?"

Kyle tented his fingers under his chin and nodded. Ryan finished his sandwich, withdrew a cigar from his pocket and rolled it between his fingers. Thoughtfully he studied the tip of his cigar before lighting it and puffing a blue cloud of smoke that circled lazily to the raised ceiling. Theatrics were part of the game, the rules of which he had learned while studying law at Yale. "As I see it, you have several options."

Kyle raised his eyebrows, encouraging the other man to continue. "You can buy out the contracts and quit using Festival completely, or you can confront the owner with your suspicions and hope that she'll back out of the contracts because of fear of bad publicity and a possible lawsuit."

"Too easy."

"What do you mean?"

"I can't do either one."

"Why not?"

"First of all, I don't have the time. I've just signed several big names to Sterling Records, paid top money for them, and I can't take the chance that the video cuts of their top hits will be stolen or reprinted. I'd not only lose the artists, they'd sue me for every cent I've got based on any grounds their agents or their lawyers might dream up.''

Ryan puffed on the cigar and shrugged. "So have the tapes produced by someone else until you get your crew together. There must be a hundred production companies that can make a four or five minute minifilm. Those videos aren't much more than advertisements for a song . . . easier, really. There's no dialogue involved.''

Kyle downed the rest of his drink and his clear gray eyes looked suddenly stormy. "That's where you're wrong. The videotape of a current song is the single most important piece of artistry put together; in some cases it's more valuable than the recording. It sells the song. A good video can beef up a mediocre record, and unfortunately, the reverse is true. Even the most marketable hits don't make it without the right video packaging. It really is an art, and Festival Productions has an uncanny way of molding music to story and coming up with an incredible finished product. They're slick. Three years ago no one had even heard of Festival Productions. Today I've got rock stars *demanding* to work with that company, to the point that it's written into their contracts. I've had entire recording deals balanced in Festival's gifted hands.''

Woods was skeptical. "What makes Festival so much better than the rest?''

"Haven't you been listening to a word I've said? It's their artistry, their interpretation of the song, their ability to give the audience a brilliant, unforgettable visual story to identify with the song.''

"I can't believe they are *that* good.''

Kyle nodded curtly. "Have you ever heard of the rock group Mirage?''

Ryan drew on his cigar and squinted. "Vaguely,'' he admitted in a stream of smoke. "I'm not up on all this new-wave nonsense.''

Kyle waved off his ignorance with a quick rotation of his wrist. "It doesn't matter. The point is, two years ago, no one had heard of them, not in the U.S. They were just one in a thousand obscure English rock groups that had never caught on, not here. They released a single and it bombed. Never broke Billboard's top one hundred."

"So?"

"So the lead singer, a kid by the name of J. D. Price, was smart enough to figure that with all-day cable video music, videotapes would be the next growth phase for rock and roll. He took all the group's money, invested in an expensive video for that same song that bombed, released the tape and presto"—Kyle's fist pounded on the corner of the desk—"Mirage was an overnight success." He paused for dramatic effect, but Ryan could feel what was coming. "Do you want to take a guess at the name of the firm that produced that videotape?"

Woods smiled as he stubbed out his cigar. "All right, you've convinced me. Festival Productions can walk on water as far as hard rock is concerned. Now, let me convince you of something. Regardless of the pirating scheme, you're better off producing your own videos. If Festival is so talented, hire the talent away from this Maren McClure."

Kyle considered the idea. "If I can," he thought aloud. "From what I understand, she's the one with the talent." His lips pursed together. "It irritates the hell out of me to think that someone would steal those tapes. It just doesn't make any sense. Festival needs me as badly as I need it."

"People will stoop to almost anything for a quick buck. I shouldn't have to remind *you* of that." Ryan had intended to say more but quickly decided to hold his tongue. He hadn't meant for his remark to have been so personal and the look in Kyle's eyes was deadly. He tried to apologize. "Don't get me wrong."

Kyle ignored his friend's attempt at amends. They'd known each other far too long to take offense at careless remarks. Besides which, Ryan was right. Kyle had been burned before, and badly. Rose had capitalized on the publicity surrounding their divorce to pad her career. He didn't intend to make the same error twice. No one was going to profit from his mistakes! He had ignored his company, but he was determined to change that, right now. The slow smile that spread across his features didn't quite reach his eyes. "You're right, Ryan." He settled back into the chair and reached for a ham and cheese sandwich while watching his friend. "Why don't you tell me exactly how you think I should handle this situation."

Ryan was pleased. At least he'd gotten through to Kyle. He considered that a major accomplishment, because in the last few months, Kyle hadn't shown much concern for his business—probably because of his kid's accident. "I think you should buy this McClure woman out. If Festival's got the reputation you claim, you buy out the company lock, stock, and barrel. Then clean house—find out if anyone there really is duplicating the tapes and get rid of him . . . or her."

"What if she doesn't want to sell?"

"Everyone has a price."

Kyle didn't seem convinced. "All right, I've told you all I know about Festival, why don't you tell me what you've dug up. If I know you, you've poked around a bit."

Ryan grinned uneasily and scanned his notes. "The most interesting thing is that Festival is run by a woman, but you already know that. Have you ever worked with her?"

Kyle nodded. He looked calm but vengeful. His expression made Ryan uncomfortable. "I've met her a few times . . . parties, social gatherings, but she's kept her distance. Most of the day-to-day office work is done between our secretaries.''

"She's something novel in the recording industry—a woman making a go of it in a predominantly man's world.'' Kyle agreed with Ryan's assessment. When he'd met Maren, Kyle had been surprised by her cool dignity and grace. He'd noticed that she was more than beautiful; she had a sophisticated manner that intrigued him. He'd been interested, but wary.

"There aren't many female executives in this business . . .'' Kyle commented absently.

"From what I understand, Maren McClure is not just any woman. This lady is a mixture of beauty, brains and artistic talent. The kind that makes men like me very uncomfortable.''

"Why?'' Kyle asked sternly.

The question was unexpected. "Because she's different, I guess. She can't be pigeonholed.''

Kyle's laughter held no mirth. "And that's how you like your women—stereotyped?''

"I didn't say I liked them that way, I said it made me feel more comfortable.''

"And you think she might sell the company?''

"It's a good guess. She's always in need of money.'' Kyle's eyes darkened. "How do you know that?''

"I talked with one of her employees. According to this guy, she runs that office on a shoestring.''

"I wonder why?''

Ryan shrugged. "Who knows?''

"I guess I'll have to talk to Ms. McClure and see if she's interested. . . .'' A wicked smile of satisfaction stole silently over the features of Kyle Sterling's famous face. He didn't understand it, but the thought of meeting with Maren McClure was pleasant . . . very pleasant.

Chapter Two

*M*aren closed her eyes and removed the clasp restraining her hair. As it fell around her shoulders she pushed her fingers through the thick auburn curls, hoping to release the tension of the afternoon. Slowly she leaned her head against the padded back of the overstuffed couch that adorned her office. Out of habit she rewound the tape for the fifth time and tried to concentrate on the mood of the song. It was difficult. Though the tempo was a light reggae, the lyrics were downbeat, a real bluesy type of song; one of those country western crossovers that always seemed to give Maren fits.

The phone rang and interrupted her thoughts. She snapped off the tape player, walked across the room and leaned over the desk to answer the call from her secretary. "Yes?"

"Kyle Sterling is on line one. Can you take the call? He says it's important," Jan explained.

Maren's elegant black brows pinched together. "I always have time for the head of Sterling Records," Maren replied. "Thanks." She sat on the edge of the desk, removed her earring and pushed the flashing button on the phone. Using her most professional voice, she spoke. "Good afternoon, Mr. Sterling. This is Maren McClure. How can I help you?" If she was nervous, it wasn't audible in the even tone of her voice.

"I'd like to meet with you, Ms. McClure."

Maren frowned to herself. His request was out of the ordinary, and from what she knew about Mr. Sterling, he usually didn't do the legwork himself. He preferred the privacy he could well afford. The one time he had been in the office concerning one of his artists had been brief and to the point. From that one experience Maren realized that Kyle Sterling was a determined man who didn't waste his time. "Is there any particular reason or problem?" she asked, remembering the as yet unfulfilled contracts on several of Sterling's top artists. Maybe that was why he was calling. He wanted to cancel. Maren nervously tapped her fingers on the desk.

Kyle didn't hesitate. He knew that discretion was in his favor. "Nothing serious, Ms. McClure," he assured her. Maren's jaw tensed and the headache that had been threatening all afternoon began to pound in the back of her head. "When would be a convenient time for you? Sometime this afternoon?"

Maren quickly scanned her appointment book. It was filled for the rest of the week. "I'm sorry, Mr. Sterling. Today is impossible and I'm afraid the rest of the week is hectic as well. If you can give me a few minutes, I'll try to make some calls and rearrange my schedule so we could meet on Monday of next week." Kyle Sterling was one of the most important names in the recording industry and a valuable client to Festival Productions. Whatever it was he wanted to discuss, it was certain to be a matter of priority. The head of one of the fastest-rising recording companies in L.A. didn't call to pass the time of day.

"Are you free this evening?" he asked, taking Maren completely by surprise.

She didn't immediately respond. She dealt with pushy people every day, and she didn't really like it. Kyle Sterling was definitely pushy—but he had to be, didn't he? One didn't rise to the heights he had reached by being Mr. Nice Guy. "I don't have any plans," she admitted.

"Then let's discuss business over dinner at Rinaldi's. I'll pick you up at the office . . . around seven. We can go to the restaurant from there." It almost sounded like a command and involuntarily Maren's lips tightened. She'd been in this business five years and still hadn't gotten used to the way big shots threw their weight around. Trying to ignore Sterling's demanding tone, she once again checked her calendar.

"Could you make it seven thirty? I have a late appointment that might run over."

"Fine."

Maren didn't replace the receiver until she had heard the sound of Kyle Sterling ringing off. She reflected on the telephone conversation. It was strange. She'd been working with recording companies for nearly five years and she could count the number of times on a single hand that Kyle Sterling had called her for what sounded like an imperative meeting. Usually any business was concluded over the phone by one of his underlings. She wanted to think that her luck was finally changing, and that the reason for the call was an offer of exclusive business, but she couldn't. Instead she was overcome by a disturbing sense of restlessness.

What could he want? She gazed out the window, past the flowering cherry trees to the hazy Hollywood hills in the distance. The soft blue slopes rose quietly out of the suburbs of Los Angeles, seeming to guard the sprawling city.

Still sitting on the desk, she rang for her secretary. Jan's voice responded quickly. In the background Maren could hear the rapid clatter of typewriter keys as Jan didn't bother to break stride in her work. The woman was amazing.

"Could you bring in all of the unsigned contracts we have with Sterling Records?"

"In a flash," the pert secretary responded.

True to her word, Jan appeared in Maren's doorway within a few minutes time. Her purse was slung over one of her slim shoulders and she was balancing a thick stack of papers in her hands. "You're sure you want all of these?" she asked dubiously as she placed the heavy pile of legal documents in the middle of Maren's desk.

Maren's blue eyes widened in amazement. "None of these have been signed?" she inquired as she shook her head and began to shuffle through the stack.

"None."

"But aren't some of these already on the production schedule?" She picked up one of the documents. "Here, this contract with Mirage, I'm sure I told Ted we'd be ready to shoot in a couple of weeks. . . ." She spotted another contract. "And what about Joey Righteous? That kid wanted to get his tape out before he started his tour of Japan, which, I think, is slated for sometime in late June."

"And it's already April."

"Precisely! What the devil's been going on, Jan?"

"I wish I knew," the thin secretary admitted. "For the last two and a half weeks, I haven't been able to get any signed contracts *or* information out of Sterling Records. I've called Angie Douglass—she's in charge of the contract department—at least twice a day since last Friday, and I haven't been able to get a straight answer out of her." Jan dropped into a side chair near the desk as Maren studied the terms of a particular contract.

"Hasn't she given you a reason?"

Jan nodded her blond head. "Oh, sure she has. The usual. You know, 'Mr. Sterling is out of town for the week,' or, 'the artist is balking over a certain clause in the agreement,' or some other lame excuse." Jan's mouth turned into a disgusted grimace and she fished in her purse for a cigarette. She looked tired and drawn, probably from too much work.

Maren pursed her lips together as she thought. "Then I take it you don't believe that Ms. Douglass is telling you the truth?"

"Not all of it." Jan lit her cigarette, tilted her head back and blew a thin stream of smoke toward the ceiling. "She's always been very efficient, and now, out of the blue, she can't seem to get her act together."

"So you've surmised that someone is deliberately telling her to stall."

Jan shrugged thoughtfully. "I really don't know. But something isn't kosher. I'd planned to let you know about it later today, after I'd given Angie one last chance."

"You should have told me about it earlier."

Jan smiled ruefully. "I didn't think you needed any more headaches."

Maren returned the smile. "On that count, I'd agree with you. But maybe I could have gotten to the bottom of this mess."

"Is that why Sterling called?"

"I wish I knew," Maren replied. "He didn't say why he wanted to see me, just that it was important. When I couldn't see him this afternoon, he insisted upon tonight. I

guess I'll find out soon enough." Her light tone couldn't
hide the worry in her eyes.

"So, you're having a hot date with the infamous Kyle
Sterling," Jan teased with a nervous smile and a twinkle
in her dark eyes.

"More like being called on the carpet, I'd guess."

"You can handle him," Jan predicted as she stubbed
out her cigarette and rose to leave.

"What makes you so sure?"

Jan pretended confusion and touched the tip of her
finger to her forehead as she winked. "What is it they say?
Something about the bigger they are, the harder they
fall?"

"Yeah, something like that," Maren agreed with an
uneasy laugh. Jan chuckled as she went back to the
reception area and Maren continued to look over the
contracts with Sterling Records. What was the hitch? Was
Kyle Sterling considering pulling his account from Festival Productions?

Her stomach knotted as she thought about the last time
she had seen Kyle Sterling. It had been her first and only
glimpse into the personal side of the man. All other
contact she had with him had been strictly business.

Nearly a year ago, feeling the pressures of social
commitments for the sake of making a name for Festival
Productions, Maren had accepted an invitation to a gala
event celebrating Mitzi Danner's recently signed multire-
cord deal with Sterling Recording Company. In a much
publicized event held at the attractive young singer's
Beverly Hills address, Maren had quietly sipped her
champagne and watched Kyle Sterling from a distance.

The man had style. Whether natural or aquired, genuine
or fake, the man had style. Begrudgingly Maren noted
that he always seemed to be the center of attention in a

crowd of the Hollywood elite. He wasn't loud, quite the opposite. It was his understated manner, brooding gray eyes and flash of a rakish smile that made him stand out.

The festivities were held in the center courtyard surrounding an oval-shaped pool. The house was a rambling, two-storied nineteen twenties home built for a silent-screen star. It was as eccentric as the gaudy young singer who now occupied it.

Kyle had seemed at home beneath the colored Japanese lanterns that were strung from the fragrant lemon trees surrounding the pool, and yet, as Maren watched him, she noticed that there was something about him . . . a rest-lessness that added to his aloof charm. Though part of the celebration, he had somehow seemed detached, as if he would rather be anywhere else than in the throng of Hollywood faces who were milling around the oval pool. In the crowd of the most famous people in Hollywood, Kyle Sterling alone had held Maren's interest. She had tried to blame it on the fact that he was a powerful man in the recording industry, but she had the disturbing feeling that she was deceiving herself.

And now, at the memory of that warm summer night, Maren was apprehensive. She searched through the large stack of legal papers on the desk for some clue as to why Kyle Sterling wanted to see her. What was happening? Festival Productions needed Sterling Recording Company and, until earlier this afternoon, Maren had suspected the reverse to be true. If Sterling decided to pull his account, it would be difficult to keep Festival Productions operational. It was true that recording stars finally had discovered Festival and business was beginning to increase, but by the same token, the costs of expansion were staggering. On top of all the ordinary costs was the large outstanding debt to Jacob Green, the original owner of Festival. The escalating payments in the contract took an ever larger bite out of an already tight budget. All of which didn't begin to touch Maren's personal expenses, which were monumental. But that was her fault, she reminded herself grimly. Her fault and her responsibility. Unfortunately there was no end in sight.

It would be no less than a disaster if Sterling Records decided to pull out. Maren couldn't let it happen. She'd worked too hard to make Festival Productions profitable, and she wouldn't let it slip. She couldn't. If not for herself, she had to at least think of Brandon. He was depending on her.

Quickly she pressed the intercom button on the phone. "Jan, could you please cancel all of my appointments for the rest of the afternoon? Reschedule them for later in the week."

"I'll give it a try. . . . What about Joey Righteous?"

Maren had to think swiftly. Joey was hot on the charts and a real pain in the neck. "Reschedule him for sometime . . . make that *any*time tomorrow and explain that I'm working with Mr. Sterling on Joey's latest solo album . . . what's the name?" Maren quickly retrieved Joey's contract from the stack. "Here it is . . . *Restless and Righteous*, can you believe that? Anyway, that should put him off for a while."

"Put him off or tick him off?"

"Probably both." Jan had a good point, but Maren persisted. "I know you can do it, Jan. You have a way of pouring oil on troubled waters."

"And you have a way of conning me into anything."

"You love it."

"Sure. Sure I do," Jan replied sarcastically. "Okay, I'll give it a try, but if Mr. Righteous comes blasting in here with one of his usual tirades, don't blame me."

"Consider yourself absolved."

Maren picked up the intricate pages of legal work,

carried them over to the couch and flopped down in her
favorite spot on the couch. She put on her reading glasses
to survey the top document, which was a contract for five
songs from the soon-to-be-released Mirage album. Maren
began to pour over the complicated legal contract, hoping
for just a glimmer as to why Kyle Sterling wasn't satisfied.
Intuition told her he wanted something more from her, but
she didn't understand what it was. Why had he been so
insistent about meeting with her tonight? It didn't make
any sense.

Jan had long since left the office and Maren was
finishing reading the final contract. Other than a few
typographical flaws, she found nothing out of the ordinary
in the documents. The small ache in the back of her head
had magnified as the hours had passed and there was still
no answer to the puzzling question regarding Sterling
Records.

She pulled herself out of the cramped position on the
couch and stretched, letting her fingers work out the
tension in her shoulders. She rotated her head as she
opened her eyes and stared out the window that over-
looked the parking lot. From her position on the second
floor she could see that the long shadows against the
concrete promised an early dusk. A slight breeze moved
through the palm trees near the entrance of the building
and a brilliant orange sun slipped lower in the horizon.

Though it was only a few minutes after seven, a sporty
silver Mercedes rolled to a stop near the building. Maren's
fingers stopped massaging her shoulders as she watched
the owner of the car with unguarded interest. When he
stretched out of the car, Maren's throat constricted with
the recognition of Kyle Sterling. As president of Sterling
Records, he held all of the cards concerning the fate of
Festival Productions in his hands. That wasn't true, she

argued with herself. Festival relied on Sterling Records, but surely it wouldn't crumble if the contracts weren't signed. Or was she kidding herself?

Apparently Mr. Sterling had ignored her request to change the time of the meeting. Though he had agreed to a time of seven thirty, he was nearly a half hour early. Convenient, she thought sarcastically to herself as a slow burn crept steadily up her neck.

He didn't bother to lock his car, but Maren wasn't surprised. What had come as somewhat of a shock to her was that he drove at all. She'd expected a man of such celebrated reputation as Mr. Sterling only to suffer the indignities and snarls of L.A. traffic behind the protective tinted glass of a chauffeured limousine. So the infamous Kyle Sterling was human after all. But she'd guessed that much, hadn't she, at the party in Beverly Hills. The woman in her had intuitively known about his nature as a man.

Kyle strode toward the building as if he were a man with a mission. He was taller than Maren remembered. Though his shoulders were broad, his torso was lean, and he moved with the purpose and grace of a hunter stalking his prey. His dress was sophisticated, but casual: tan corduroy slacks, an ivory sweater and a brown tweed jacket. The tabs of a pale blue collar showed against the neckline of his sweater, but there was no evidence of a tie.

For some strange reason she couldn't completely understand, Maren smiled. It was comforting to think that Kyle Sterling rebelled against the formal convention of a tight silk tie knotted at his throat. It made him seem more real—less of a legend. As he approached the building he made no effort to straighten his jacket or comb his slightly unruly dark hair. It was as if he really didn't care much about his appearance.

When he passed out of view, Maren hurriedly ran her

fingers through her hair, put her glasses in her purse and snapped the contracts into her briefcase. She heard the sound of his footsteps on the stairs. Was that how he kept himself slim—by avoiding elevators? The door to her office opened after a brief knock. She had just tossed her jacket over her arm.

It was when she lifted her eyes to meet the uncompromising gaze of Kyle Sterling that the full impact of the man and what he represented hit her. From a distance his eyes had been interesting, a bold gray set deep into his head and guarded by thick black lashes and brooding ebony brows. Within the proximity of the small room, they were more than commanding or masculine, they held a controlled power that threatened to become unleashed at the slightest provocation.

"Mr. Sterling," Maren managed to say, meeting his severe gaze squarely and ignoring the challenge in his eyes. "You're early."

His gaze swept the room. "And you're alone . . . Miss . . . excuse me, *Ms*. McClure. Sometimes I forget that we live in liberated times."

"Intentionally?"

The hint of a smile tugged at the corners of his mouth. "If it serves my purpose," he admitted.

Maren inclined her head and smiled stiffly. She extended her hand. "Please call me Maren. It makes things simpler." Her smile softened and seemed sincere. It allowed Kyle the tantalizing glimpse of straight white teeth and a small dimple. For an uncertain moment he had the feeling that hers was the most honest smile he had ever seen. Her handshake was firm, her fingers warm. He released her palm reluctantly.

She was more beautiful than he had remembered. He'd met her twice. There had been once in this office for only a few minutes and he'd noticed that she was good-looking. He hadn't really thought much about it because he met many good-looking women on a daily basis. But there had been the party at Mitzi Danner's. He'd sensed at that time that she had been staring at him, but by the time he'd had the opportunity to confront her, she was gone. He had never pursued her, knowing instinctively that it could prove dangerous.

But now, as he stared into Maren's mysterious blue eyes, he could imagine himself drowning in their intense indigo depths. The blue color was cool, but Kyle suspected it warmed easily for the right man. Delicate black brows and a slightly upturned nose gave her an innocent look that contrasted suggestively with her elegantly sculpted cheekbones and full lips. Maren McClure was an enigma . . . a provocative enigma.

Kyle shifted his weight and pushed his hands deeply into his pockets, never once releasing her from the power of his gaze. "I thought you had a late appointment."

"I did. I managed to cancel." Once again he was rewarded with the trace of a smile.

"Even though you thought I'd be here later?" he asked skeptically.

"I wanted to be prepared."

"For what?"

A fire sparked in her icy blue eyes. "For whatever it is you think is so important."

His brows rose slightly. "And are you?"

Was it her imagination, or was he toying with her? "I hope so, Mr. Sterling."

"Kyle," he interjected.

"Kyle." The word seemed to stick in her throat, but she managed to ignore the familiarity his first name engendered. "I assume you want to talk to me about the unsigned contracts between Festival Productions and your firm.''

His jaw tightened and he walked across the room. After a quick glance out the window, he balanced his weight on the ledge, supporting himself with his hands, his long legs extended on the floor. He seemed entirely at ease, as if he owned the place, and yet he avoided her question. "That's part of the reason I'm here,'' he finally allowed. "We should clear up a few of the problems with the contracts."

"I wasn't aware there were any."

"No?" He was dubious; mocking. It made Maren uneasy, but she contained her case of nerves under a thin, tight smile.

"No." She crossed her arms under her chest. "You keep hinting that we have a problem. Let's quit beating around the bush. What exactly is wrong? I read all of the contracts this afternoon and they seem in perfect order. Is there any particular clause to which you object?"

"Several. We'll discuss them later."

"Along with the other part of the reason you're here," she pressed.

"Of course." His gaze dropped from her eyes and slid past the gentle slope of her shoulders to the swell of her breasts hidden annoyingly by the tie of her blouse. Abruptly his eyes returned to meet her gaze. "There's something more important to talk about."

"More important than the contracts?" she repeated, as a puzzled expression crossed her finely sculpted features. "Such as? . . ."

"For one thing, the relationship of Festival Productions with Sterling Records."

"Is it in jeopardy?" she asked calmly.

"Not really, but there are a few things I'd like to change."

"Major things, I take it."

His smile was sincere and there was a gleam of satisfaction in his eyes. "You don't miss much, do you?"

"I hope not."

"But you did have a bit of trouble here," he prodded, and for a strange reason Maren felt as if her back were against the wall.

"What do you mean?"

"A couple of our videos were duplicated and put on the black market."

This was a subject she had hoped to avoid. Kyle Sterling didn't seem to miss a trick. "That's true," she agreed hesitantly. We had a dishonest employee—he's no longer with us."

He watched her intently. Was it his imagination, or was there just a trace of doubt in her clear eyes? He pushed himself away from the window and walked toward the door. "Are you ready?" he asked, positioning his body against the door in order to allow her to pass.

"As ready as I'll ever be," she whispered, picking up her briefcase and puzzling over his cryptic comments concerning the relationship between her company and his. Apprehension knotted her stomach. They walked down the stairs and out of the building into the emerging evening. In the dusky twilight, Maren slid a secretive glance in Kyle's direction.

His was a hard face. A face that had once been in the nation's eye. A face that had been posed perfectly onto the record jackets of more than a few albums. A face that represented the American dream: A poor boy from the back hills of the Blue Ridge Mountains makes good. Perhaps it was the shadowy twilight that made his features appear more rugged than they had earlier, or maybe it was the years of living on the road that made his face seem strained. Whatever the reason, Kyle Sterling was still an attractive man and despite the webbing of crow's-feet near

his eyes or the hint of gray at his temples, he conveyed a
raw masculinity that was lacking in most of the men
Maren had met in her lifetime.

He opened the car door for her, but she paused before
taking a seat. He stood on one side of the silver door, she
the other. She met his gaze levelly, but her brow was
furrowed, as if she were reading an unfathomable pas-
sage. "My curiosity has the better of me," she confided,
noting his uplifted brows. "Just what is it that you want to
change? It's not every day that the president of Sterling
Records comes begging for my company."

"Maybe tonight will change all that," he replied
cryptically.

"Oh?"

"We'll see. I've got a proposition for you, if you're
interested."

"Is it related to that enigmatic statement in the office—
you know, about the duplicating of the tapes?"

"Only slightly. That's not why I had to see you
personally. The black market will always be there, no
matter who Sterling Records does business with."

She slipped into the soft leather seat of the expensive
car and waited while Kyle got into the Mercedes and
maneuvered it speedily down the freeway. Though she
worried over his mysterious remarks, she held her tongue,
deciding it was better to bide her time and let the cryptic
man sitting next to her make the next move. She was
conscious of every movement he made as he drove.

Without looking in her direction, Kyle slipped a tape
into the cassette recorder on the dash. The interior of the
car was filled instantly with soft-rock music. "Do you like
it?" he asked, referring, of course, to the driving beat and
sultry lyrics of the song.

She concentrated for a moment, knitting her dark
brows. "It's all right," she said a few moments later. The

last thing she wanted to do was offend this man. She knew that he was playing some obscure game with her, but she wanted to understand the rules before she committed herself to what was apparently a test.

"Ever heard it before?" The question seemed innocent enough. Kyle's eyes never moved from the darkened freeway and the endless taillights of the cars speeding west through the sprawling city of Los Angeles.

Maren's nerves were stretched more tightly than piano strings. It had been a long day and she wasn't up to guessing games with a man who could very well decide her future. She tried to focus all of her attention on the recording. The beat was unfamiliar. "No."

She shook her thick copper-colored hair and cocked her head thoughtfully. The blend of voices and musical instruments was distinctive. "I don't think I've heard it, but the group sounds like Mirage."

"It is. The song is the title track from their next album."

Maren nodded noncommittally. It was the album for which Festival didn't have a signed contract. Was Kyle toying with her? Why? She sensed that he expected something more from her, but she didn't understand what. The entire situation added to her unease. She shifted uncomfortably in the seat and turned her attention to the view from the window of the car.

The city was alive. Motorists and pedestrians crowded the concrete streets. Several popular restaurants sat on the edge of the boulevard and traffic snarled as cars attempted to squeeze into parking spaces.

The people were as diverse as the city itself. Maren smiled to herself as she saw punk rockers dressed in outrageous leather outfits walking next to couples conventionally attired in silk dresses and conservative business suits. Only in L.A., she thought. It was a city of glitter

and serene beauty, home for the very rich or the incredibly
poor, a city caught between the sea and the mountains in
an incongruous collection of communities joined together
in four hundred and sixty-five square miles. Where else
could you drive from the Pacific Ocean to the Mojave
Desert, or tour through Beverly Hills and Hollywood in
the beautiful Santa Monica Mountains? Maren had lived
in southern California all her life and had never grown
tired of the warm climate or the ever-changing city of Los
Angeles.

As they continued to travel west on Wilshire Boulevard,
Maren eyed the bold skyscrapers of the business district of
L.A. Lights from the man-made towers illuminated the
night. Grand hotels built in the flourish and style of the
twenties stood next to the more austerely constructed
office buildings of the seventies.

Elegant palms swayed in the wind moving inland from
the ocean. The air was clear and warm, adding to the
feeling of electricity in the air. It was the kind of
California evening that Maren had learned to love. If not
for the tension within the confines of the car, she could
envision herself enjoying this evening.

When the song ended, Kyle ejected the tape. The
silence in the car became oppressive. His fingers rubbed
over the smooth plastic surface of the cassette, as if he
were rolling a weighty decision over in his mind. "Here,"
he finally stated. "This is your copy of the music." He
placed the black rectangle in her hand. "Five of the
thirteen cuts on the album are on that tape. We plan to
release them as singles about every four to six weeks,
depending on how they do on the charts. The first song is
scheduled for the end of May."

"Next month?" she inquired, accepting the cassette
and wondering why it felt so cold.

"That's right."

"Not much time," she thought aloud. "I don't know if we'll be able to produce a video that would be ready for release in six weeks."

"You'll have to," he retorted sharply.

"Then I guess you intend to sign the contract."

"Of course."

Maren pinched her lower lip between her teeth. Finally she shook her head and turned it toward him, in order that she could watch his reaction. "You're cutting it too close."

His voice softened. "I'm sure you can work it in," he suggested, knowing full well how dependent she was on his company's business.

Carefully turning the black cartridge over, Maren ran her fingers along the smooth plastic casing. It was as if the fragile relationship between Festival Productions and Sterling Recording Company rested between her palms. "Is there something significant about these songs?"

"Yes."

"I thought so."

Kyle turned off Wilshire and headed south on the Coast Highway. Night had deepened the color of the ocean to a purple hue and only a faint ribbon of magenta colored the horizon where the sun had settled into the serene waters of the Pacific. A few dark images of distant boats sailed on the quiet sea.

They traveled the rest of the distance in silence, each consumed with private thoughts and vague speculations of what the night would bring.

Rinaldi's was located in Manhattan Beach. The stucco two-storied building sat on the edge of the white sand and had an impressive view of the ocean. The walls were painted a soft apricot color, and a balcony off the second story was supported by columns of marble imported from a rock quarry near Naples.

A parking attendant opened the door for Maren. She got out of the car and dropped the cassette into her purse, knowing that Kyle's dark eyes missed nothing of her actions. He was scrutinizing her; watching her every movement.

Several minutes later they were seated at a private table on the balcony. The waiter had poured them each a glass of Cabernet Sauvignon before disappearing into the restaurant for their orders. One small candle stood in the center of the table, its flame flickering dangerously in the slight breeze.

Kyle took a sip of wine and set the glass on the table. He rested his elbows near his plate and supported his chin on his clasped hands. His eyes never left Maren's face. "First of all," he said quietly, "everything I'm about to tell you is very confidential and I expect you to keep it that way."

Her blue eyes didn't waver. The candlelight was trapped in their mystic depths. "Of course."

"I can't afford to take the chance that the competition might find out what we're doing because we're working on an entirely new concept." It sounded like a warning. His eyes had deepened to a threatening gray in the gathering dusk.

"I understand." She took a sip from the wine to clear her throat. A warm breeze lifted her hair away from her face and the candlelight caught on the burnished strands. "What is this *new concept?*" She couldn't mask the interest in her voice.

He watched her carefully. "What we want from you is a thread of continuity in all of the cuts from that one album. For example, the first song, the one you just heard in the car, is about a young man who finds out that his live-in lover has been unfaithful and that she's leaving him for the other guy. All in all the lyrics are pretty basic: melancholy rock and roll.''

Maren nodded. Nothing he had told her was out of the ordinary. Not yet. But apparently he thought he was offering her the opportunity of a lifetime. She could read it in his intense gaze.

''Okay. In the following song, this same man is out on the streets, looking for another woman. He's still alone, but instead of hoping his lover will see her mistake and come back to him, he's relieved that their affair is over.''

''So much for love everlasting,'' Maren noted cuttingly.

The corners of Kyle's mouth quirked as if he might smile, but he seemed to think better of it. ''The point is that I want to see some part of the original tape cut into the second and quite possibly the third. I want a visual image that carries through the entire five-song story. For example, the actress who plays the lover on the first tape should also appear in the following sequences. I don't care if she's just an elusive memory, or if he actually sees her again. I'll leave that part of it up to you. But I want the visual story to flow smoothly and be not only a story in itself, but also to contain a vital part of the five-chapter song.''

''And the reason you're doing this is so that one side of a video disk will display a twenty-five-minute movie that you can sell.''

Kyle smiled and the lines of his face seemed less harsh. ''One reason,'' he agreed slowly. Ryan had tried to tell Kyle about Maren McClure's intelligence, and the man had been right. The lady was definitely not easy to pigeonhole. Kyle wondered why a man would even want to try and stereotype Maren. Her air of mystique intrigued him; her keen mind beckoned him . . . Maren broke into his dangerous thoughts.

"So you're looking for a record of something like a television miniseries."

"You could look at it that way," he acquiesced. The woman with the icy blue eyes and flaming hair was quick, there was no doubt about it. "The principal characters of the plot would, of course, be members of Mirage."

Maren held back the sigh in her throat. Teaching rock stars to act was one of the largest stumbling blocks in the making of videotapes. The musicians were great when called upon to lipsynch the words to a studio recording while playing their instruments, but when called upon to act, very few could perform without a considerable amount of coaching. Fortunately J. D. Price, the lead singer for Mirage, was handsome and had some acting experience—two big plusses. It made Maren's job considerably easier.

"So you expect me to outline all of the action on storyboards for all five cuts and have the first tape ready to be released by the end of May?" Kyle nodded as the tuxedoed waiter brought steaming platters of Italian scampi to the table. After refilling their glasses, the waiter once again left them alone on the balcony. Maren thought about the work ahead of her, should she accept Kyle's offer. "That's a tall order."

"I'd pay you for your trouble."

She considered his proposal as she ate the tangy seafood. Though the meal was excellently prepared, Maren had little appetite. She remembered the cassette in her purse. It represented a fortune, and she needed money badly. It was a tempting offer, one that she hated to turn down. Though she tried desperately to mentally allot the time needed for the project into her schedule, it was impossible. The next six weeks were already crammed with appointments and deadlines.

All the while she was lost in thought, Kyle watched her. He witnessed the silent play of emotions clouding the elegant lines of her face. Something was bothering her, he was sure of it. But *what?* He hadn't even broached the subject of buying out Festival Productions, and he was sure that she was being honest when she stated that the pirating of videotapes was a problem that no longer existed.

Shadowy light from the candle played upon her hair, streaking the rich auburn color with bursts of fiery red. The silken strands framed her face in thick curls that were cut in several fashionable layers and finally rested just below her shoulders. Though she was dressed in a smartly tailored business suit of cream-colored linen and the collar of her turquoise blouse tied over her throat, Kyle knew that she was the most seductive woman in the restaurant. It wasn't what she was wearing that added to her attraction, it was the sophisticated manner in which she carried herself.

"It's a tempting offer, Kyle, and I really do wish that I could take you up on it, but I just don't see where I'll be able to find the time to do everything you want by the end of May. I'm already behind in the production of several tapes—some of which are Sterling Recording Company's releases."

"You're turning me down?" His jaw tightened and he couldn't hide the sarcastic bite to his words. After reading the financial statements of Festival Productions, he had been sure that she would gladly accept his offer . . . along with any others he might make concerning the business at hand.

"I'm not turning you down, Kyle, I'm being honest with you." She smiled slightly, displaying just the hint of white teeth. "My first instinct is to say yes and agree to anything you want, but that would be unfair, not only to Sterling Recording Company, but also to some of your artists who are expecting my services."

Kyle rubbed his thumb under his chin and his dark brows drew together in a deep scowl. "Whom?"

"There are several," Maren admitted. "The first one who comes to mind is Joey Righteous. I'd hoped, in fact I'd almost promised him that his videotape would be completed before he started his tour of Japan. I don't think I can just push him aside for a special project, and I'm not sure that I'd want to."

Kyle felt the muscles in the back of his neck begin to tighten. "Have you already started working on his tape?"

Maren let out a long breath. "I've got the idea on paper, pending Joey's and Sterling Recording Company's approval." She pushed her plate aside and ignored the rest of the meal. "We could start shooting as early as next week, except for one major hang-up."

"And what's that?"

She was suddenly dead serious, her blue eyes arctic. "The fact that I can't get anyone at Sterling Recording Company to help me. Joey's contract, along with about seven others, hasn't been signed by anyone of authority at your firm."

Kyle's mouth tightened into a firm hard line. "I'm prepared to correct that."

"Fine. I happen to have the contracts with me." His eyebrows arched in interest and she forced herself to continue. "But that doesn't help my production schedule, does it?"

"You're asking for more time?"

Maren shook her head. "I'm trying to explain that you're asking the impossible."

Kyle felt his teeth grinding together in frustration. So this was what Ryan Woods had attempted to warn him about: Maren McClure's clever way of turning the game around to suit her needs. Just when he had expected her to jump at the juicy morsel of bait he had offered her, she had turned him down flat, not accepting it until some other business had been accomplished. He would have staked his life on the fact that Ms. McClure would do practically *anything* for the contract he was offering her. He had been wrong; seriously wrong.

"All right, Maren, I think we can stop playing games."

She managed a thin smile over the rim of her wineglass. "Good. It's getting a little cumbersome, isn't it?" Had she pushed him too far? She couldn't afford to offend the head of Sterling Records; too much was at stake. Her heart began to pound, but her gaze remained outwardly calm.

Kyle twisted the stem of his glass in his fingers. "I know that J. D. Price of Mirage thinks that you're single-handedly responsible for the group's success. And, for whatever it's worth, I'm sure he's at least partially correct. Without that first videotape of "Danger Signs," the song might never have hit the charts."

Maren disagreed. "It was a good release."

"It was a bomb. No one bothered to listen to the record until your video hit cable TV."

Maren smiled at the memory of making that tape. The dusty on-location shooting of the videotape for "Danger Signs" had run over budget, had several lighting flaws in scenes that had to be reshot and everything that could have gone wrong did. But it had been the beginning of Festival Production's fame. "We were lucky."

"Maybe. But the point is that J. D. Price will have no one but you and your company produce this series of videotapes for Mirage's album."

"Is that right?" she asked with a satisfied smile.

"What do you think?"

"I think I need more time to come up with what you want."

Kyle Sterling smiled despite the uncomfortable feeling that he was being manipulated. "And I think you drive a hard bargain."

"Just wait," she volunteered. "We haven't begun to talk money."

"I was just coming to that."

She inclined her head as she took a swallow of wine, encouraging him to continue.

"Actually, it's not the money that's the problem," he allowed. She waited, sure that he was finally coming to the point of this intimate business meeting. "You see, I think it would be better if Sterling Recording Company had more control in the making of the videos."

Her eyes narrowed as she put her empty glass on the table.

"More control?" she repeated. "How?"

"We're considering producing the tapes in-house."

Maren somehow managed to smile faintly. "I don't understand. You just offered me a very specific and expensive piece of business."

"That's because I was trying to make my offer attractive to you."

"What offer?" Her pulse was racing and she had trouble keeping her voice even. The bottom was falling out of her world and Kyle Sterling was the man responsible.

"I want to buy out Festival. . . ." He read the look of disbelief and dismay in her cool eyes.

"Why?" She swallowed back the apprehension rising in her throat.

"Because I want you to work for me. You would still

have complete discretion concerning the making of the videos, and you would be paid very well.''

"But I would only be able to work with your artists."

"That's true," he agreed. "But you would be able to work with *all* of them, and from what I understand Sterling Recording Company is your major source of income."

His last statement was the final nail in the coffin. He knew how desperately she needed his business. He knew it was a matter of life and death for her small company. If she could only hang on a few more months, business was beginning to turn around and come from other sources than Sterling Records. But right now, she needed the contracts from Sterling desperately.

"I'll be honest with you, Kyle, I've never really considered selling Festival Productions, and I'm not sure I'm comfortable with the idea. I like working for myself and being my own boss."

"Do you like the headaches of keeping Festival afloat?"

She smiled distantly. "It's all part of the game, I guess. A challenge. I don't know if I'm willing to give it up."

"You don't have to. . . . We can even use the location of your offices until your lease is up and we've made room for you downtown."

"What about my staff?" she asked, her blue eyes trying to read the gray depths of his.

"The staff is up to you . . . within a reasonable budget."

"And you're the one who decides what is 'reasonable.'"

He settled back in the chair and returned her inquiring gaze. "Ultimately, yes."

"If I decide against this . . . what happens to the unsigned contracts?" she asked.

"They'll probably remain unsigned. This is important to me, and if we can't get your cooperation, then I'll have to find someone else. I'm giving you first opportunity."

"Because J. D. Price and a few other artists will insist upon it."

"Right."

"I'm not crazy about the idea," she conceded.

"And you feel forced into it?"

"I think 'coerced' is the term I would use," she replied thoughtfully. "I suppose you want an answer tonight."

"It would make things easier for me."

Maren felt as if her world were falling apart. Festival Production Company was little security, but it was all she had in the world. It would be hard to give up. "I'll have to think about it," she whispered. "And of course I'd want to see a firm offer with an employment agreement attached to it in writing." He waited, expecting other demands, but there was only the one. She stared at him evenly, without the slightest evidence of anxiety. "The only way I would consider your offer is if in the purchase price you included shares of Sterling Recording Company stock."

His eyebrows raised in surprise and the corners of his mouth pulled into a tight frown.

"It's not unrealistic," she pointed out. "I want to make sure that I have some say in what goes on."

"And you think by owning stock in my company, you will?"

"We'll find out, won't we?" she countered, hoping that her bluff would remain uncovered. What did she have to bargain with?

He noticed the deadly gleam in her eye and couldn't help but smile. After running his fingers through his sun-streaked hair, he shook his head and smiled. His laughter was low, rich and infectious. It seemed to relieve the tension in the air. "Lady," he said with his amused grin familiarly in place, "I have the distinct feeling that I've been had." He refilled his glass and chuckled.

"That makes two of us," she confided with less enthusiasm. If the situation weren't so serious, she, too, might be inclined to laugh. As it was, she could barely manage a smile.

The cool wine slid down her throat and Kyle winked at her. "Lighten up," he instructed with a sly smile. "Things can only get better. You may as well enjoy yourself."

"I suppose you're right," she replied and a spark of interest danced in her clear blue eyes.

Kyle Sterling was certainly an interesting man, she thought to herself . . . a very interesting man.

Chapter Three

$\mathcal{T}$he remainder of the evening passed quickly. The uncomfortable tension had eroded and though Maren wondered how she was going to handle Kyle's proposition, she felt herself relax in Kyle's company. Though the conversation centered around business, the intimate restaurant provided a warm, quiet atmosphere that created a sense of familiarity. All too soon the waiter had served the final cups of cappuccino and the conversation lagged.

Moonglow shimmered on the dark sea and the soft waves broke into white foam as the tide caressed the opalescent sand. Maren wondered at the feeling within her; she felt almost as if she had known the enigmatic man with her for most of her life. And she had, really. During Maren's early twenties, Kyle Sterling was a household word, his life an open book, edited carefully by his press agent. What Maren had known of him then was only what she and the rest of the record-purchasing American public were supposed to see.

There had been glimpses of the private Kyle Sterling that even his smooth-talking agent hadn't been able to hide. Rumors of a stormy marriage to a beautiful country singer, a child born, the marriage crumbling, and more recently, a near-fatal accident had continually headlined the scandal sheets. Conjecture ran high as far as Kyle Sterling was concerned. Maren had discounted the stories, knowing from personal experience how easily the press could misrepresent the facts.

As she stared across the small table into the bold eyes of the famous man, she felt as if she could trust him with her life. It was strange. She could sense that he didn't completely trust her, but she chalked it up to the fact that it had been only hours since they had really met on a personal level.

"Where can I take you?" Kyle asked as he rose from the table and tugged at the lapels of his jacket. His eyes never left hers and for a heart-stopping moment, Maren imagined a seductive glint of passion in their mysterious depths. What would he say if she responded that he could take her anywhere he pleased? A tinge of scarlet touched her cheeks at the wayward thought—what was happening to her? In one evening she was willing to push aside all of her morals just to feel the touch of this one man. It was a disturbing thought, completely out of character, and she wondered if she was turning into one of those brash, lost souls called groupies.

With obvious embarrassment she regained her fragile poise and managed to smile. "My car is at the office."

He helped her with her jacket and the warm tips of his fingers brushed the back of her neck. For a dizzying second they seemed to linger and leave a heated impression on her skin.

They walked to his car in silence, listening to the sounds of the night: the quiet lapping of sea against sand, the muted chatter of guests in the restaurant and the hum of cars moving about the city. Maren noticed the lovers walking on the moonlit beach and she felt an urge to reach for Kyle's hand and lead him to the water's edge. It had been so long since she had felt this way about a man. It was a dangerous, yet exhilarating sensation.

While driving toward the office, Kyle had become pensive, lost in thoughts that seemed miles distant. Maren was aware of nothing other than Kyle. She could smell the scent of his cologne lingering in the air, see his hard profile as he squinted into the night and feel the unleashed tension building within him. She knew now how he had been so successful as a country singer: There was a raw magnetism about him that contrasted to the quietly aloof image he attempted to project, a fire burning beneath the ice that enticed Maren. Kyle Sterling was captivating, and just being with him was risky.

Soon they were back at the office. He made no move to help her out of the car. Instead he continued to grip the steering wheel and stare into the black night.

Maren reached for the door handle.

"Don't go," he commanded. "Not yet." His voice was hushed and raw. It forced Maren's heart to her throat.

"I wasn't looking forward to this meeting," Maren admitted cautiously. She felt the urgent need to explain herself.

"Neither was I."

"But I guess I should thank you for your offer to purchase Festival. I realize that *you* think it would not only be in your best interests, but mine as well."

"Oh, Maren, haven't we talked enough business for one night?" His hand moved from the steering wheel to touch her cheek. It was a gentle caress and quickly withdrawn, leaving Maren suddenly cold.

"Are you asking me to leave?" she asked haltingly.

"What do you think?"

Maren sighed. "Truthfully, Kyle, I don't know what to think."

"You're the most interesting woman I've ever met." It was a flat, emotionless statement and it almost sounded as if the admission disgusted him.

"I guess I should consider that a compliment."

Kyle's eyes found hers in the darkness. They drove deeply into her soul. "You should, lady, because I meant it to be one. I find you incredibly alluring. You're beautiful, I suppose you know that much. But . . . it's not your looks that make you so damned captivating . . . it's more than that. A lot more."

"And you don't like it," she finished for him.

Kyle's smile was grim. "I don't know how to handle it."

"I find that hard to believe."

"I suppose you do, but then you don't know me very well, do you?"

Honesty flashed in her clear blue eyes. "Not as well as I'd like to."

"Now that's the problem, isn't it?" he whispered. "Because I want to know you better as well . . . a whole lot better. You know it and it scares you." His voice had lowered to the point where it was barely audible. His eyes searched her face and she knew in that instant that he was going to kiss her.

His hand reached under her hair and gently pulled her head toward his. She offered no resistance. She could feel the warmth of his breath fanning her face, heating her cheeks. He groaned when his lips first touched hers and conveyed the depth of his need. Liquid sparks of passion raced through her blood as his arms tightened over her body, crushing her to him with a savagery that bespoke hours of restraint. She closed her eyes and let him part her lips with his tongue. Hungrily he tasted the sweetness of her mouth and felt her soft, teasing body pressed against his.

His lips moved over hers, gently coaxing the warmth within her to flood her senses. She felt devastatingly feminine, and the womanly ache within her began to grow as it spread upward through her body.

"Oh, Maren," he moaned, kissing her eyelids and letting his fingers twine through the thick fiery strands of her hair. "Let me be with you tonight. Come home with me." His breath was ragged against her ear. It softly beckoned her to respond. Her throat became dry, her emotions torn.

Against the persuasive touch of his fingers on her skin, she slowly pulled herself out of his tender embrace. A thousand reasons to go with him filled her mind, but she ignored them. "I can't," she whispered. He heard the regret in her words.

"Why not?" He attempted to take her into his arms again, but she held his hands away from her body. Her hair was tousled, her breathing ragged, her heart pounding.

"This . . . this has nothing to do with desire or want," she attempted to explain. "I just need some time to sort out my feelings about you." Her blue eyes, darkened by the night and her passion, pleaded with him to understand. "Until a few hours ago, I hardly knew you, and now I want to fall into your arms without so much as a thought to the future. I can't do that, Kyle. Not yet. Now that we may become business partners . . . or maybe not . . . I don't think it would be wise to become . . . involved."

"I'm not asking for a lifelong commitment."

"And I'm not ready for a relationship."

"Is that what you think I want?" The question, like a silver blade, cut through the silent emotions stretching between them.

She shook her head. "I don't know what you want, Kyle, but I know that neither one of us would be satisfied with a one-night stand." She watched him cautiously, her head tilted upward to meet his impassioned gaze. Without a word she dared him to deny the truth.

A lazy smile stole over his rugged features. "How do you know so much about me?" he asked, as he gently pushed an errant copper lock out of her eyes.

"I don't. Not yet. But I hope to God that any man I'm attracted to isn't interested in one lonely night of passion just to fulfill basic sexual needs."

His dark brows raised. "You really lay it on the line, don't you?"

"It comes with the territory," she sighed, trying to calm her racing pulse. Why did she feel compelled to explain herself to him? Why did she *care?* "I've worked hard to get where I am, and it hasn't been easy in a predominantly man's world. If I had become sexually involved with any of the men I've worked with, I'm sure the business would have suffered. And to me, it's just not worth the price." She could see his eyes narrowing in disbelief.

"Are you trying to convince me that you're a hard-nosed business woman who puts her company before everything, including her own pleasure?" he asked dubiously.

"Considering the circumstances, I think you should be pleased."

"What I am is unconvinced." Just what kind of a woman was he dealing with?

The hint of a smile teased her lips. "Good. Because I'm trying to point out that to me, sex is more than just pleasure."

"A commitment?"

"Yes."

He paused and the silence in the car weighed heavily on Maren's shoulders. How much of her soul could she afford to bare? "Is that what you expect from me—*a commitment?*"

Maren grinned at his obvious discomfort. "No. What I'm trying to tell you is that *I'm* not ready to give one," she explained.

Kyle let out a gust of air and ran his fingers through his hair. He chuckled despite the uneasy feeling in the atmosphere. "I'm afraid that meeting you might turn out to be the biggest mistake of my life."

"And why is that?" Her heart seemed to miss a beat. She knew that he was joking, but there was an undercurrent of truth beneath his words.

"Because not only are you going to cost me a fortune in videotape production, but you're also going to frustrate the hell out of me!"

"You're breaking my heart," she teased with a wicked gleam lighting her eyes.

"If only I could," he muttered, almost to himself.

The smile on her face faded. "Then why don't you try being honest with me—*completely* honest."

"I have been."

She pursed her lips and shook her head, dismissing his statement as a careless lie. "I don't think so. It doesn't take a genius to figure out that something's up—something big."

"Such as?"

"I wish I knew, Kyle," she replied, a sad smile resurfacing. "I've been in this business for nearly five years and I can sense when someone's not leveling with me."

"I don't know what you're talking about."

"Then let me take a guess . . ."

"All right."

"Does this have anything to do with the pirating of your recordings?" she asked.

"I thought you explained all that."

"So did I. But for some reason, I feel that there's still an element of trust missing in our conversation. If it doesn't hinge on the tape duplication, I'm at a total loss as to what it might be."

She looked at him and the moonglow seemed entrapped in her eyes. Kyle hadn't counted on the depth of Maren's perception. Ryan Woods had warned him about her, but Kyle had been convinced that he could handle any woman, including Maren McClure. But, once again, he'd been proven wrong . . . dead wrong. The thought was an irritating thorn in his side, and the worst part of the situation was that Kyle was attracted to her—more attracted than he had been to any other woman in his life. The situation was rapidly getting out of hand and he had no one to blame but himself.

"If there is a problem," he replied as he pulled on his lower lip, "I think it's that I had no intention of becoming attracted to you."

"Then you're not concerned about the pirating?" she asked dubiously.

"Of course I'm concerned. I have to be. Someone is duplicating our recordings, and the videotapes as well. They're being distributed on the black market several weeks before the albums are released." He had her full attention and to his relief her eyes remained clear, unclouded by fear.

"And you think that someone at Festival might be involved?"

"You said the problem was corrected."

"But I'm not sure that you believe me."

Kyle weighed his words carefully. "I'm convinced that you're not involved." In one short evening his opinion about Maren McClure had changed and taken a hundred-and-eighty-degree turn. Kyle would be hard-pressed to believe that Maren knew anything about the duplicated tapes, other than what she had told him. It was the honesty in her eyes that arrested him, and he found it impossible to think her a consummate liar. He frowned at the irony of it. Maybe he was more of a fool than he knew. The last thing he would have expected this evening was to be taken in by a woman.

"But you still think that someone at Festival Productions might be on the take. That's it, isn't it? That's why you want me to come to work for you—to tighten your security! And I was gullible to think that it was my talent; but it's only because the *artists* are insisting on working with me! This way you can kill two birds with one stone!" Her small fist clenched and pounded against the pliant leather seat. "Damn!"

"I haven't accused anyone at Festival of anything . . ."

"Yet!"

"And you think I might?" he asked warily.

"You don't have to!" She sank back against the cushioned upholstery. "I didn't mean to react so violently," she apologized. No matter how angry she became, she couldn't forget who this man was and what he represented. She had to keep her pride in perspective. "Maybe I did jump to the wrong conclusion. I hope so."

"You act as if you *expect* me to accuse Festival

Productions of having a part in the pirating," he said evenly. "Do you?" Dark gray eyes held her transfixed.

The lie slid easily over her lips. "Of course not." It was impossible to explain her unfounded suspicions about her own company. If Kyle Sterling lost faith in Festival, he could take away his offer and start his own in-house production company, robbing Festival of the business it so desperately needed. If he found out about the internal problems at Festival, Kyle would never sign a contract with Festival again. It would be a crippling blow, considering Festival's poor cash-flow position. The last risk Maren could take was to lose this man's trust, and for all she knew, everything at Festival *was* above board, and the missing cassettes had been found. The entire incident had been cleared up in a matter of two hours, and yet it still made Maren uneasy.

"I guess I'm a little sensitive," she amended, "because of the trouble we had a few months ago."

Was it his imagination, or had she paled? "But you're sure it no longer exists."

"Positive." Maren placed her hand on his arm. She felt his muscles tense. "I think it's only fair," she began nervously, "since you've offered me such a unique opportunity, that I be straight with you. I know that you still have some suspicions about Festival, and I don't know how to convince you otherwise. The only thing I can do is promise you that if we have any more trouble, to let you know immediately. That's the best I can do."

"Am I to assume that you're declining my offer?"

"I'm just going to need a little time . . ."

She felt the warmth of his fingers over hers. "All right, Maren, but I'm not a patient man."

Her breath caught in her throat. "Should I take that as some kind of warning?"

A wicked smile twisted the thin line of his lips. "I would never threaten you, Maren . . . but you might be able to convince me to make promises . . ."

"That you wouldn't keep," she supplied, reading his impassioned thoughts.

His face was so close to hers that she could feel the warmth of his skin. His eyes roved restlessly over her face and his voice became a hoarse whisper. "All I know at this moment is that the only thing I can think about is you and what I would like to do to you."

The night seemed to close in on her and she swallowed with difficulty. "Those kinds of promises can be dangerous."

"Only if you let them." He squinted into the darkness as he surveyed the seductive curve of her lips. He traced the pout with the tip of a finger. "Besides, unless I miss my guess, you're the kind of woman who loves to flirt with danger."

"You're wrong," she denied, aware only of the raw masculinity of his strong features and the power of the hand that held her bound to him. Strong but gentle, coarse but kind . . . if only she could let him touch her. . . . She refused. "You're wrong about me," she repeated.

"Prove it." Before she could protest further, he lowered his head and his lips touched hers softly. She gasped and his mouth pressed against hers, hard and demanding, claiming her lips in a kiss that warmed her body and promised to find her spirit. Though she tried to fight it, she felt her body melting against his, becoming alive beneath his persuasive touch. The heat of desire in his body flowed into hers and she yearned for more of the sweetness his touch inspired.

"This is crazy," she whispered, when finally their lips parted. Her dusky blue eyes were glazed with a hunger, deep and anxious.

"It's not crazy; it's right." He kissed her again, letting her know of the throbbing passion buried within him.

His fingers found the tie of her blouse and tugged slowly on it until it loosened and fell open. Maren's heart hammered loudly within the confines of her rib cage, her blood pounding incessantly in her eardrums. The silky fabric parted, exposing the soft white skin of her throat and shoulders. Kyle's lips touched her neck, and his tongue left a dewy impression near her shoulder. Maren felt the warm moisture cool in the night air and she sighed with the consuming need beginning to awaken within her. His lips lowered to her neck and he kissed the delicate hollow of her throat, leaving his moist imprint on her delicate bone structure.

Maren tilted her head, exposing more of her throat to him. Her dark curls touched his neck in an intimate caress known only to lovers. His lips touched her skin and dipped lower, closer to her breasts. Maren swallowed against the bittersweet yearnings and her senses became confused in the once-forgotten passion rising within the deepest core of her. "Don't," she managed to whisper when his finger slid a button through the hole. His hand flattened against her chest, feeling the warm skin rising and falling with each shallow breath she managed to take. The only sound in the darkness was the desperate beat of her racing heart.

"You want me," he whispered as he felt the fluttering irregular cadence.

"Yes," she admitted.

He groaned and moved closer to her, pressing her into the soft leather cushions. His shaking hand gingerly cupped her breast, rubbing the silky texture of her blouse against her skin, until she thought she would go insane with frustrated longing. She swallowed to moisten her throat and had to force her hand to restrain his wrist. "Please . . . don't."

"You can't deny it . . . you want me as much as I want you."

"I . . . I haven't denied anything. But it's not enough."

"What is, Maren?" he asked, his lips brushing the silk over her breast. He felt the tautness of her nipple straining against the flimsy fabric and found that he was unable to cope with the frustration burning within him. "What is enough?"

His hot breath against her breast encouraged a thin layer of perspiration to collect between Maren's shoulder blades. "I don't know," she conceded with a sigh.

He clenched his teeth together to stem the tide of desire rising in his body. Reluctantly he pulled his head away from her swollen breast. Without considering her actions, she placed a protective hand over her heart.

Regarding her through half-closed but penetrating eyes, he spoke. His words were punctuated with his uneven breathing. "Sure you do," he accused, "you're just not willing to admit it. You said you weren't ready for a commitment, and I believed you. Hell, we had barely met!" He clenched his fists to fight against the emotional and contradictory feelings battling within his mind. "But you still want something from me, don't you? You want to hear words of love, whether they have meaning or not."

Maren bristled. "You're wrong, Kyle. I'm thirty-three years old, and I've learned not to confuse sexual attraction and physical desire with love."

"Then what is it you want?" he asked raggedly, hoping to understand just a little part of her.

"Time." She pulled out of his embrace and reached for the handle of the door. "I don't think it's an unreasonable request considering the circumstances.'' She opened the car door and slid outside. He followed.

A gentle breeze blew through the two stately palm trees that stood near a lone lamppost, forcing the leaves to dance in the air and cast moving shadows in the ethereal gray light. That same soft wind lifted the parted fabric of Maren's blouse and made it difficult to rebutton. Caught in the moving air, the silk tie and the copper strands of her hair fell away from her neck and throat. Her eyes shimmered in the lamplight, changing from deep indigo to an intriguing shade of silver-blue. She seemed strong and yet vulnerable, innocent and wise; a bewitching creature who turned his head around.

She was still fumbling with the tie when Kyle reached her. He lifted her face with his hands and gently kissed her trembling lips. ''Promise me that you'll see me again,'' he coaxed. His fingers slid against her throat and rested upon her shoulders. She wondered what it would be like to be controlled by those persuasive hands.

''I will,'' she hesitantly agreed, aware only of his fingers softly tracing her jawline. ''We have business—''

''Shhh . . .'' He placed his finger against her lips. ''Not business. I want to see you again.''

''I don't know.'' Once again her heart was racing. What was it that scared her so?

He wouldn't be put off. ''I want you to come to my home in La Jolla for the weekend. I want to walk on the beach with you. I want to show you where I live. I want to get to know you . . . all of you.''

''You live alone?'' she asked breathlessly. She was afraid of the answer and she prayed for any excuse to avoid the intimacy they had shared this evening. It was much too perilous. She couldn't afford to fall in love with Kyle Sterling and she realized that it would be easy . . . too easy.

"My housekeeper is gone on the weekends."

"But . . . I thought . . . don't you have a daughter?"

His silvery eyes darkened in pain. "My ex-wife has custody."

"Even on the weekends?"

His jaw tensed and his eyes hardened against the bitter memories. "I don't see my daughter very often. Holly prefers it that way."

"I'm sorry . . ."

"Don't be. It's not your fault."

For the first time that evening Maren had some insight into another, more private side of Kyle Sterling. It was a part of his life that was shielded from the press and definitely brought him torment. Maren was surprised to understand that he, too, had suffered at another's hand. She saw it in the set of his jaw and the shadows under his eyes. All of his money and fame hadn't bought him happiness. "I . . . I didn't mean to pry," she said, avoiding his gaze.

He dismissed the subject with a frown. "It's all right." His fingers pressed more warmly against her shoulders. "Will you see me again?"

She forced back the lump that had swollen in her constricted throat. "I don't know . . . if I want to get . . . involved with you," she replied, attempting to control her ravaged emotions. "There's a part of you that seems so remote . . . so untouchable. Not only are you wealthy, but you're famous . . . really famous . . . and you own the company that is the single largest account of Festival Productions. It's all so overwhelming . . ." Her voice faded into the night. It wasn't like her to be indecisive. Kyle was disturbing her equilibrium. She wasn't thinking rationally.

"I'm a man who just wants to spend some time with a very interesting woman. Can't you understand that?"

She smiled wistfully. "I suppose so. I just don't know what to do about it."

"Trust me." The words echoed dully in her brain. She'd heard them in the past and they had betrayed her.

"I want to," she allowed.

"But you can't?"

She smiled despite the unwanted tears burning in her throat. Had she really come to the point where she could trust no man? "I guess I'm just not a trusting soul."

His hands slid down her arms and she felt the pressure of his fingers gently holding her wrists. "Because you were hurt by someone else?" His features contorted with anger. Despite the threatening tears, she looked upward at him defiantly. The silvery glow of the streetlamp reflected in the unshed teardrops. She brushed them away with the back of her hand, refusing to cry because of painful memories.

"I don't think I know you well enough to discuss what has happened to me—anyway, it's not all that interesting."

He looked down at her hopelessly. "You're hiding something from me. What is it?"

"It has nothing to do with you . . . or your company."

"To hell with the company. Something's bothering you." If only she would open up to him, perhaps he could help. He had the urge to protect her.

"It's none of your affair," she replied, her eyes once again dry. "And none of your concern."

She shook her head against the insistence of his furrowed brow, but the fingers over her wrists tightened. "Tell me," he demanded.

"I can't."

"Why not?" His voice was rough.

"Because . . . because . . ."

"Because you're ashamed?"

Blue eyes blazed and she jerked her arms free of his possessive grip. "Because I don't want you to know everything about me. I don't want my personal life to become entangled with my business—"

"Another man hurt you!" he accused, refusing to believe her lie. His body had become rigid, his eyes accusing. "A man whom you loved very much!"

"It's over," she snapped back. Her entire body was shaking from the ordeal. Why, tonight, was she reminded of Brandon?

"You still love him." He waited for her denial, silently counting the condemning seconds as they passed. When the silence remained unbroken, he turned on his heel and walked to the car.

Her hands came up to cross over her breasts as if to ward off a sudden chill, but her head remained regally high. She watched him leave and ignored the urge to call out to him and tell him her deepest secrets. Those silent thoughts were better left unspoken.

Chapter Four

Sleep was elusive and the night stretched endlessly before her. As she lay in the darkness on her bed, she tried to rest, but painful memories made her restless. Kyle's image with its dark brooding gray eyes couldn't be erased. Nor could she forget the warm feel of his fingers when they caressed her skin. Her response to him had surprised her; she had thought her desire had been buried so deeply it would never resurface.

Haunting memories of another man destroyed her warm thoughts of Kyle. Trapped in her mind were painful thoughts of Brandon, a man to whom she was hopelessly bound. She wondered if she would ever be free of him. She doubted it.

The nightmares of Brandon disturbed what little sleep she managed to find. It had been three years since the divorce was final, but she still bore the scars from her passionate but brief marriage. It had ended because

Brandon was a man who couldn't abide the restrictions of a monogamous relationship, and Maren couldn't bear the torment of wondering who was warming her husband's bed. She had hoped that the divorce would release her from him. It hadn't. Theirs was a relationship that couldn't be broken easily, and even though they both knew it to be a mistake, they had once considered reconciliation.

It had been that weekend at Heavenly Valley that had altered the course of Maren's life. Brandon was a natural athlete and had been showing off on the slopes, attempting to race down the most dangerous runs at breakneck speeds. Maren's insides had twisted as she watched him put tougher demands upon his body. He ignored the fact that he was obviously tired and pushed himself to the limit. His last chilling run had ended in tragedy. The fall should have killed him, but it didn't. Maren had witnessed his loss of control of the skis and the jump that had ended in a body-wrenching dive against the packed snow and ice. Her strangled screams had brought the rescue team to Brandon's side within minutes. Somehow he had managed to survive, though he only recovered partial use of his legs.

Maren shuddered at the memory and pulled the blankets more tightly around her neck. She could remember the emergency room of the stark hospital and the fear that had gripped her in its cold grasp when she had first understood that Brandon might never walk again. The doctors had been grim, but persistent. If it hadn't been for a succession of expensive operations, Brandon would still be confined to a wheelchair. As it was, he could now walk painfully with the aid of a brace. In time, the orthopedists were predicting, he could recover, if he could somehow manage to get over the emotional trauma of the accident. Brandon had not only lost his ability to walk in that terrifying leap, he had also lost his career as a tennis pro and his self-esteem as a man.

As the first golden streaks of dawn began to lighten her room, she thought about Kyle's vicious accusation. Could he have possibly been right? Did some small part of her still love Brandon? Could she still love a man who had thought so little of her while they had been married? She had quit asking herself that question after the divorce had become final, and she had vowed to forget both him and his endless affairs with younger women. But that had been before the skiing accident at Heavenly Valley, and before Brandon had become financially dependent upon her.

She shook her head, turning it slowly against the pillow, hoping to dislodge her unpleasant thoughts. The past was dead and gone. Her love for Brandon had withered years ago, but regardless of the fact that she no longer loved him, she couldn't turn her back on him; not yet, not while he still needed her. She was the only scrap of family he had, and if she had to imprison herself to give him the emotional security he needed, so be it.

Though it was barely six in the morning, Maren dragged herself out of bed and headed for the shower. Rather than concentrating on problems she couldn't begin to solve, she would push herself ever deeper into her work. She had to make things work for her, and she had to seriously consider all the ramifications of Kyle Sterling's offer. Just at the thought of him, she felt a blush rise to her cheeks.

She let the bathrobe slide to the floor and stepped into the hot shower, lounging under the soothing spray. She tried to think of anything other than Brandon and the guilt she carried because of him. How many times had she attempted to convince herself that his accident wasn't her fault? And how many times was she left with the same condemning conclusion: If it hadn't been for Maren,

Brandon would never have gone to Heavenly Valley. It had been her suggestion that they spend the day on the snow-laden slopes; he had only complied, and in so doing, ruined the rest of his life.

"Stop it!" she told herself fiercely. "You can't blame yourself!" She plunged her head under the spray and let the water run over her. Her wayward thoughts turned to Kyle Sterling and without realizing it, Maren began to smile. Kyle was such a puzzling man; so unique.

While lathering her shoulders, she reflected on the events of the previous evening. Despite the fact that it had turned sour, last night had been the single most inspiring evening she had spent in years, and the man she had shared it with was more fascinating than she could have ever guessed. His intrigue was more than the fact that he was a wealthy man with a colorful and famous past. It was his energy, his sensuality, his gentle touch, that had captured her. The quiet sound of his low laughter had entrapped her in its honesty. She knew intuitively that he was a man who didn't laugh often, and that knowledge made the short time she had spent with him all the more endearing.

She had just reached for a towel when her thoughts turned dark. Kyle had sought her out only because he wanted Festival Productions, and very badly. His primary motive in seeing her was to try and force her into a position to sell Festival to him. There was also the pirating scheme to consider. Kyle had been trying to ferret information from her, and though he said he was satisfied, he seemed a little uneasy about it. Could he really suspect someone, at Festival, or was he merely being cautious because of the fact that he intended to purchase the company at whatever the cost? She shook her head and water from her hair beaded against the sides of the shower stall. No, if he had really been suspicious, he would never have made the offer. Then again, he hadn't signed the contracts, had he?

The full impact of her thoughts hit her with the force of a slap in the face. She slumped against the wet tile when she realized that she had left her briefcase, with the contracts, in Kyle's car. In her fumbling efforts to dissolve the growing intimacy between them, Maren had hurried out of the car with her purse, forgetting the briefcase and the valuable contracts therein. Maren rolled her eyes skyward. This wasn't like her, not at all. She usually wasn't a bundle of nerves with a man, nor was she forgetful. But Kyle Sterling wasn't just any man, and his image continued to play havoc with her reason. If she had indeed left the contracts with him, it wasn't the end of the world, but it would certainly make her seem irresponsible, and that was the last impression she wanted to leave with Kyle Sterling.

Disgusted with herself, Maren scrambled into her bathrobe and raced through the small apartment, leaving a wet trail on the carpet as she confirmed with her eyes what she had mentally discovered. Her briefcase was missing. It wasn't in the closet, nor under the hall tree, nor near the foot of the bed, nor tossed recklessly on the kitchen table. After checking the usual spots, she began to search the obscure ones. It was gone. Muttering an oath at her own carelessness, she dialed the offices of Sterling Recording Company and was politely informed by a prerecorded message that the normal business hours for the company did not begin until eight o'clock.

She began to dry her hair, going through the motions without bothering to check her reflection in the steamy mirror. Several minutes later, when the condensation from the shower had disappeared and she looked directly into the blue eyes of her mirror-image, she questioned her motives. Had she left the briefcase in Kyle's car with a purpose? Subliminally, she might have created a convenient excuse to see him again. But she didn't need an excuse, she argued with herself. Kyle had made it crystal clear that he wanted to see her again. All she had to do was summon the courage to call him. If she wasn't able to do that much, she would certainly see him soon regarding the buy-out . . . if there was going to be one.

She considered calling him in the time it took to dress and drive from the apartment to the office, but she decided to wait until Sterling Recording Company had opened its doors. She didn't want to appear too anxious by tracking him down. She needed to find out that he had the contracts, but certainly it could wait until he had made it in to his office.

As was usual, Maren was the first employee of Festival Productions to arrive. It was the bookkeeper's day off, and the production crew was on location. For the past few weeks Jan had been arriving at the office late in the morning. Jan was always apologetic and managed to get her work done, so Maren didn't force the issue. Maren had come to suspect that Jan was having trouble with Jacob again.

It was well after nine when Jan finally got to the office. Maren had already begun working on the layout for the first song on the Mirage album. She had listened to the song "Yesterday's Heart" until she could sing the lyrics along with the band. Over the sound of the sultry music, Maren heard Jan arrive.

For a moment she tried to continue working, but couldn't. She sighed as she took off her reading glasses and got up from the drafting table in the corner of her office. After she switched off the tape player, she walked slowly into the reception area.

Jan was already at her desk and the meticulous mask of

makeup couldn't hide the dark circles under her eyes or the pallor of her skin. Maren poured Jan a cup of black coffee, which the blond woman accepted gratefully. Jan took an experimental sip, grimaced and blanched.

"Bad night last night?" Maren asked cautiously as Jan lit a cigarette with unsteady hands.

The secretary managed a weak smile and set the coffee aside. "Not the best," she admitted. "But I did manage to finish all of this correspondence." She blew out a thin stream of blue smoke before handing Maren a sheaf of typewritten pages. Maren could see in one quick glance that the papers were letter-perfect.

"You don't have to work after hours," Maren offered, sitting on a corner of Jan's cluttered desk.

"I know. But I've been getting in later and later . . . and . . . well, I feel guilty about it."

"You shouldn't."

"It's not your fault that I can't seem to get my act together." She avoided Maren's probing gaze and picked up the steaming coffee. Uncomfortably she stared into the black brew.

"Jan, is something wrong?" Maren asked gently.

Jan froze before stubbing out her cigarette and quickly lighting a replacement. She had to blink back her tears as she inhaled deeply on the cigarette. "Nothing really," she replied.

Maren didn't move. "You're sure?"

Jan nodded, afraid to trust her voice.

Knowing she was getting nowhere, Maren patiently waited. She cared too much about Jan to see her become a shell of her former self because of a contemptible man like Jacob Green. "Would you like to take your vacation early this year?"

"Look, I'm all right. *Really!*" Jan snapped angrily.

"I'm sorry. I didn't mean to pry." Maren got up from

the corner of the desk, straightened her skirt and started toward the door leading to her office.

"Maren . . . wait," Jan called. Maren turned to face her friend. Jan looked miserable. "I'm sorry," the secretary whispered. "I don't know what's gotten into me . . . no, that's a lie. I do know."

"You don't have to talk about it."

"Maybe I should," Jan murmured. "At least I owe you an explanation as to why I've been getting in late . . ." Maren leaned against the doorjamb. She didn't really want to hear about Jan's personal problems, but she needed to help her friend, if she could.

"I trust you, Jan. If you get in late, I know you've got a good reason."

Jan seemed to wince under Maren's kind words. Tears threatened to spill from her large brown eyes. "Look, I'm a little upset, that's all." She breathed deeply. "We had another fight last night."

"You and Jacob?"

"Right." Jan nodded and pursed her white lips together. For a moment Maren thought she would break down, but Jan squared her shoulders and bravely fought against the tears.

"I take it that it was bad."

"Are there any good ones?"

Maren frowned into her empty coffee cup. "No, I guess not. But some are worse than others."

"It sounds like you've been there."

A wistful smile formed on Maren's full lips. "I've got a few scars," she conceded. "Anyone who's managed to reach the age of thirty-three has seen her share of battles."

"So, are you here offering advice?" Jan asked with just a hint of sarcasm.

"I don't know if I'm qualified to give it. Do you want to hear my opinion?"

"I don't know what I want . . . not anymore," Jan sighed. "You see, there's more to it than just a simple fight." Maren waited, watching grimly as she witnessed the tortured play of emotions distorting Jan's usually cheery features. Her admission came slowly. "I think I'm pregnant."

Maren swallowed and closed her eyes for a moment. "How do you feel about it?" she asked.

For the first time that morning, Jan's smile was genuine and illuminated her pale face. "I'm happy, I think. Can you believe that, the girl who said she'd never have any kids?"

"I think it's wonderful," Maren said with heartfelt enthusiasm. "Congratulations!"

Jan seemed partially relieved. "That's one of the reasons I've been getting in later. . . . I haven't felt all that sharp in the mornings."

"Don't worry about it. It's all right; you certainly have a good reason, and from what I understand, morning sickness doesn't last forever."

"Thank God," Jan murmured fervently.

"How did Jacob take the news?" Maren asked and immediately regretted her question when Jan's face sobered.

"I haven't told him yet," Jan replied, warding off Maren's surprised stare with a wave of her hand. "I told you that we haven't been getting along very well, and that's an understatement. We fight all the time. I'm afraid he'll think I'm using the baby to trap him into marriage."

Maren silently agreed, but decided it was best not to voice her fears. "Give the guy some credit, will you? We're talking about a child—*his* child. I bet he'll be thrilled by the news."

"I doubt it."

"Jan, you've got to tell him sometime."

"I know and I will, once I go to the doctor and find out that I really am pregnant. I have an appointment scheduled for next week." Jan lowered her eyes and fidgeted at the desk.

"You're sure you're happy about this?" Maren prodded.

A shadow of doubt clouded Jan's dark eyes. "Yes, I'm sure. About the baby, that is. But I'm worried about Jake . . . he's changed, Maren . . . a lot. I . . . I don't know how he's going to take the news."

Maren understood Jan's concern, but forced herself to smile. "Don't borrow trouble. You don't know, the man might be ecstatic at the prospect of becoming a father."

"He has grown children and never sees them," Jan replied tonelessly.

Maren winked with feigned enthusiasm. "Maybe *this* one will make the difference."

"I hope so."

Maren turned toward her office, but Jan's whispered voice kept her in the room. "Maren?"

Maren looked over her shoulder, but Jan was no longer facing her. Apparently she had changed her mind. When Jan did meet Maren's inquisitive eyes, the secretary's face was pulled into a tight knot of confusion. "Forget it," she said, reaching for another cigarette. Maren noticed that the second one was still burning unattended in the ashtray near the typewriter. "I'll . . . I'll talk to you later," the secretary said dismissively.

"All right . . . and you'd better check with your doctor soon. I'm afraid he's going to suggest you stop smoking."

"Great. That's just what I need," Jan muttered to herself.

After casting a worried look in Jan's direction, Maren went back into her office and closed the door. Finally she understood the young secretary's behavior. For the last few weeks Jan had been edgy and forgetful, and Maren had suspected it had something to do with her on-again, off-again romance with Jacob Green. Now that her suspicions were confirmed, Maren could at least understand Jan's actions and her reticence to discuss her problems.

Jan and Maren had always been friends, but over the past year, during the time in which Jan had become involved with their former employer, Jacob Green, the relationship between the two women had suffered and sometimes been strained. Maren knew that she was more than partially to blame because she had never liked Jacob, and that fact was transparently clear to Jan. Both Maren and Jan had worked for Green before Maren had purchased Festival Productions fr om him. Now that he was no longer in the business, Maren tried her best to avoid him.

There was something about the man that had always bothered her. Maybe it was because he had made a pass at Maren years ago when she had still been married to Brandon. Since that time, she had never completely trusted Jacob Green. The man was shifty. If it hadn't been for the contract on the business and the fact that she still owed him nearly eighty thousand dollars, Maren would have made it a point never to see him.

And now, to complicate things, Jan was carrying Jacob's child. Maybe a baby would change him; make him realize what was important in life. Maren seriously doubted it, but for Jan and the baby's sake, she pushed her forebodings aside and hoped for the best.

The intercom beckoned her and Maren answered the call. Jan's voice, once again cool and professional, greeted her. "Kyle Sterling is on line two, returning your call."

Maren's pulse jumped. "Thanks, Jan." She sat in the desk chair for a moment to steady her nerves. Why was she so jittery? No man had ever affected her like this, and it was damned unsettling. Resting her forehead in her palm, she cradled the receiver between her shoulder and her ear and pressed the flashing light on the telephone. "Hello."

"Maren? My secretary said you wanted to get in touch with me." His voice was cold and distant. Gone was the intimacy of the night.

"Not an easy thing to do," she allowed.

"I instruct my staff not to give out my telephone number."

"Not even to business associates?"

"To no one."

"I'm sorry to bother you," she replied evenly, though her heart was pounding an irregular cadence in her chest, "but I think I left my briefcase in your car last night."

There was a weighty pause on the other end of the line. "You're sure about that?"

"Yes." Maren couldn't hide the strain in her voice. "Didn't you find it?" Her dark brows drew together. What was he trying to do—scare the devil out of her? The briefcase had to be in his car.

"Wait a minute. I'll check."

"Kyle—" But he was gone. Her mind revolved backward in time, recalling the events of the evening. She remembered putting the briefcase in the backseat. It had to be there. Certainly Kyle had noticed it when he'd driven to work—unless of course he took another car. Maren tapped her fingernail nervously on the desk. The only other alternatives were dismal: Either her briefcase had been stolen, lost, or Kyle was deliberately withholding it from her, though for what purpose, Maren couldn't begin to guess.

"Got it." Kyle's voice broke into her thoughts. "You were right. It was in the backseat."

Maren felt a wave of relief wash over her. "Good. I'll send someone over to pick it up early this afternoon."

There was a deep-throated chuckle on the other end of the fragile cord linking her to him. "Oh, you will, will you?" Why did he sound so amused? Maren's tight nerves got the better of her.

"Is there a problem with that?"

"Not for me. I plan to be here the rest of the week."

"The rest of the week? But it's Friday . . ." Suddenly a dim light dawned in her worried mind. "Kyle, where are you?"

"San Diego . . . I drove down last night after . . . our discussion. I didn't think about your briefcase."

"Neither did I," Maren admitted. "So you're at your home in La Jolla?"

"Uh-huh." Maren could imagine the seductive twinkle in his silvery eyes.

"Great." She glanced at her watch. Though it was still before noon, the drive to San Diego would take over four hours round-trip. It was pointless and a waste of time, except for the fact that she had planned to work over the weekend. She needed her case. Damn!

"Do you need the contracts immediately?"

"It would help—especially considering your proposal."

There was an awkward silence. "I can't bring them to you, Maren."

"I didn't expect you to."

His voice became low and all-too-familiar. "Why don't you come down for the weekend? You can get the contracts and we can work out a few ideas for the Mirage album . . . besides which, I could talk you into selling Festival to me."

"You think so?"

"Sure of it."

The sound of determination in his voice made a chill skitter up her spine. "I'd love to Kyle, but . . ."

"You're afraid." He was angry. She could hear it in his sharp accusation.

"I didn't say that."

"You didn't have to. What is it, Maren? Are you committed to another man? Was last night just an idle flirtation? All that talk about one-night stands and commitments, was that just sophisticated hype?"

"Of course not." Her voice had begun to shake. She had to sink her teeth into her lower lip.

"Talk is cheap."

"What do you mean?"

"Prove yourself. Come down here tonight."

Despite her anger, she forced herself to remain calm. "I don't have to prove anything to you other than that I can produce the best, most artistic and marketable videotapes on the market today."

"You're right, if what you want from me is strictly business. Last night I was left with a different impression."

"I wish I knew what I wanted from you," she admitted.

His tone softened, and when she closed her eyes, Maren could imagine the look of frustration on his rugged face. "Let's find out," he suggested. "We're two adults, and I won't force you into anything you don't want."

"I know that much," she conceded. It wasn't his needs that frightened her; it was her own.

"Then what d'ya say?"

She couldn't help but smile. "All right—why not?" she asked, laughing at the folly of it all. This whole idea bordered on insanity. "I'll need your address and telephone number, just in case I get lost."

"Or have second thoughts."

Her lips pursed into a provoked frown as she scribbled his hasty instructions on a memo pad. After hanging up the telephone, Maren wondered if she had the courage to take him up on his offer, or would she, as he had intimated, back down?

A thousand excuses for avoiding the trip filled her mind, and just as many reasons for going refuted them. It was foolish to get involved with Kyle Sterling. She knew it as well as her own name. And yet, she was enticed by him, drawn to him as a moth to flame.

Chapter Five

The phrase that came to Maren's mind when she first drove through the gates and caught a glimpse of Kyle Sterling's home was "la casa grande." The house was magnificent. Wrought-iron gates and a stucco fence guarded the estate, keeping the curious sightseers at bay. Softly arched palm trees and fragrant hibiscus lined the circular drive leading to the two-storied Spanish home. The exterior of ivory plaster gleamed in the sunlight and contrasted to the angular red-tile roof. Long narrow windows had taken on the hue of the lowering sun.

The house stood proudly on a cliff overlooking the calm blue-green waters of the Pacific Ocean. Maren parked her car near a sprawling garage and tried to ignore the fact that the house and well-tended grounds reflected the image of the man living on the estate—private, wealthy and powerful. She hesitated before getting out of the car and wondered if this weekend might become the single largest mistake of her life.

It wasn't that she hadn't been around wealth. In the recording industry, it was impossible not to run across a young overnight success story who ran through money as if it were water. But dealing with Kyle Sterling was entirely different. Though Maren had often rubbed elbows with the Hollywood elite, she had meticulously avoided being swept up in the Hollywood social tide. It was too fast-moving and dangerous for her. She had refused to get involved with any man since Brandon, and now that she was becoming emotionally entangled with Kyle Sterling, she felt twinges of doubt. What did she really know about the man? Business with a man as powerful as Kyle Sterling was one thing, but a one-on-one relationship was quite another.

Calling herself a fool, she walked up the flagstones leading to the courtyard and tried to bolster her wavering confidence. Don't let all of this overwhelm you, she cautioned herself. Remember that he's only a man. Ah, yes, her worried mind tossed back at her, but a man who wants the one thing you have: Festival Productions!

Maren couldn't ignore the fact that Kyle wanted very much to own Festival Productions and, for that matter, herself as well. He knew that she was the artistic force behind Festival, and there was no doubt that he would do just about anything in his power to entice Maren into selling him her production company. More than anything, she had to keep a level head while in his company. She couldn't allow herself the luxury of trusting him completely, because she understood his motives. How much of his affection for her was sincere and how much was just a part of the game? Was his interest in her merely a well-rehearsed act carefully planned to seduce her into selling Festival? She wanted desperately to believe that he really did care for her, but her common sense instructed her to tread warily.

After stiffening her backbone, she pressed the doorbell and braced herself for another meeting with him. Poise and control were the order of the day. Why then was her pulse racing in anticipation?

Lydia was gone for the weekend and Kyle had awaited Maren's arrival impatiently, watching the clock as the slow hours passed and cursing himself for his own impetuosity. Right now, the last thing he needed cluttering his life was an entanglement with Maren McClure. Why then was he so anxious to see her again?

There was something damnably seductive about that woman. It had captivated him last night and ruined his sleep. He had lain awake for hours, frustrated by urges he hadn't felt in years. It was as if he were compelled to see her again, forced to confront her. He only hoped that the frustration would soon end; that they would become lovers and his lust for her would be satisfied. It would be better for everyone involved if his fascination for her would die a quick death. A quick affair would serve his purpose. He could convince Maren to sell out Festival to Sterling Recording Company, satisfy his physical needs and then be back on track. It had been a long time since he had been with a woman. Maybe that was his problem.

The chimes alerted him of Maren's arrival. Without realizing it, he smiled and the deep furrows of concentration that had lined his brow softened. He opened the door and stared into Maren's incredible blue eyes. Sunlight filtered through the fronds of the palm tree and caught in the dark strands of her hair, streaking the rich auburn color with fiery bursts of burnished gold.

Kyle's smile broadened to touch his eyes as he wedged

himself between the heavy door and the wall. "So you made it," he greeted.

"Were you afraid I wouldn't find the place, it being so small and all?" she returned, showing off just the hint of a seductive dimple.

He cocked an appreciative dark brow. "I try to keep things simple," he responded with a hearty laugh. Moving out of the doorway, he pushed the door open and silently invited her inside. "I'm glad you're here," he admitted, with only a trace of reluctance. His knowing gray eyes were warm and tempting. "I assume you're planning to stay . . ."

"I don't think that would be wise."

"Why not?"

It was difficult dissuading him. He noticed the hesitation in her eyes. "You *are* having second thoughts."

"Maybe. I'd prefer to think of it as considering all of the alternatives and carefully deciding what's the best course of action."

"Boardroom double-talk," he muttered as he motioned her inside the house. "Are you always so . . . poised and careful, Ms. McClure?" he asked as he followed her inside the hacienda and closed the door behind him. That single action seemed to cut the two of them off from the rest of the world.

Maren managed to hide her unease with a composed smile. "I'd like to think that I am," she replied, ignoring the sarcastic bite to his words. "And I would think that you, above all people, would understand my caution, and appreciate it."

"That's the problem. I don't understand, not at all."

She paused for a moment, waiting until her eyes had adjusted to the dim light of the interior, and hoping that she could somehow convey her feelings to him. It seemed important that he understand her.

Once inside the plushly carpeted sunken living room, Maren turned to face the solitary man who made this estate his home. "I don't know you very well," Maren conceded, cocking her head and letting her hair fall away from her face. "In fact, I wasn't sure that you would be here, alone . . . or that you would meet me at the door. I really didn't know what to expect." The expression on Kyle's face was still puzzled, and Maren realized that she wasn't making much sense. She started over.

"Look, Kyle, I know that you run with a pretty fast crowd." His thick brow quirked, indicating that he had heard her. The rest of his face was set in an intent expression as he regarded her silently, patiently waiting for her to continue with her explanation. Fascinating slate-colored eyes held her stare.

"And you don't . . . run with a fast crowd?"

"Right. I'm a little . . . no, make that *very* uneasy with the idea of spending a weekend with a man whom I barely know, and a business associate to boot. I'm not like Mitzi Danner or any of those other glamorous Hollywood types who change lovers as easily as they change shampoos." She shook her head and held her palms skyward in a supplicating gesture. "I'm not apologizing for my sense of values, but I thought you should know that this sort of thing is just too casual for me—not my style . . ."

"Thank God," he murmured, obviously relieved and slightly amused. The laughter in his eyes fueled her unexpected anger.

"I don't even really know what I'm doing here," she admitted. "I shouldn't have agreed to come and should have told you to put the briefcase in the mail!"

"What is it that you're afraid of? Is it me—or men in general?" he asked.

"Fear has nothing to do with this—"

"I think it has everything to do with it," he argued, his

eyes darkening dangerously. "The conflicting signals I get from you lead me to believe that something about me scares you—more than just a little. Now it could be that I intimidate you because I own Sterling Records and Festival strongly depends on its relationship with my company," he suggested calmly. "Or, it might be that you're *afraid* of any kind of relationship with a man, because you let yourself get involved in a bad relationship in the past."

"Or it could be," she said loftily, "that all my instincts tell me that spending a weekend with you might end up to be one monumental mistake!" Unwanted scarlet crept up her neck. "I'm not afraid of you . . . but I'm not . . . easy, either, and I'm not comfortable with the idea of spending a weekend with a man I don't know. Is that so hard to understand?"

Impatience flashed in his eyes. "Damn it, woman," he whispered as he shook his head in disbelief. "How many times do I have to tell you that I like your 'style'?" After crossing the room, he reached for her and traced the ridges between her wrist and fingers with his strong hand. He captured her gaze in the warmth of his stormy gray eyes.

She was still wary. "Does my 'style' include my production company?" she whispered. "Isn't that what you really like about me?"

A muscle near the back of his jaw began to tighten and his eyes bored into hers. "I admit that I'm interested in Festival Productions. You know it, and I haven't tried to hide the fact. I thought I put my cards on the table last night. I'm very interested in your production company." She was about to interrupt but he held a finger to her lips. "But that is *not* the reason that I invited you down here."

"But on the phone you said—"

"It doesn't matter what ploy I used to get you here." He saw the argument forming in her eyes and warded it off. "It won't change things to accuse me of being underhanded," he warned with a rakish grin. "I've heard it before." He took both of her hands in his, forcing her to face him squarely. "I don't want to get involved with you anymore than you do with me, but it seems to be in the cards, wouldn't you say?"

Gently he kissed her palm. Her teeth sunk into her lower lip at the intimacy of the gesture and her heart began to beat in a syncopated rhythm. "I just hope the deck isn't stacked against me."

Again his eyes drilled into hers. "Would I do that?"

"I don't know. Why don't you tell me?" she replied, her voice becoming ragged. He was getting to her, just as surely as if she had willingly let him in to her heart.

"Let's not argue," Kyle suggested, releasing her hand. "I've had enough of that for one day."

Maren was perplexed. "From me?" The sudden tensing of his body warned her that she was prying into forbidden territory.

His gaze clouded. "No." He didn't elaborate and Maren didn't press him. The private battles he was fighting were none of her business and she knew intuitively that the less she became entwined in the personal aspects of Kyle Sterling's life the better. "Can I offer you a drink?" he asked abruptly, effectively changing the subject. When she nodded, he strode over to an ornately carved wooden sideboard that had been converted into a bar.

While Kyle was mixing the drinks, Maren took the time to examine the living room. It was expansive, with an open-beamed ceiling rising a full two floors. A polished tile floor was covered with a tightly woven cream-colored carpet. The furnishings were modern pieces in variegated hues of brown and rust with clean, strong lines. A bank of tall windows facing west opened to a commanding view of the restless azure Pacific Ocean. A few potted plants were casually arranged near the heavier pieces of furniture and watercolors of dusky mountain ridges adorned the walls.

When Kyle turned his attention back to Maren, she was struck by his overwhelming masculinity. She suspected that it wasn't an image he attempted to cultivate, but the power surrounding him couldn't be disguised. He was dressed in faded blue jeans and an open-throated shirt. His arms were bare and bronzed, and when he handed her a glass of amber liquor, his arms flexed to display lean, corded muscles that moved smoothly under his dark skin. He was more ruggedly sensual than any man Maren had ever met, and he wore his masculinity with a pride and near-arrogance that fascinated the woman deep within her. Though she tried to think of him as the opposition and not as a man, she found it impossible.

"Is brandy all right?"

"Fine," she responded, taking the glass. "I try to keep things simple, just like you." She was rewarded with his amused smile. His eyes were warm and seemed to caress her skin. For an awkward moment there was silence. She sipped the drink before motioning toward the watercolors. "Did you do those?"

His smile broadened. " 'Fraid not. My artistic ability is limited to a twelve-string guitar."

"And sheet music."

"Some people would beg to differ on that point."

She smiled and relaxed a little. "But they couldn't argue with your success."

He seemed about to say something, but thought better of it. His eyes became guarded. "That was a long time ago," he whispered.

Realizing that she had touched a sensitive nerve, Maren changed the subject and forced her attention back to the watercolors. The brandy slid easily down her throat as she concentrated on the varied hues of purple and blue. She inclined her head in the direction of the most distinctive work of art. "Do you know the artist?"

Kyle shrugged. "Not really. I met him once and liked his work. He was working on a series of watercolors of the Blue Ridge near the town where I was born. I bought the entire series."

"So this is where you grew up?" Maren asked, eyeing the pictures with new interest.

Kyle corrected her. "You might think so if you listened to my agent for very long. He seemed to like to perpetuate the old rags-to-riches story about a good ol' boy from the Blue Ridge."

Maren focused her attention back on the man. "Isn't that the way it happened?"

"Not exactly . . . you see, my parents moved out here when I was pretty young. I've been a Californian ever since. My agent and my manager didn't think having a client from southern California was nearly as interesting as a genuine country boy from the South. My agent thought it would add to my . . . image. I went along with him."

"And it worked. You convinced the record-buying public that you were the real thing."

"I was. What did it matter where I grew up? They wanted country songs—and that's what I gave them. That's the business we're in, Ms. McClure, or have you forgotten?" He drained his drink and set the glass on a nearby table. "There are a lot of things about me that you don't know—or maybe even have misconstrued. Why don't you take a chance and get to know me better? Stay with me."

He was standing only inches from her. The warmth of his body seemed to touch her skin. "I try not to make a practice of taking chances," she said softly, never letting her gaze waver from his. "They could become dangerous."

"And you're trying to convince me that you aren't attracted by risk?" he asked dubiously. Before she could respond, he continued. "Don't bother to waste your breath. No woman could have achieved what you have without taking a few gambles along the way."

"And the chances I have taken didn't include sleeping with someone to get what I wanted." She tilted her head upward, daring him to pursue the subject.

"I know that. Neither have I."

She smiled in spite of herself. "No female executive ever got you in a compromising position?" she asked.

"Not until now."

Maren's heart seemed to skip a beat. When she raised her glass to her lips, her hands were trembling. There was something disturbing in his quiet gaze and in an instant she realized just how desperately he wanted her. "This is very difficult for me," she admitted, her voice suddenly rough.

"That makes two of us."

The air between them was tense. Maren knew that if Kyle were to touch her, she would fall willingly into his arms. She wanted to believe that his desire for her was more than just physical; she needed to know that there was more involved than lust. The idea of spending the night with a man she barely knew made her uneasy. Things were moving much too rapidly, and it was difficult to keep her feelings for Kyle in perspective.

"I think there are a few things we should get straight," Maren volunteered as Kyle shifted and walked toward the fireplace. He rubbed the back of his neck as if to erase the tension developing between his shoulder blades.

"Ground rules?" He captured her with his questioning gray eyes.

Her smile was frail. "I suppose you might call them that," Maren allowed.

"Okay, shoot." He leaned against the rough stones of the fireplace and crossed his arms over his chest. The fabric of his shirt strained against the muscles of his shoulders and back. One foot was poised on the raised hearth. Maren noticed that his thigh muscle was tightening. Kyle's pose was obviously seductive, and Maren wondered if it were spontaneous or contrived.

"I talked to my lawyer today," Maren began.

His gaze never faltered. No trace of emotion threatened to distort the even features of his face. "And?"

"She advised me—"

"*She?*" he interrupted. His jaw tightened and his eyes seemed to darken dangerously.

"Elise Conrad. My attorney." Maren could read the suddenly wary look crossing his eyes. "This *is* the nineteen eighties, Kyle. There are such things as female lawyers." For a reason she couldn't define, Maren felt defensive.

"Don't I know," Kyle returned evasively. He lowered his chest to his knee, still keeping his gaze fixed on Maren. "What did this woman, pardon me, *your attorney*, suggest?"

"Nothing out of the ordinary. Elise said that you should give me a firm offer for Festival in writing, and that I shouldn't sign *anything* until she has had the chance to go over it."

"Sounds like an attorney," Kyle muttered angrily.

"It sounds fair."

"Then I guess you'd better tell me exactly what you want for your business," he decided aloud. "And I'll want a full financial report on Festival. Then you'd better determine whatever other terms you want: cash outright or contract? Employment agreement? Anything else. I think *my* attorney will insist upon them." His face had hardened menacingly and in a fraction of an instant Maren witnessed a transformation in Kyle. One minute he was a sensitive man intent on seducing a woman, the next he was a ruthless executive bent on only one thing: getting what he wanted for his company.

"You act as if this transaction might get a little vicious."

He shook his head and frowned. "You're the one who brought in an attorney," he reminded her.

"You expected me not to?" She was incredulous. "What kind of an idiot do you take me for?"

His frown disappeared as he gazed into her eyes. "I think of you as a lot of things," he admitted. "But an idiot? Never! I hope that we can accomplish the purchase of Festival without shedding too much blood, but it doesn't hurt to be prepared."

"Are you always so calculating?"

"Only when I have to be, and I'd say that with you, as far as business is concerned, I'm going to have to be careful—damn careful."

"And that bothers you?" she guessed.

He lifted his shoulders and shook his head. "Not really. I just don't want to spend the rest of the weekend arguing about dollars, cents and Festival Productions."

"No?" Cocking her head to the side, she smiled, showing the flash of even white teeth. "Why don't you tell me exactly what it is you want to do?" There was an alluring invitation in her seductive indigo gaze.

Though Kyle was several feet from her, she felt as if they were nearly touching. His eyes caressed her and held her gaze in an intimate and familiar embrace. As he rose and crossed the room, Maren felt her heart begin to pound mercilessly in her chest. His masculinity unnerved her; his self-assured power disturbed her equilibrium. "I just want the chance to get to know you . . ." he replied, reaching her and touching her shoulders lightly. The warmth of his fingers permeated the light fabric of her linen jacket, leaving a torrid imprint on her skin. "Why can't you understand that?"

"I do," she admitted.

"But?" His dark eyes coaxed her.

"But I can't help but think that the owner of Sterling Recording Company might have ulterior motives for seeing me."

"You expect me to seduce you into selling Festival?"

"I expect you to *try*."

"Then what's to worry—since you're onto my game plan?" he mocked, with a twinkle of expectation lighting his eyes. He lowered his head and his lips hovered over hers for a breathtaking instant. "What I wouldn't do for just one chance," he sighed as his lips touched hers in a kiss as warm as it was sensual. Maren didn't move, but felt as if every muscle and bone within her body were melting. Strong lean arms wrapped possessively around her, and Kyle's hand slipped under the hem of her jacket to touch the bare skin exposed by her backless sundress. At the touch of his fingers against the sensitive skin, she shuddered, and she felt his muscles tense. He groaned in frustration as his tongue traced the soft flesh of her lips before probing the warm recesses of her mouth.

A soft sigh escaped her as she hungrily returned the fervor of his kiss. Her heart was beating mercilessly in her eardrums, and a warm ache was uncoiling deep within the most secret part of her. Never had she felt desire so molten; never had she so boldly responded to a man.

"Stay with me," Kyle encouraged as he dragged his lips from hers and kissed the column of her neck. Shivers of anticipation raced down her spine.

With all the effort she could muster, she gently pushed him away, placing her palms on the hard muscles of his chest. "I'll think about it," she agreed.

"What are you trying to do to me?" he demanded, his breath as ragged as her own. "One minute you say no, the next yes. What do you expect from me?"

"Time—"

"I'm not made of stone," he replied. "And neither are you. Do you get a kick out of teasing me?"

"That's unfair, Kyle. Teasing is for children and teenage flirts. I'm only trying to be sensible and go slowly. I don't want to do anything either of us might regret."

His hands fell to his sides. Frustration darkened his eyes. "You don't have to play games with me, Maren. I thought we understood at least that much from our conversation last night. I don't expect you to pretend to be a born-again virgin, for God's sake."

Maren's lips pursed. "Virginity isn't the issue—and really, neither is sex."

"Forgive me, I'm missing the point."

"Casual sex is what I'm worried about."

"You could have fooled me."

She ran her fingers through her hair. How could she make him understand? "You're a very famous man, Kyle. You're used to fan adulation, and groupies—"

"And casual sex," he finished for her.

"Yes!"

"You've been reading too many trashy movie magazines," he accused, "and you haven't listened to a word I've said in the last forty-eight hours." He stalked away from her angrily, only to turn and face her with accusing, omniscient eyes. Every muscle in his face had hardened. "But this really isn't about me, is it? This cat-and-mouse game and talk about commitment has to do with the man who hurt you." She didn't respond and his fist clenched angrily at his side. "If I ever have the misfortune to meet the bastard, I'll personally destroy him," Kyle promised.

The telephone rang impatiently, and Kyle answered it gruffly. The anger seething within him continued to rage. It was a one-sided conversation, punctuated only by Kyle's pointed remarks. "Just who do you think you are?" he asked. "Don't you think you ought to consider Holly's feelings. . . . I wish I could talk you out of this. . . . Take this as a warning; I'm not about to bail you out, not this time, not ever . . ."

Rather than eavesdrop on the personal conversation, Maren decided to leave Kyle and whoever was on the other end of the line in privacy. Earlier she had noticed a door leading from the living room to a covered deck, and when she tried the handle, she found the door unlocked.

Kyle's anger continued to rage, and the last statement Maren heard before the sound of the sea drowned out the remainder of the conversation was ". . . you know that I'm never too busy for Holly," Kyle conceded, disgust audible in his voice. ". . . You'd better believe that you're in for the battle of your life . . ." The rest of his warning was lost to Maren as she quietly closed the door behind her and stood near the wrought-iron railing surrounding the porch. Far below the rugged cliffs was the sea. Maren breathed deeply of the salty air and listened to the roar of the surf as it crashed against the buffer of dark rocks protecting the lonely stretch of sand.

The sun had lowered into the sea, coloring the aquamarine water with streaks of gold. Maren was leaning on the railing, staring at the distant horizon and the dark silhouettes of sailboats when she heard Kyle approach. "I didn't mean to listen in," she apologized, still staring out to sea.

"You didn't." He stood next to her and focused his

attention on a craggy jetty to the north. "Rose always has had an incredible sense of timing," he muttered. At the mention of Kyle's famous ex-wife's name, Maren's stomach knotted. Of course—why hadn't she guessed that he was talking to the petite blond country singer? As if to dismiss his ex-wife completely, Kyle touched Maren on the cheek. "Come on, let's go inside and I'll show you where I work."

Kyle led Maren to the far end of the deck. Opening the door, he escorted her into a room that appeared to be his office. "This is the den," he explained as they entered the oversized room. "When I'm not in L.A., this is where I spend most of my time."

The desk was cluttered with papers. The walls were covered with gold records and pictures of a girl with dark hair and intense green eyes. Maren suspected the portraits were of Kyle's child. The furniture was expensive but slightly worn, and Maren could picture Kyle very much at home in the comfortable, eclectic room with its expansive view of the sea.

Maren's briefcase stood near the desk. She was surprised to note that it seemed to belong in this private room. Dismissing the thought, she picked it up and turned to face Kyle. "I think I should go now," she stated, clutching the briefcase in a death grip.

"You have what you came after?"

She hesitated slightly. "Yes . . ."

"The least I could do is offer you dinner." His voice was low and seductive. The shadowed room began to close in on her.

"You did that last night, and I appreciated it."

"I have reservations at a nearby restaurant, and I'd much rather dine with you than spend the evening alone. It's your choice . . ." He smiled engagingly and Maren knew she'd lost the battle. More than anything else, she wanted to stay with this enigmatic man with the mysterious gray eyes.

A small smile graced her face. "You've convinced me," she agreed. "I'd like nothing better."

The restaurant wasn't far from Kyle's house. The ancient structure had originally housed an order of monks but had fallen into disuse until recently, when it had been renovated into a secluded restaurant and hotel. The original gardens had been restored to lush grandeur, and the ancient woodwork had been polished to a warm luster. The smooth stones of the floor were only partially covered by new carpets, and electricity illuminated the rooms where only candles had burned in the past. Waiters dressed in somber brown robes brought the dishes to the table, and Maren felt as if she had been thrust backward in time.

"Do you come here often?" she asked, taking a final sip of burgundy.

"When I can," Kyle replied. "I like it here; maybe because it's so quiet."

"A strange statement from a man in your profession," Maren observed.

"Not so strange. Everyone needs a little solitude in his life. Especially a person who is a public figure." Candlelight flickered in his eyes, and Maren noticed a deep pain lingering in his gaze. She had the uncanny sensation that she should comfort him, but refrained from putting her hand on his by telling herself to wait and try to remain objective. The feelings beginning to well within her would only complicate her life. She couldn't afford to feel obligated to another man; not now, when she was still tied to Brandon. The fact that she wasn't married to him wasn't the issue: Brandon still depended upon her financially.

Kyle drove back to the house without speaking, and Maren was content to stare into the black night. The silence gave her time to think and consider the situation. She was tempted to stay with Kyle, to spend a weekend of pleasure with this captivating man—and yet, she was wary.

When Kyle parked the car, he withdrew the keys from the ignition before turning to face her in the darkness. His eyes were as dark as the night. "Would you like a cup of coffee?" The question was simple, but another, deeper, unasked question lingered between them. Gently his fingers touched her chin, and her eyes closed.

"Yes," she whispered, accepting anything he could offer and knowing it to be an incredible mistake.

She felt his nearness as he helped her from the car. Though he didn't touch her as they walked toward the house, she could feel his eyes caressing her, and she found herself wanting to know what it was like to be touched by Kyle Sterling.

Upon entering the kitchen, Maren relaxed slightly. In the blaze of the electric lights, the seductive spell woven in the ancient monastery was broken. The kitchen was airy and light. Maren glanced appreciatively at the warm clay-colored tiles and the contrasting hand-painted tiles glazed in rich hues of blue and gold. Green plants were clustered near the windows, and shining brass pots hung from the ceiling.

"A gourmet's delight," Maren commented, running her fingers against the cool tiles.

Kyle smiled as if amused at the thought. "I don't know how gourmet she is, but Lydia seems to like it in here," Kyle observed as he heated the coffee.

"Lydia?" Maren's tongue nearly tripped over the unfamiliar woman's name.

"My housekeeper." Kyle poured the coffee into cups and added a little brandy to the steaming brew. "Actually, she's more than just a housekeeper." Maren swallowed with difficulty. "She helped raise me when my parents moved here from North Carolina. She's a Mexican-American who's lived with me off and on from the time I was nine."

"So much for your country image."

"Just don't let on to my agent."

"You still have one?"

Kyle shook his head. "No. Thank God those days are gone." He frowned into his coffee cup, as if calculating how much of his life story he should divulge to Maren. "Lydia came to work for me after Holly was born . . . but Rose never cared much for Lydia. When Rose and I were divorced, Rose got custody and refused to let Lydia stay on. So Lydia came here to take care of the place."

Rather than dwell on the personal aspects of his story that seemed to make him uncomfortable, Maren changed the subject. "One woman looks after all of this?"

"I let her hire the help she needs."

"Isn't this house a little overpowering for one man?" Maren asked. "Especially when it's your second home?"

Kyle frowned and looked out the window into the darkness. "I guess you could say that," he acquiesced. "I certainly didn't buy it with the intention of letting it sit idle." He set his cup on the table and concentrated on the night. "But, at the time, I didn't know any better. I always thought I would fill it with a lot of kids . . ." He shrugged. "It just didn't turn out that way." His voice and eyes seemed distant, as if he were locked in a past he couldn't accept.

Maren shifted uneasily and set her empty cup next to his. His brooding silence was as uncomfortable as a tight-fitting shroud, and just as bleak. "I didn't mean to pry," she offered, wondering at the pain he silently bore.

"You didn't."

"It's none of my business."

Without hesitation, Kyle crossed the room to wrap his arms possessively around her waist. He was standing behind her and his warm breath fanned the back of her neck. Without thinking about the consequences of her actions, she folded her arms over his, tightening the embrace. His voice was low and persuasive. "I asked you to come and stay with me. I expected you to inquire about personal aspects of my life. It's only natural."

"For some teenage groupie maybe—"

"Shh. . . . For anyone." He kissed the back of her neck and felt the air rush out in a sigh from her lungs. "There are things I'd like to know about you," he admitted, gently tugging on her jacket and removing it.

"Such as?"

"Everything." He tossed the jacket over the back of a chair and guided her toward the door leading to the porch. "Let's take a walk."

"Now?"

He flashed a charming smile—the same smile she had seen in numerous promotional posters when he was still the nation's most-photographed country singer. Slowly he released her waist and took one of her hands in his. "Come on."

He helped her down the worn steps running along the face of the cliff, and when they finally reached the bottom of the stairs, he kicked off his shoes and encouraged her to do the same. "This is the best time of day," he announced with a wicked smile.

"It's night."

"Yes, but the sand is still warm even though the sky is dark."

He coiled his fingers over hers and gently forced her hand into the pocket of his pants. Through the soft lining of the pocket, Maren could feel the movement of his thigh muscles with each of his strides. "So I take it you're a night person," she observed, trying to concentrate on the conversation and ignore the warm flesh straining beneath her fingertips.

He frowned pensively into the incipient night. "I don't sleep much," he admitted. "When I was on the road, late nights were common. I guess I never got out of the habit."

They walked near the ocean's edge. The sand was wet but firm, and their feet left soft impressions near the frothy waves. Occasionally the sea would rush over Maren's bare feet, splashing against her legs and threatening to dampen the hem of her sundress. The first stars began to wink above the fading streaks of light from the sunset.

"I think I owe you an explanation," Kyle decided aloud.

"About what?" Maren noticed the change in his voice. He seemed to be tossing something around in his mind. She slid a glance in his direction and noticed that his frown had deepened into a black scowl. In the darkness his features appeared more severe—as if he had suffered wounds too deep to bear.

"I know that you overheard part of my conversation with Rose."

Maren braced herself. "Not intentionally."

"I know." Kyle smiled sadly. "It doesn't matter. The point is that now that you're here with me, you're entitled to know what's going on."

Maren stopped dead in her tracks, forcing Kyle to do

the same. How much did she want to know of this man? She didn't want to hear anything that might endear him to her further. Her blue eyes held his. "You don't have to tell me anything you don't want to," she whispered. "You're not obligated to say a word about that conversation or any part of your private life. I didn't come here to intrude—"

"Why *did* you come?" he demanded, surveying her with renewed interest. "And don't give me that garbage about Festival Productions; there's more to it than that!"

He took his hand from his pocket and drew her to him. The sea breeze ruffled his thick near-black hair. Danger sparked in his intense gray eyes. His fingers coiled tightly over her bare arms, his jaw clenched threateningly. "Why can't you admit that you came here to be with me? Is that so difficult?"

"Of course I came to see you—"

"Because you want me!" All of the pent-up frustration was tearing at him. He had been patient with Rose, with Holly and now with Maren. But the strain of the last six months was tearing him apart, and he couldn't deal with another woman who wouldn't face the truth.

Anger sparked in her cool blue eyes. "I'll admit that I want you, Kyle, if that's what you want to hear. But I loathe the idea of being compared to one of those starry-eyed teenagers who see you as a God. Country Singer, Record Mogul, Songwriter, *God*."

"I'm only asking that you look at me as a man." His voice was as low as the softly rushing tide. "And that frightens you."

Her lips trembled before she steadied herself. She leveled her gaze upward, giving no hint of the quivering emotions erupting within her. "It would be easy to say that I'm not afraid of you or what you represent, but that would be a lie, Kyle. I am afraid. I'm not used to dealing with men who are so pushy and forward. And I don't know how to react to you!"

"Reactions should be automatic," he replied, pushing his body against hers, fitting his legs around hers, pressing against her, muscle to muscle. The thin fabric of her sundress was a frail barrier against the hard power of his muscular frame.

"When reactions are automatic, and no logical thought controls actions, one person is lost to another." She tried to still the hammering of her heart; attempted to ignore the warm pressure of his hands against the small of her back.

"I wish I understood you," he moaned.

"Try, damn it, just try! Can't you see? I'm trying desperately not to confuse physical lust with mental attraction."

"Is there a difference?" he growled as his lips touched the crook of her neck and a shiver of anticipation skittered up her spine.

"I hope so," she answered. "Dear God, I hope so . . ."

His fingers splayed against the bare skin of her back. The rose-colored halter dress was little defense against the warmth of his palms. His lips touched her eyelids and slid over her cheeks. In a voice that was raw with tortured emotions, he whispered against her ear: "What is it you want from me?"

A lump rose in her throat. "I need to know that this is not just physical need. . . . I . . . I have to know that some of the attraction is mental."

"Oh, God," he swore as if the breath were torn from his lungs. "Can't you see what you do to me? Don't you know that the agony, the frustration, is as much in the mind as the body? Contrary to what you might think, Maren, I'm not a horny teenager chasing anything that

moves. I haven't wanted a woman for some time now."
His broad shoulders slumped with the weight of this
admission. "But with you, it's different. I haven't been
able to think of anything but you since I left you last
night." With one hand he pulled her head away from him,
twining his fingers in the long dark strands of her hair and
compelling her to look into his passion-glazed eyes. *"Last
night was the loneliest night of my life."*

If only she could believe him. She wanted with all of
her heart to think that she alone would make such a lasting
impression on him, but she was realistic enough to
understand that his words were gentle words of seduction.
Their meaning was lost in the warm, enticing mystique of
night.

"Let me make love to you," he coaxed. His head
lowered, and his lips brushed tantalizingly against hers.
"Let me make you feel like the woman you are."

In silent invitation her lips parted and she felt his moist
tongue slide between her teeth. The tongue invaded her
mouth, arousing within her feelings she had thought dead.
She could taste his need; sense the urgency with which he
held her. Warm damp pressure was placed against her
back. His hands kneaded the soft muscles and traced the
length of her spine. A warm flood of prickling desire ran
in her veins, and she sighed against him.

"I want you so badly," she conceded, the ache within
her beginning to burn.

"Don't fight it . . ." His tongue rimmed her lips,
teasing her until she groaned in frustration. Her heart
pounded as loudly as the restless surf, the emotions
grinding within her making her pulse race erratically, the
arguments in her mind slowly dimming. She wanted this
man. With more desire than she had ever before experienced, she wanted Kyle Sterling. Nothing else seemed

important. If she were to fall in love with him, so be it.
Let fate cast her what it would. It had been so long since
she had been with a man . . . so long.

His lips warmed a path from her cheek to her neck. She
rolled her head to the side, exposing more of her throat to
his tantalizing exploration. Her heart threatened to explode within her and a film of perspiration clung to her
skin. His hands moved slowly up her back, tracing the
muscles until he reached under her hair, to her neck, to the
single ribbon that held the bodice of her dress in place.
"Let me undress you," he pleaded hoarsely as his fingers
freed the ribbon. The soft fabric dropped, and the cold
breath of the sea embraced her naked breasts.

"Oh, God," Kyle groaned as he stepped backward and
watched the silvery moonglow caress each of the supple
white mounds. Maren's nipples hardened under his intense stare. Goose bumps rose on her flesh as the sultry
wind brushed over her naked torso and caught her hair,
ruffling it away from her face.

Standing alone, one hand clasping the dress as it draped
over her lower body, her eyes turning silver with the
moonlight, Maren didn't move, but returned Kyle's unguarded stare. Surely he could see the hint of love
lingering in her gaze; surely he knew that she would
willingly give him what she had denied so many.

Kyle raked his fingers through his hair and pondered
whether she was the most regally beautiful woman he had
ever met. He closed his eyes for a second, hoping that
with that one gesture he could stem the rising passion
taking hold of his entire body. Desire throbbed in his
eardrums and heated his loins.

When he opened his eyes, Maren took a step nearer to
him and let go of her dress. It fell limply to the sand,
leaving her naked except for her lacy underwear.

Kyle tried to hold back the passion threatening to take

him over, body and soul. "If I didn't know better, I might think you were seducing me," he whispered, just as she reached him and stood on her toes to press her mouth against his lips. Her arms encircled his neck, and her fingers caught in his hair.

"Isn't this what you wanted?" she asked, trying desperately to understand him.

His throat was dry. "Yes," he whispered, "Oh, yes, but Maren, don't do this to *please* me." The blood was rushing through his body, his fingers sinking into the soft skin around her waist.

"The only person I'm pleasing is myself," she lied, hopelessly lost to the fires he ignited within her.

He groaned against her ear. A deep savage noise erupted from his throat and pierced her soul. His thumbs moved upward, tracing each of her ribs until his hands found the weight of her breasts. She sighed as he fondled her and the aching in her breasts was soothed as his hands traced their shape as if he were sculpting her.

"Undress me," he commanded, taking her hand and pushing it beneath the fabric of his shirt. "I want to be closer to you." Her fingers pulled the shirt over his head, feeling the strength of each of his rippling muscles.

The hard flat wall of his chest crushed against her breasts, and his lips kissed hers heatedly. Gently he lowered her to the sand and managed to kick off his pants. The cold sand pressed against her buttocks and shoulders while the warmth of his body heated her chest and abdomen. "You're more beautiful than any woman has the right to be," he confided. He traced the hollow of her throat with his fingers before letting his tongue rim the delicate bones. The heat in her veins sparked when his tongue flattened between her collarbones and then licked downward to rest between her breasts. His hot breath warmed her skin, the smell of the sea permeating her senses, and his hands, God, his loving hands, stroked her skin, softly kneading it until she thought she would go mad with longing.

Fires raged deep within her; aches demanded to be satisfied. His tongue encircled first one nipple and then the other, teasing the dark points until they were rock-hard and bursting to be soothed. He pressed his mouth over the brown circle and took the entire nipple in his mouth, suckling her with the bittersweet pleasure of his moist affection. Unconsciously she arched upward to meet his body, and her fingers dug into the hard muscles of his back. She wanted more from him—all of him.

In a deft movement he removed her underpants, and she lay naked against the sand. She moaned her need, but he pulled away, taking one last look at her slim nude body on the sand. Moonlight mingled with passion and tinged her eyes an insatiable shade of blue. Her hair was tousled away from her face, and two points of color pervaded her cheeks.

"You do things to me that I can't explain, love," he admitted, moving over her and poising his body atop hers. "I feel as if I've waited all my life for this moment." He lowered his head and bestowed urgent kisses upon her mouth. His body hovered over hers until his weight began to press her down into the cool sand. His legs parted hers slowly, as if by his restraint he could stretch the magic out a little longer; prolong the anticipation until just the right second.

"Make love to me," she pleaded, unable to restrain herself any longer. "Make love to me, Kyle, and never stop."

With a moan of surrender, he claimed her, and her sigh of contentment was lost against the sound of the relentless sea. She felt the heat of his passion, his explosion of desire and her answering shudder of surrender. The weight of his body fell against hers, and she knew the supreme ecstasy of resplendent love. Her body melted against his, and she became aware of his uneven breathing against the shell of her ear. Dear God, Maren thought to herself, how easy it is to love this man!

Chapter Six

The quarter moon cast a thin shifting ribbon of silver on the purple ocean. Stars winked conspiratorially in the blackened sky. Slowly Maren's rapid heartbeat became normal, and she sighed with contentment as she lay in the protective cradle of Kyle's strong arms. His features were shadowed with the night, but the soft moonglow caught in the slate-colored depths of his eyes, making them appear a ghostly silver.

Maren reached upward with her hand and lazily traced the line of his jaw. It was a tender gesture that silently expressed the feelings of love growing within her. He captured her hand with his fingers and kissed her soft fingertips.

"I could get used to this," he admitted roughly.

"So could I."

He pulled on his pants before reaching for her dress and gently easing the rose-colored garment up her legs. It was a natural feeling to have him dress her. As natural as it had been for him to remove her clothes. She lowered her head and lifted her hair off her shoulders, allowing him to retie the ribbon. Her skin tingled where his fingers brushed against the back of her neck. It was a strange seductive feeling—one she had never previously experienced. The few times Brandon had helped her dress had been from necessity only. It had never been an erotic experience. But with Kyle, anything he did with her became sensual. Maybe I've been too long without a man, she worried, but managed to push the unlikely thought aside. Long ago she had learned to live without a man, and although many men had been eager to help her forget Brandon's betrayal, Maren hadn't been interested in anything they had to offer. Until she had met Kyle. Whether she wanted to admit it to herself or not, she was beginning to fall desperately in love with Kyle Sterling; and love was the one emotion she had vowed to avoid. Falling in love with Kyle could only end in disaster, not only personally but professionally as well.

"I said earlier that I owed you an explanation," Kyle said softly as they walked back toward the worn staircase.

"It's not necessary," she replied. She paused to pick up her sandals and slip them onto her feet before taking the hand he offered and climbing the stairs.

"I usually don't talk about my marriage, not to anyone."

"I'm not asking any questions," Maren pointed out. "Just because we made love doesn't mean that I need any explanations or confessions from you. You don't have to tell me anything about your life. What happened between us doesn't change that."

"There are things I would like you to know."

"Not now," she sighed as the cool wind touched her back and the full force of her actions taunted her. Why had she let the intimacy growing between Kyle and herself get so far out of hand? Why had she so willingly offered herself to him? "I don't think we should discuss what happened between you and Rose—at least not for a while."

He hesitated on the steps, and she felt the warmth of his hands on her waist. Rotating to face him, she looked into his eyes. "What are you running from, Maren? What is it about me that scares you?"

"I'm not scared," she asserted, her chin lifting defiantly, "but I'd be a liar if I didn't admit to being overwhelmed . . ." A look of genuine confusion darkened her clear indigo eyes. ". . . I don't know if I'm ready for all of this . . ." she gestured with her upturned palm toward the rambling hacienda and the sea far below.

"Because of your ex-husband?" His voice was low and deadly.

She wanted to lie and tell Kyle that Brandon had no control over her. She needed to explain that her love for her ex-husband had died before ever really blossoming, but the words wouldn't come to her. "I don't love Brandon, if that's what you're inferring."

Leaning insolently against the worn railing, Kyle's gray eyes accused her of the lie. "Then what is it with you? One minute I get the feeling you want me and the next I sense that you're pulling away. It's as if you won't let me get too close."

"I'm just not sure how involved I can be right now," she sighed. The words were difficult to say. "Maybe it would be better if I just left . . . now."

His eyes darkened dangerously as he climbed the two steps separating their bodies. "I want you to stay . . ." Gathering her into his arms, he pressed his lips urgently against hers. His reawakening hunger, savage and raw, was imprinted upon her skin. Her flesh quivered expectantly under his fingertips. "Don't go," he whispered roughly against her ear. "Stay with me." Once again his lips found hers in an urgent kiss that silently conveyed the depth of his passion. Warm fingers splayed against her back, and the reasons for leaving him faded into the night.

She dragged her head away from his, hoping that she could find the strength to deny what she so desperately wanted. "I think it would be better if I returned to L.A. tonight. I need time to think things through."

"I'm not asking for a commitment for the rest of your life," he reminded her gently.

"I know." She pulled out of his embrace and felt a pang of regret when he didn't attempt to stop her.

"I'm not a man to beg," he stated, dark brows drawing over his eyes.

"Good. That will make it easier, won't it?" she managed to reply, hoping to hide the reluctance in her voice. "I'll get the briefcase—" She hurried up the remainder of the steps and raced into the den. By the time he caught up with her, she had the briefcase tucked safely under her arm. "I'll let you know about my decision concerning the sale of the production company after I talk to my attorney."

He nodded curtly, responding as if he were in a boardroom, with no hint of emotion registering on his rugged features. Handing the jacket to her, he let his fingers touch hers for a moment, but still his face showed no sign of feeling.

His jaw was tight. "And I suppose that you'll do your best work on the series of videos for Mirage."

"You can count on it," she responded, her clear blue eyes holding his gaze evenly.

"So that's the way it is—all business with you."

"When it has to be."

A shadow of frustration blackened his eyes, but was

quickly disguised as she turned toward the door. ''Good night, Kyle,'' she called over her shoulder, not expecting or receiving a response. He began to follow her, but stopped at the front door and frowned to himself as he watched her leave.

Maren slipped into her car and hesitated only slightly before pushing the key into the ignition and putting the car in gear. Caught in the reflection of her side-view mirror, the well-lit Spanish house stood proudly in the night, silently watching her leave. A sadness settled into her heart as Maren realized that she had just abandoned the most interesting man she had ever met. The darkness of the night seemed to taunt her as she remembered Kyle's warm, inviting embrace.

The remainder of the weekend passed uneventfully for Maren, and though she hoped that Kyle would call, she was disappointed. She tried to keep herself busy and concentrated on ideas for the Mirage videos, but she couldn't put thoughts of Kyle or their short time of lovemaking out of her mind.

When Monday morning finally came, Maren was up at the crack of dawn. As Maren walked through the doors of Festival Productions, the real world came crashing back to her and the distant thoughts of Kyle were replaced by her concern for the production company. When she sat down at her desk, she realized that time had stopped for Festival Productions and the same nagging problems she had left behind her on Friday were still waiting to be solved. Added to her already weighty work load were her concerns about the company. Kyle had insinuated that Festival might still have a problem with pirated videotapes. Though Kyle's manner had been unsuspicious and casual, Maren had been left with the impression that he was concerned about the problem and had brought up the bootlegged tapes as an obscure warning.

As she considered the conversation about the piracy, Maren took the cassette from her purse and placed it in the tape player. Rather than dwell on Kyle's cryptic remarks, she decided to tackle the work ahead of her. Slowly an idea for the Mirage videos was beginning to form in her mind. She pressed the play button on the tape deck and within a split second the inflamed lyrics of "Yesterday's Heart" filled the small office. Maren leaned against the back of her chair, closed her eyes and tried to study the words of the song, but she was unable to block out Kyle's strong image. Would he be like the unfaithful lover in the song? Dear God, she hoped not. Despite her brave words of the night before, Maren prayed that Kyle's lovemaking was a form of commitment.

Would it be possible for a man of Kyle Sterling's wealth and reputation to love her with even a fraction of the emotion she harbored for him? She shook her head and pressed her eyelids tightly closed, trying vainly to dispel her love. If she sold the production company to Kyle, she would have to work for him and see him frequently. Was it possible to be an employee by day and lover at night? What would happen if she sold her equity in Festival Productions and Kyle decided that he wasn't interested in her? Could Maren, like the hero in "Yesterday's Heart," pull herself back together?

The disturbing questions rattled around in her mind, nagging at her until the final strains of the song faded. Without thinking, Maren quickly rewound the tape and listened to the song again. The idea for the video began to expand and she envisioned an action sequence during the final refrain. Absently she started jotting notes to herself as she heard someone arrive in the outer office. Just as the throb of the music disappeared, Jan entered Maren's office with two cups of steaming coffee.

"Mirage?" Jan inquired, placing a cup on Maren's desk. Maren smiled gratefully at the blond secretary. There were deep circles under Jan's brown eyes, evidence of more than one poor night's sleep.

"Yes." She took a sip of the coffee. "Thanks," she murmured, as she set down her pencil and leaned back in the chair. "It's a song called 'Yesterday's Heart': the first single to be released from Mirage's next album."

Jan held up her palm. "Slow down," she suggested. "The last I heard, Festival didn't have a signed contract on that album." Before Maren could respond, the secretary caught on. "Don't tell me—let me guess, the infamous Kyle Sterling, as I predicted, fell at your feet like a penitent lover."

Maren was forced to smile at Jan's graphic image. "Not quite," she replied, "but I did manage to get him to sign a few of the contracts."

"The gentle art of persuasion," Jan surmised.

"I think we're back in business, at least for the time being," Maren admitted with obvious relief.

Jan withdrew a cigarette from her purse. "I just hope that one of the contracts belongs to Joey Righteous. That kid's been driving me crazy . . ." She inhaled deeply on the cigarette and blew a thin stream of smoke toward the ceiling. Some of the tension left her wan features.

"Unfortunately for Joey, we're going to have to concentrate on the Mirage videos first," Maren asserted, regarding her friend with worried eyes. Jan looked as if she hadn't been able to rest for over a week.

"Joey's going to be fit to be tied," Jan predicted.

"Isn't he always?"

The secretary chuckled and nodded her blond head in agreement. "Yeah, I suppose he is."

Maren took another sip from her cup and tapped her pencil nervously on the desktop. She was concerned about Jan and hoped the secretary would open up to her. Even though Maren considered Jan a friend, she hated to pry into her personal life. "Has anyone from production managed to make it in today?"

Shaking her head and blowing out a cloud of blue smoke, Jan frowned. "Not yet, but Ted thought he'd be in around eleven. He's helping edit the final takes of the Mitzi Danner release—"

" *'Going for Broke?'* " Maren guessed.

"That's it."

"Is there a problem with it?" Maren asked, her dark brows pinching together in worry. The last thing she needed was a problem with Mitzi Danner, whose hot temper was as well-known as her sensual songs. "I thought that tape was supposed to be finished last week."

"It was."

"So there was a problem." Maren experienced a sinking sensation.

"What do you think?"

Smiling at the private joke, Maren looked questioningly at Jan. "Okay, so fill me in—what happened?"

"Don't panic—it wasn't anything *too* serious," Jan said with an amused laugh. "There were a couple of outdoor shots that came out too dark—probably because the sun had already set by the time Mitzi managed to get herself ready. The final scene of the song was supposed to be backdropped by a setting sun—"

"I remember."

"Anyway, when Ted realized that the scene was too dark, he convinced Mitzi to reshoot over the weekend."

"I bet she loved that," Maren observed sarcastically.

"Well, according to Ted, Mitzi managed to pout throughout the filming." Jan laughed aloud at the image.

"Actually, Ted was pleased; Mitzi's petulant look was perfect for the take."

"Thank God for small favors." Maren leaned her head against the back of the chair and ran her fingers through her hair thoughtfully. "Let's hope the final takes were okay. I'd hate to be the one to have to call Mitzi and explain that we had to do it all over again."

"Amen," Jan agreed, with a frown. "You've never been too crazy about her, have you?"

A fleeting image of Mitzi draped over Kyle's arm near a swimming pool flashed through Maren's mind. "Are you kidding?" Maren replied lightly. "I've got every record she ever released."

"You're hedging," Jan accused.

"And you're right. I really don't have any problem with Mitzi. She's a good client, and she has a tremendous talent for picking the right songs to complement her style."

"But," Jan coaxed.

"I could do without the prima donna routine."

"You and me both." Jan stubbed out her cigarette and slowly pulled herself out of the chair. The color drained from her face as she straightened.

"Are you all right?" Maren asked with genuine concern. She noticed the expression of pain on Jan's tired features.

Jan offered her boss a tentative smile, hoping to ease Maren's mind. "As well as can be expected."

"I assume that means you've seen a doctor."

Jan's nervous smile broadened, but there was a catch in her throat when she tried to speak. "I went this morning. It's official: I'm going to have a baby early in November."

"Jan! That's wonderful!" Maren exclaimed, expressing her heartfelt enthusiasm. "Have you told Jacob yet?"

Jan took in a deep breath. "No," she admitted reluctantly, "but I will, tonight or later in the week. He's been pretty moody lately, so I think I'd better wait until just the right moment before I spring it on him."

"You might be surprised by his reaction."

"I doubt it," Jan confided, pursing her lips together in order to hold back the tears burning behind her eyes. Visibly straightening her shoulders, she managed to slip her poise back into place by turning the conversation away from Jake and the baby. "So tell me, how did you manage to get Mr. Sterling to sign those contracts?"

"Careful negotiation," Maren joked, hoping to lighten the somber mood that had settled on Jan's slim shoulders.

"Negotiation?"

"That's right. It seems that Sterling Recording Company is very interested in buying out Festival Productions. Kyle wants me to sell my interest to him and continue to run the operation from the recording company. It would be an easy way for Sterling Records to start producing their videos in-house."

Jan looked as if she'd been struck. "But surely you're not considering his offer—"

"It might be the answer to our problems," Maren stated. Why was Jan so distressed? The poor girl actually looked as if she were frightened of something. Maren noticed the trembling of Jan's lower lip and the widening of her dark eyes.

"But you've worked so hard to make it on your own!" Jan protested vehemently. "Are you going to give up all your freedom, your artistic license, all this . . ." With her arm she made a sweeping gesture to encompass the furnishings of the office.

"I'm considering it," Maren stated evenly, trying to understand Jan's uncharacteristic paranoia.

"Why?"

"First of all, I wouldn't be giving up that much; I'll

have everything I want written into the contract of sale, and secondly, Festival needs a more secure future. How much longer can we survive living from contract to contract?''

''But things have just started to turn around! I know for a fact that J. D. Price will have no one but you handle his videos. Even Joey Righteous thinks you're divine, and that's a mighty big compliment from someone who considers himself a deity.''

Maren tried to placate the anxious secretary. ''Jan, what's wrong? Nothing is going to change—at least, not significantly. Everyone in production will still work under me. It's just that Sterling Records will be my employer. We'll all be a lot more secure, and that includes the record company. Kyle feels that he needs tighter control on the videos.''

Jan's entire body tensed. ''Why?'' she whispered, looking as if she expected the roof to collapse.

''Videos are big business. They've turned the recording industry slump around. Sterling Records wants to cash in on them now, while they're hot. No matter what *I* do, Kyle Sterling is determined to produce the videos in-house. I'm just lucky that he wants to work with me instead of edge me out of the business.''

Jan leaned against the wall, and her brown eyes narrowed suspiciously. ''Don't you think that's exactly what he's doing?''

Maren smiled, trying to hide the doubts forming in her own mind. ''No, I think he's sincere.''

''Then why didn't he sign *all* the contracts?''

''I didn't press him, I guess.''

Jan's expression hardened. ''That doesn't sound like you. What's happened to you, Maren? You've never let a man push you around before.''

''I don't think I'm being pushed, Jan.'' It was Jan's

tone of voice more than her accusation that made Maren uneasy.

"Don't tell me that you've started to fall for the guy . . ." When Maren didn't immediately respond, Jan rolled her eyes expressively toward the ceiling. "Don't do it, Maren. Don't let that guy get to you. He has a reputation as long as my arm for using women. Don't you remember what a field day the press had covering his divorce from Sterling Rose? And then, what about all the women and men he stepped on to get where he is today! Even Mitzi Danner didn't get away from him unscathed."

"Look, Jan," Maren interjected, hoping to quell the tide of anger welling within the secretary. "I told you I was considering his proposal to buy out my interest in Festival. Until I see a firm offer in writing, I won't make up my mind."

"It sounds as if you already have," Jan stated weakly.

"For the time being, nothing's changed," Maren assured the young woman. "And I just wanted to let you know what was going on. I didn't mean to upset you. You don't have to worry about your job."

"How can you be so sure of that?" Jan charged. "What do you know about Sterling Recording Company and the way it handles its employees. Kyle Sterling has a reputation for being a very shrewd and ruthless businessman. He'll step on anyone who gets in his way. There're just no two ways about it, the man's an A1 bastard!"

Maren stood her ground. Her blue eyes were determined; her soft voice was calm. "I've heard about his reputation, Jan. I haven't gotten where I have by hiding my head in the sand. But I've also met the man, and I think he's going to play fair with me."

"How do you know that? You're talking about everyone who's involved with Festival. All of our futures are at stake!"

"And I won't let anyone, including Kyle Sterling, pull a fast one on me. If you don't trust me, certainly you can rely on Elise Conrad, Festival's attorney. Everything will be reviewed by her office before I make a final decision. Don't worry," Maren urged with an indulgent smile. "Everything's going to work out very well."

"Since when did you become an optimist? Since meeting Kyle Sterling?" Jan asked, still visibly shaken. "What exactly happened between the two of you?"

"Not much," Maren evaded. "We met and talked business and got to know a little more about each other."

"Oh, Maren," Jan sighed, seeing through Maren's words. Jan hesitated in the doorway and stared at the floor before raising her dark eyes to meet Maren's questioning gaze. "What you do with your personal life is none of my business," she began uneasily, "but I just hope you're careful. I'd hate to see you become another one of Kyle Sterling's conquests. From what I understand, he'll destroy anyone or anything he considers a threat." The secretary attempted a smile and failed miserably. "Don't get into anything you might regret later," she advised.

"Such as enter a relationship with Kyle Sterling?"

"Such as getting involved with the wrong man." Without another word, Jan left Maren's office, leaving her employer to wonder if Jan was offering advice from her own experience. But why the absolute hatred of Kyle? From the look on Jan's face, Maren could tell that Jan's relationship with Jacob Green hadn't improved. Perhaps that was the cause of Jan's distress. If her situation with Green was insecure, the pressure of the pregnancy coupled with a change in job status might account for the young woman's concern about the sale of Festival. But it didn't explain Jan's angry remarks about Kyle.

Maren tried to shake the uncomfortable feeling enveloping her and concentrate on the storyboards for the

Mirage videos. The theme tying the separate cuts of the album together was taking shape in her mind, and she worked furiously on her sketches for the rest of the day, pausing only during lunch to discuss her idea with Ted Bensen, who was in charge of the production crew.

It was nearly five when she received the call from Kyle.

"Kyle Sterling's on line one," Jan announced with audible reluctance.

"Thanks," Maren replied before pressing the lighted button on the telephone.

"Maren?" Kyle's rich voice called to her before she had a chance to answer. The sound of her name reminded her of the night she had lain in his arms. The moon had cast its silvery glow over the sea before resting in Kyle's gaze. He had lain over her, whispering words of love into her ears. Her heart hammered mercilessly in her rib cage.

"I was beginning to think I wouldn't hear from you." Her tone was light and carefree and disguised the misgivings that had plagued her. Jan's warning echoed in her ears: *"He'll destroy anyone he considers a threat."*

"I've been busy," was the abrupt reply. "But I did manage to call my attorney. He promises that you'll have an offer for Festival within the week."

"And I assume that you want an immediate response."

"As quickly as possible." There was a moment of hesitation. "You can get hold of me here. I doubt that I'll be in the office for a couple of weeks."

"What about the other contracts—there were a few you didn't bother to sign."

"You can bring them with you, with the sales agreement."

"You expect me to bring them to La Jolla?" she asked incredulously.

"If you want them signed. I won't be back in L.A. for a while."

"I'll have to have my attorney look over the sales contract," Maren stated, slightly unnerved by his totally businesslike tone.

"I realize that. Call me when you've made your decision."

With his final words, he hung up the phone, and Maren was left with the disturbing feeling that Jan's warnings were about to come true.

Chapter Seven

One week stretched into two and Maren had had barely a moment to herself. The days at the office were a whirlwind of paperwork, meetings and production schedules. Maren drove herself at a furious pace until late each night. Somehow she managed to keep up with the bookkeeping, correspondence and client relationships, along with creating a complete set of storyboards for each of the five cuts on the Mirage album. J. D. Price had tentatively approved her story lines and had only offered a few bits of advice about changing a couple of action sequences. The next man to tackle was Kyle. As far as Maren knew he was still in La Jolla.

The short nights crept by at a snail's pace. Though Maren felt dead on her feet by the end of each day, she was unable to fall asleep promptly when she finally crawled under the covers and collapsed in a weary heap. Thoughts of Kyle crowded her tired mind, and her body ached for his gentle touch. Memories flooded her senses when she thought of the one night she had spent with him, and she wondered if she would ever feel the warmth and power of his arms around her again. Or had that one solitary night meant nothing to him?

Thursday morning the ringing of the phone jarred her out of her restless sleep. Muttering angrily to herself, she reached for the telephone and knocked the receiver on the floor before summoning enough dexterity to grasp the slippery instrument. "Hello?" she mumbled ungraciously into the phone.

"Maren?" Kyle asked. "I realize that it's early—"

"I guess." Maren smiled and yawned. It felt good to wake up to the sound of his voice. "What time is it?" She forced her gaze to focus on the digital display of the clock radio near the phone. "Six o'clock!" She rubbed her hands over her eyes before raking her fingers through the tangled strands of her hair. "No one in his right mind calls at this hour," she accused with a sigh.

"It was now or never. I doubt that I'll be near a phone for the rest of the day and I wanted you to know that I'll be in L.A. late this afternoon." There was a weighty pause in the conversation. "I was hoping that we could meet to discuss the Mirage videos and my offer on Festival. You have made a decision, I assume."

"Not until Elise Conrad approves," Maren hedged.

"Has she seen the offer?" Kyle's voice had become strained. Maren could hear it in the sharpness of his words.

"I sent it to her on Monday."

"Good. Then maybe we can tie all the ends together tomorrow before I have to return to La Jolla."

"I doubt if it will be that easy," Maren replied.

"I don't have much time."

Maren's lips pulled into a frown. Why was he pushing

so hard? Was he afraid she might back out of the sale? Was it *that* important to Sterling Records? "This is a big decision for me, you know."

There was an exasperated sigh on the other end of the connection. "I understand that, Maren, but I'm caught between a rock and a hard spot. The sooner this sale is complete, the better for everyone involved, including you. Right now, I can't afford not to produce the videos at Sterling Records. If you're not going to accept my offer, or at the very least negotiate a deal, then I'll have to hire someone else to establish Sterling videos on the market. As I said before, I don't have a hell of a lot of time to waste while your attorney nitpicks through each clause of the contract."

"You don't like the idea of attorneys being involved in this, do you?" Maren charged.

"I've dealt with quite a few in my time—"

"And obviously been burned," Maren interjected angrily before managing to regain control of her temper. Kyle Sterling was too important a client to infuriate, and regardless of her conflicting emotions toward the man, she had to remain rational and calm. "Look, Kyle," she said more calmly, "I'll see what I can do. I'll call Elise this morning and find out what she thinks about the offer."

"I'd appreciate it," he responded curtly. "Can you meet me at my office?"

Maren mentally reviewed her schedule. "I think so. What time?"

"How about four?"

"I think that will work out. I want to bring along the storyboards for the Mirage videos: It's time we put "Yesterday's Heart" into production."

"I'll see you then." He paused for a moment, as if he might have something more to add. Maren waited while her heart pounded in anticipation. If only he could let her know that what they had shared together was more than just an idle afternoon of passion. . . . "Good-bye."

"Good-bye," Maren whispered as she heard him sever the fragile connection. A dull pain twisted in her heart. She set down the phone and leaned back into the pillow. What had she expected, anyway? Maren knew that Kyle's primary interest in her was Festival Productions; he'd admitted as much. She also realized that he was attracted to her and probably, in his own sophisticated way, cared for her. But the love she felt for him could never possibly be returned. It just wasn't possible, no matter how desperately she wanted to believe that he loved her. "No sense in deluding yourself," she mumbled miserably as she tossed back the covers and compressed her lips into a line of disgust. Knowing that falling back to sleep was completely out of the question, Maren reached for her robe and decided to go into the office early. There were still a few details she had to straighten out on the first Mirage video, and she wanted everything in perfect order when she met with Kyle later in the day.

The parking lot was usually empty. This morning was an exception. The warm morning sunlight reflected brightly off the sleek imported sports car parked in front of the building housing Festival Productions.

Maren parked her car and approached the building. As she neared the silver import, Jacob Green extracted himself from the vehicle. He was a slim man of medium build with perfectly combed sandy-colored hair and an equally manicured smile. Maren knew that Jake had to be pushing fifty, but he managed to keep himself fit and looked a good ten years younger than his age.

"Hi, Maren," Jacob greeted, falling into stride with her as she headed up the concrete steps.

Maren forced an uneasy smile onto her face. "Good

morning." After unlocking the glass door, Maren stepped inside the building. Jacob Green was quick to follow her, and Maren felt an uneasy sensation take hold of her.

"If you're looking for Jan," Maren said, picking up the newspaper that had been forced through the mail slot near the door, "she's not here yet." Certainly Jacob knew of Jan's whereabouts, Maren thought; Jan was living with him.

"Actually," Jacob replied smoothly, "I wanted to see you."

"Oh?" Maren lifted her eyes from the front page of the *Los Angeles Times,* and started up the stairs. "What's up?"

"I thought you and I could discuss our contract on Festival," Jake suggested.

Maren was instantly wary, and her back stiffened. "Is there a problem?"

"Not yet." His words were cryptic, and they made her uneasy. It took every ounce of civility within her to hang on to her poise.

"Good. Why don't you wait for me in my office," Maren suggested as she mounted the stairs. Jacob was only a couple of steps behind her, and she had the uncanny feeling that he was eyeing her hips as she climbed the stairs. "I'll get us each a cup of coffee."

"Great!" They reached the second floor and Jake started toward Maren's office. "Don't forget the sugar." He disappeared into the other room.

"Wouldn't dream of it," Maren mumbled to herself. There was just something about the man that made her anxious and unnerved. It didn't help matters to know how unhappy Jan had been recently. Jan had never mentioned telling Jacob about the baby, and Maren had never pried. It was evident that something was eating at the poor girl, but the one time Maren had commented on that fact, Jan had told her nicely but firmly that it was really none of her concern. Rebuffed and slightly embarrassed, Maren hadn't mentioned the situation again.

"Here you go," Maren announced, setting a cup of coffee along with several sugar cubes next to Jake's chair. "Now tell me, what is it you want to discuss?"

Maren took a seat behind the desk, feeling more comfortable with the large piece of furniture separating her from Jacob. The barrier, however frail, gave her some sense of strength. Jacob stirred his sugar into his coffee and took a long swallow. When he looked up at Maren he hoped his smile seemed sincere.

"You always could make a great cup of coffee," he stated with a slippery grin.

"And you've been known to beat around the bush. I'm really very busy today, Jake. In fact, I've got a nine-o'clock appointment. So why don't you tell me what it is that's bothering you about the contract?"

"It's no big deal, really," he said, shrugging his shoulders. Maren could tell by the way he avoided meeting her gaze that he was lying. Whatever it was, it was very important to Jacob Green. Something was up. Something big. "I was hoping that you could make the May *and June* payments on the fifteenth."

Maren regarded him silently for a moment. She would like nothing better than to pay him his money and send him packing. Dealing with him had always been difficult. Her blue eyes narrowed as she considered the possibilities. Finally she shook her head. "I'm sorry, Jake, but I just can't swing it. If I remember correctly, the June payment escalates by another thousand dollars. There's just no way I can stretch my budget right now, at least not until I get some cash from the April billings, and they just went out."

Jacob's friendly smile faded, and he set his cup on the

table. "Can't you work something out, Maren? I'm really strapped right now." He stood from the chair and pushed his hands into his back pockets as he faced her.

Maren managed to conceal her surprise. She had always assumed that Jacob was well-heeled. Not only had he received a large amount of cash when she had purchased Festival, but she paid him monthly on the contract. The last she had heard he was working at Sentinel Studios. Where could his money be going?

"I just can't handle a larger payment this month."

Jacob's eyes traveled around the room, noting the few but expensive pieces of furniture. From what he could discern, Maren's operation was doing well—very well— and the gossip in the industry indicated that her services as a producer of videotapes were in considerable demand. He changed his tactics.

"Jan tells me you might be selling the business."

The hackles on Maren's neck rose. She had expected her secretary to hold her tongue. But that might not have been possible, considering Jacob's link to Festival. "That's right," Maren conceded unwillingly. "I'm considering the possibility. Nothing more."

"Jan seemed to think it was all wrapped up." Once again Jacob took a seat. He felt as if he had unwittingly gained the advantage in the discussion. Lines of worry creased Maren's normally smooth forehead.

"I'm still thinking about it," Maren hedged. As far as she was concerned, what she did with Festival Productions was none of Jacob Green's concern as long as she paid him off.

"You still owe me about eighty thousand dollars," Green pointed out with a bitter smile.

"I realize that."

"I just wanted to remind you that the contract is nontransferable. I want my share in cold hard cash."

"And that's what you'll get," Maren assured him. "If and when I decide to sell."

"Damn it all, I never thought that videos would take off the way they did," Green admitted with a trace of disgust. "If I had, you can bet I never would have sold this operation to you!"

"When I bought Festival, you were concentrating mainly on commercials," Maren observed. "I don't think you had even thought of doing videos."

"Yeah, well, maybe that's true. But you can bet that I would have changed course once I'd figured out how hot those videos would become. They're a goddamn gold mine!"

"I told you that before you sold the business to me," Maren pointed out. "You didn't listen."

Jacob waved off her words with the back of his hand. "How was I to know they weren't going to be some overnight flash-in-the-pan fad that was here today and gone tomorrow. Son of a bitch!"

Jan entered Maren's office, and her dark brown eyes took in the scene before her. Maren was surprised and grateful for Jan's arrival. "Jacob?" Jan asked uneasily, her thin lips pulling into a tight smile. "What're you doing here?" Her liquid brown eyes accused Jacob of something Maren couldn't understand. It was probably another lovers' quarrel and none of Maren's business, she decided, trying to find an excuse to leave the two of them alone.

Jacob was immediately defensive. "I was just havin' a chat with Maren, babe," Jake replied with an uncomfortable grin. He rubbed the back of his neck after setting his coffee cup aside. "You know," he cajoled, seeing Jan's obvious distress, "it's about that time again. The rent's due, so to speak." A flush of scarlet crawled up Jan's neck, disguising her wan pallor.

Trying to pull herself together, Jan ignored Jacob for

the moment and looked toward Maren. "Joey Righteous will be here at nine," she reminded her employer as she crossed the room and placed a stack of neatly typed letters on the corner of Maren's desk.

"Should I have my attorney present?" Maren joked, and Jan forced a laugh despite the disturbing situation. Jacob looked from one woman to the other, not completely understanding the private joke.

"I don't think it will be necessary today," Jan said, relaxing slightly.

"Good." In an effort to get rid of Jacob Green, Maren pulled the checkbook from her file cabinet and wrote a check for the May-fifteenth contract payment. Jacob took the check and stuffed it into his wallet while Jan effectively ushered him out of Maren's office.

Angry portions of the argument between Jan and Jacob filtered through the closed door. Though Maren switched on the tape player and concentrated on the third song to be released from the Mirage album, she couldn't shake the feeling of concern overtaking her. Maren cared for Jan, and it was apparent that the secretary was very unhappy. Something wasn't right between Jan and Jacob, and Maren suspected it was more than just the pregnancy. Jan hadn't been herself lately. She was nervous and jittery. Perhaps it was because of the pregnancy, but Maren doubted it. Maren had never known Jan to attack anyone; she was a reserved girl who usually kept her opinions to herself. But the other day, without provocation, Jan had verbally assaulted Kyle. It was unusual. Obviously Jan was under a tremendous amount of pressure from Jake.

Maren's musings were cut short when Joey Righteous burst into the room. He was sporting a black leather jacket, dark sunglasses and tight-fitting red leather pants. He looked the part of an overnight R & B sensation. "Hey, Mama, what's happenin'?" he asked as he sprawled into one of the chairs. His charming smile spread evenly across his dark skin, exposing perfect white teeth.

Maren returned the smile. Despite his infamous hot temper, Joey Righteous boasted a certain charisma that couldn't be denied. "Save the 'bad, black and beautiful' routine for someone who'll buy it," she returned with a knowing laugh. "You might be able to convince the record-buying public that you're just a poor ghetto kid from the streets of Chicago, but I know for a fact that you graduated from Stanford."

Joey exaggerated his cringe and put his finger to his lips. "No more of that talk," he whispered. "You'll destroy the image."

"Impossible." She eyed the gaudy outfit and grinned in amusement. "No one would ever believe that you graduated with honors in math."

"Shame on you," Joey accosted, lifting his dark glasses and giving Maren a glimpse of his sparkling black eyes. "You been checkin' up on me."

"Just doing my homework—same as you."

Joey, anxious to get down to business, slapped his broad palm on the desk as if to change the subject. "So how's my video comin'?"

Maren leaned back in her chair. Her blue eyes never left Joey's dark gaze. "I'm afraid it's been put on hold for a little while."

"*What?*" he shrieked. "What you talkin' 'bout?" Anger sparked in his dark eyes.

"Your contract with Festival hasn't been signed by Sterling Records."

"Why not?" he demanded.

"It's nothing serious," Maren said, holding up her palms as if physically attempting to soothe him.

"Oh, yeah? Tell me about it!"

"I'm taking your contract with me today. I have a meeting with Kyle Sterling. I'm sure he'll sign the contract, and we can proceed with the video. Then I expect there will be no further delay."

"Sounds like double-talk to me," Joey complained. "Or honkie bull . . ."

"Not from me, Joey. We've done business for a couple of years now, and we haven't had a problem, have we?" She didn't wait for his reply. "I promised you that the video would be complete before your tour of Japan. I'm sure Sterling Records will agree."

"You ain't jivin' me?" Joey asked, unconvinced.

Maren shook her head, keeping her warm smile intact. "No, but if I do have a problem with Sterling, which I don't anticipate, I'll let you know immediately. What do ya say?"

Joey frowned pensively, and his head bounced to an angry beat. "I don't know."

Maren pushed away from the desk, stood and walked over to her long cabinets. Bending on one knee, she pulled open a drawer and extracted her sketches. She handed them to Joey. "Here are the storyboards for 'Restless Feelin'.'" Joey balanced his sunglasses on the top of his head as he studied the drawings. "What do you think?" Maren asked when Joey raised his head.

"You sure know your business," he admitted with a low whistle.

"I try."

Plopping his shades back onto his nose, he rose from the chair and towered over Maren. "What's this I hear about bootlegged videos?"

Maren's smile froze. "What do you mean?"

"Didn't Festival have trouble a while back?"

"There was a problem. It's been corrected."

"I hope so," Joey whispered. His dark face seemed suddenly threatening. "I wouldn't like it if my video was pirated."

"Neither would I."

Rubbing his chin, Joey smiled again. "No, I suppose you wouldn't. Hey, now, you'll call me if the record company gives you any trouble 'bout signin' that contract?"

"As soon as I find out," Maren assured him.

With his lower lip protruding speculatively, Joey seemed at least partially mollified. "Okay, Mama. I be expectin' your call." He sauntered out of the room with a disjointed stride that promised the rhythm and soul of his popular songs.

Maren walked with him to the door and accepted his palm along with his collusive wink. When Joey was gone, Jan turned from her typewriter, her worried eyes accosting Maren. "Trouble?" she guessed.

"Not much," Maren replied, hiding her concern over Joey's remarks about the video pirating. Within the last few weeks, the subject of pirated videos kept haunting her. Maren tried to shake off her unease and answer Jan's probing gaze. "Joey was pretty laid-back . . . for Joey, that is."

"Telling me that Joey is 'laid-back' is like saying a hurricane is a gentle breeze." Maren laughed and Jan released a troubled sigh. Her serious eyes clouded unhappily. "I should apologize for Jacob's behavior," she said, reaching for her cigarettes.

Maren waved off Jan's attempts at amends. "Don't worry about it, Jacob and I have business together. It wasn't a big deal."

As Jan lit the cigarette, Maren noticed that the blonde's hands were shaking. "I told you he's changed," Jan reaffirmed, inhaling deeply on the cigarette and leaning back in the chair to blow the smoke toward the ceiling. "I don't understand him sometimes."

"We all need a little extra cash now and again," Maren observed, not knowing how to console Jan. "I know that as well as anyone."

"I suppose," Jan agreed reluctantly and closed her eyes. "I finally told him about the baby." She turned to face Maren.

"And?"

"Nothing." Jan shook her head, as if to clear the cobwebs of mistrust. "He didn't say anything. He just stood there and looked at me as if I'd completely lost my mind. I know this sounds crazy, but I think it would have been better if he had gotten angry."

Maren disagreed but kept her thoughts to herself. She'd been on the receiving end of Jacob Green's vehement anger once in the past. It had happened when a take for a commercial had to be scrapped and reshot. Jacob had been so angry that he had thrown his paperweight through the glass door of the building. "Maybe the prospect of becoming a father again came as a shock," she suggested.

Jan leaned her chin into her hand. The cigarette was poised near her cheek, and smoke curled lazily up to the rafters as she considered Maren's words. "It was more than a shock, I'd say, but at least he didn't try and talk me into an abortion . . . not yet, anyway."

Maren was sickened at the thought. "Give him a while to get used to the idea of having a baby around," she suggested. "This might not be easy for him. His other kids are grown."

Jan sighed and looked away from Maren. "Yeah, well, we'll see, won't we?"

"Things have a way of turning out for the best," Maren predicted, knowing her words sounded lame.

"I hope so," Jan thought aloud. "God, I hope so."

Chapter Eight

$\mathcal{L}$ ocated just five blocks north of the famous intersection of Hollywood and Vine stood the Sterling Records Building. The modern structure was smaller than the nearby circular Capitol Records Building, but distinct in its own manner. Rising from the ground like a silver wedge, the three-sided building was a unique architectural triumph constructed of gray concrete slabs and reflective glass.

Maren had visited the building many times but had never ceased to be awestruck by the magnificent edifice. As she walked through the carpeted hallways, she realized that soon, if Kyle had his way, she might have her own office somewhere in the building. She wondered how it would feel to work with Kyle on a day-to-day basis and how it would affect her relationship with him. If she were to agree to the sale, would she lose all the freedom and respect for which she had fought so diligently? And what was to prevent Kyle from tossing her out, should he become unhappy with her? A simple clause in a contract was little consolation. Sterling Recording Company had lawyers and capital at their disposal that Maren couldn't begin to match. Once Festival Productions was his, Kyle could do just about anything he pleased with it.

A disturbing sense of dread ran down her spine as she followed a plump well-dressed woman to Kyle's office. After a quick rap on the door, the secretary pushed it open, allowing Maren to enter Kyle's domain. Taking her cue, Maren strode into the room, her eyes sweeping the cluttered interior of the office. Kyle was seated at a modern chrome and glass desk, the top of which was littered with papers. A quick glance at the rest of the spacious room indicated that it was in no better shape than the desk. Maren guessed that the room was lavishly furnished, though it was difficult to discern. Filled boxes, pictures, awards and various memorabilia were strewn haphazardly over the floor and furnishings. "Mr. Sterling," the complacent secretary announced just as Kyle looked up from the desk. "Ms. McClure is here."

"Thank you, Grace," he replied, dismissing the secretary.

Grace nodded curtly, seemingly oblivious of the disarray in her employer's office. She walked past an overflowing wastebasket, and with as much professionalism as she could muster, softly closed the door behind her.

"What's going on here?" Maren asked, eyeing Kyle suspiciously. "It looks like you're cleaning house, but I doubt that you made the trip to L.A. just for that."

"I came up here to see you," he said pointedly as he rose from behind the desk. "We have unfinished business." He was wearing slacks and an oxford cloth shirt. The sleeves had been rolled away from his wrists, and his tie was tossed carelessly over the back of a chair near his discarded sport coat. His bare arms crossed over his chest, and his gray eyes held hers fast. His body was lean and tense, as if he had been waiting for her, anticipating what was to come.

"I'm moving," he stated as he circumvented the desk and walked over to her.

"*What?*" Her sea-blue eyes swept up to meet his determined gaze. "Moving? Where? To another office?" She stood as if rooted to the floor, the confusion on her face demanding answers.

"I'm moving the things I need back to La Jolla," he replied. Without further explanation, he dusted his hands on his slacks and then pressed his fingertips against his neck as if trying to alleviate muscle strain in his shoulders. Maren managed to hold on to her frail smile, but disappointment welled within her. *He was leaving*—leaving the position of running the company on a daily basis to one of his vice presidents. Inexplicably she felt betrayed, as if he had lured her into nearly selling Festival Productions to him, only to abandon her and the production company to some faceless underling. For the first time since the start of negotiations for the sale of Festival, Maren realized that if she did indeed sell, she might not end up working for Kyle at all. Perhaps he intended to remain only the figurehead of Sterling Recording Company, or, worse yet, maybe he intended to sell the entire operation, lock, stock, and barrel. Included in the various holdings of Sterling Records would be Festival Productions. At the thought an uncomfortable knot formed in Maren's stomach.

"I'm glad you're here," Kyle admitted, a reluctant smile forming on his lips. He came across the room swiftly and folded Maren in his strong embrace. Powerful arms held her prisoner as his lips found hers. The kiss was bold and demanding. Maren sighed as she closed her eyes and felt a delicious swirl of excitement course through her veins. Her tormented doubts disappeared when he whispered her name softly against her ear, and her entire body felt as if it could melt into him.

His hands were warm where they splayed familiarly against the small of her back. The soft fabric of her jersey dress was only a frail barrier between his hands and her body. His lips brushed against her neck, and she moaned at the warmth he inspired. His fingers reached for the buttons at her shoulder.

"Kyle, wait," she murmured, the taste of him still fresh on her lips. She attempted to extract herself from his commanding embrace.

"I have," he admitted, once again kissing the soft column of her throat and letting his tongue gently probe the sensitive skin near her ear. "Too long . . ."

Gathering in a breath of fresh air to clear her senses, Maren managed to press her palms against his chest and force his head away from her. His eyes, when he raised them to meet her confused gaze, had darkened to a smoky gray. She could read the torment of restrained passion in their smoldering depths.

"Listen," she whispered, trying to ignore the desire infecting her. "I need to know a few things . . . what is all this?" Her upturned hand made a sweeping gesture to include the scattered contents of his office. "What do you mean you're moving to La Jolla? You're not resigning, are you?"

"Me? Resign? What are you talking about?" Pain lingered in his eyes, and his voice was edged with the frustration that had been building in him for nearly a week.

"I don't understand, Kyle. Who's going to run the company?"

"I am."

"From La Jolla?" she asked incredulously.

"Yes."

"Why?"

"There are a lot of things you don't know about me," Kyle replied. "I tried to explain some of them to you when you were in La Jolla, but you didn't want to hear them. I have personal reasons for staying near San Diego." Slowly Kyle released her, and it was evident that he was willing his desire to ebb. He raked impatient fingers through the sun-streaked strands of his dark hair.

Kyle knew that Maren was disturbed about something —something involving him. His throat went dry with dread. Just yesterday a bad copy of Mitzi Danner's as-yet-unreleased single had been discovered in a raunchy San Francisco nightclub. The pirated tape had to have come directly from Festival Productions—perhaps that was what Maren wanted to discuss. She had promised to let him know if the pirating problem resurfaced.

"I still don't understand. Who will be responsible for the day-to-day decisions of running the company?" Maren didn't ask about his personal reasons for staying in La Jolla. She suspected they might have something to do with his ex-wife, and she couldn't bear the thought of competing with Sterling Rose or sharing Kyle with any woman.

Kyle leaned against the edge of his desk, his long legs stretched in front of him, his fingers curling around the chrome frame of the desk to aid his balance. Thoughtful lines of worry creased his tanned forehead. "Several people will run the various departments, just as they do now. If a problem develops that a department head isn't able to handle, Ryan Woods will either make the appropriate decision or contact me in La Jolla . . . at least until I return."

"Then you do plan to move back here?" Maren's dark brows arched inquisitively.

Returning her direct stare, Kyle shrugged. "Circumstances permitting . . ."

"That's ducking the question."

"You were the one who didn't want to get involved in my personal life. Remember?" he charged, his temper flaring.

"That was before I realized that your 'personal life,' as you refer to it, influences what happens to me and everyone else associated with Festival Productions. You're asking me to make a decision about selling my company *and* my talent to Sterling Recording Company and you might not even be involved with Festival once the sale is final!"

"What does that have to do with anything?"

"I like to know where I stand before I sign on the dotted line," she snapped. "Whoever runs Sterling Records will be making the decisions regarding my future . . ."

"And you might not trust whoever I appoint?"

"Or sell Sterling to."

His smile was bitter, his gray eyes determined. "I have no intention of selling the record company." He crossed his arms over his chest, and his eyes bored into hers. "For once you're going to listen to me." Before she could voice the protest forming in her throat, he strode across the room. He touched her, and his fingers tightened over her forearms. His gaze was deadly from the tension holding his muscles taut. "I have to stay in La Jolla because of my daughter, Holly. There's a chance that I might gain custody of her. If I do, I won't be coming back to L.A., at least not until she graduates from high school. Her entire life is centered near La Jolla, and I'm not about to drag her to Los Angeles and disrupt her life any more than it has been already."

His daughter! The child Rose gave him. So that was

why he was moving to La Jolla. Maren witnessed the pain
in his eyes, and her heart bled for him. Her concerns for
the business seemed insignificant when compared to his
worries over his child.

"Listen, Kyle," Maren whispered, her throat suddenly rough with emotion. "You don't have to tell me anything about Holly. It's . . . it's really none of my
business . . ."

The hands encircling her arms clenched more tightly
and jerked her roughly against him. She could feel the
muscles of his thighs touching her dress, pressing the soft
fabric against her legs. Her breasts were crushed against
the firm expanse of his chest. He shut his eyes so tightly
that the webbing of crow's-feet at the corners disappeared.
For one tense moment he held her, and then slowly
released his grip. "Oh, Maren," he sighed, almost to
himself. "What is it about me and my daughter that scares
you so?"

She stood her ground and slowly let her gaze travel
upward to meet his condemning stare. "I'm not afraid,"
she protested in a throaty whisper. "Just cautious. I don't
want to get myself into something I can't get out of."

"What's that supposed to mean?"

Her thoughts returned to Brandon and the monetary
bond that still shackled her to him. Would she ever be
released—free to commit herself completely to another
man? Her voice was hoarse, and the shadow of regret
darkened her eyes. "It means that because of our negotiations over Festival, I can't afford to get too involved with
you—"

"I think you already have, wouldn't you say? Or was
our night on the beach just a solitary moment of weakness?"

"You know better than that."

"Do I? Why do you run so hot and cold with me? One minute I think I understand you, the next I'm not so sure."

"Maybe we've both got too much at stake because of the business," she lied, unwilling to bring her hopeless relationship with Brandon into the argument.

"You're evading the real issue," he charged, his eyes narrowing contemptuously.

"I don't think so. You know as well as I do that the production of videotapes pulled record sales out of the cellar. The entire recording industry was slumping pitifully until video came along and put it back on its feet. The point is, Sterling Recording Company needs Festival Productions as well as the reverse."

He lifted a finger and pointed it accusingly in her direction. "Stop it, Maren. Business isn't the issue here. Our relationship is. Are you trying to let me know that you don't want to see me except when we have to work together?" Every muscle in his body tensed for her reply. A small muscle in his jaw tightened until his teeth clenched together.

Her voice was low and unsteady. "I don't know what I want," she admitted. "At least not with you. And I'm not sure that what I want is what would be best for either of us." She laid bare her heart in an uncontrolled moment of weakness. "We've both been through bad marriages . . ."

"I'm not asking you to marry me, for God's sake. I'm only asking for a little of your time. Is that so hard to accept?" His anger was replaced by confusion, and when Maren stared into his perplexed eyes, she felt her heart melt. *He cared.* It was evident in the concern on his face. Jan and all the others who judged him by the scandal sheets or industry gossip were wrong! This man really cared.

"I guess not," she replied, forcing back the tears threatening to pool in her eyes.

The rigidity of his muscles relaxed. "Good. Then let's get down to the business at hand and get it over with. We have more important things to do," he declared cryptically.

Ignoring his seductive remark, Maren reached down and picked up her briefcase. She was grateful for the change in mood in the office and relieved that their argument had subsided, at least for the present. It had been much too long since she had seen him, and she didn't want to spend her time with him doing verbal battle. She put the briefcase on the cluttered desk, opened it and extracted her preliminary sketches.

"These are still a little rough," Maren warned, clearing a space on the desk and laying the drawings face up on the glass surface. "What I've decided to do is use the same principal characters in each video for the Mirage album, just as you suggested. But the interesting twist will be that each song will be set in a different time period. For the first cut, 'Yesterday's Heart,' I've started with the Depression. With each successive song, I've moved forward by fifteen to twenty years. The final cut will end in a futuristic world."

Kyle frowned as he sifted through the large sketches. His thick brows drew downward in concentration as he stared at the images. When he didn't comment on the drawings, Maren was forced to continue the one-sided conversation.

"I hope you approve of this idea, because I've already hired the dancers and a couple of bit-part actors for the action sequences on the first three cuts. The costumes are being designed, and the only problem so far is that the actress who agreed to do all five songs broke her leg while roller-skating in Venice last week."

Kyle raised his thoughtful eyes to meet hers. "Have you been able to find a replacement?"

Maren nodded. "I think so. I'm still waiting to hear from her agent. I doubt if it will be a problem." Maren waited anxiously as Kyle returned his gaze to the sketches. She was unable to decipher the dark frown on Kyle's features. "Well," she prodded, more than a little exasperated that he couldn't even make a comment. "What do you think?"

"They look fine to me," he conceded.

"Just fine?" She couldn't hide the frustration in her voice. "Those storyboards represent nearly two solid weeks of blood, sweat and tears."

His gaze hardened. "I expected the best from you, and I'm not disappointed. What more can I say? I'm not very good at visualizing the finished product until I see it on film. As a matter of fact, this is the first time I've ever seen the artwork for a video. Someone else usually handles it." He pointed a long finger at the top sketch. "These drawings don't mean a hell of a lot to me until I can actually hear the music and watch the action. That's why I hired you and why I want to purchase Festival." He read the slightly rebuffed expression on her elegant features. "What did you expect from me? I'm not the kind of person who hands out effusive compliments for a job well done, at least until it's finished."

"I just thought you might show a little more enthusiasm," Maren replied with a widening grin.

"Look, Maren, I hired you because you're the artist." He slapped his palm on the first drawing. "If you tell me that his action sequence will work, then I'll believe you." He leaned over the desk, both arms supporting his weight as he looked up at her. "Now, tell me, do you foresee any problems with production?"

Maren shook her head, and the light from a lowering

sun caught in the coppery strands. "I don't think so. J. D. Price and the rest of Mirage have approved; the location sites have been selected; the choreographer has worked up two of the dance sequences . . ." She raised her shoulders elegantly. "Barring a strike from the musicians' union, we're right on schedule."

"*If* you can sign the actress."

"I don't think it's anything to worry about. The girl I want is relatively unknown, and she sees this as her chance at the big time. Ever since Cindy Rhodes, whom Sly Stallone reportedly first spotted on Toto's 'Rosanna' video and later cast opposite John Travolta in *Staying Alive,* made the transition into movies, videos have become relatively easy to cast. The girl I want is Janie Krypton," Maren hesitated, and Kyle shook his head, indicating that the actress' name meant nothing to him. "Janie's a big fan of Mirage, and I'm sure she'll work out well opposite J.D."

"Good." Kyle handed her back the sketches. "Then you think you can make the deadline?"

"I think so. The actual filming will take a couple of days for the first song, but the editing will require another week or so. Unless something unforeseen happens, we'll make the June-first deadline." She searched her briefcase once again. "In fact, I think I can even squeeze Joey Righteous' video of 'Restless Feelin' into production, if you'll be so good as to sign the contract." Placing the storyboards neatly into the briefcase, she waited for Kyle to sign and return Joey's contract.

He hesitated. If Ryan Woods had been correct, the latest Mitzi Danner video had already been duplicated. How could he take the same chance with Joey Righteous? The Mirage album was already a very costly gamble.

"Don't you think you should concentrate on Mirage first?" he suggested.

She could feel the undercurrents of tension quietly charging the air. Something was wrong. "We can handle all of it, and I promised Joey that the video would be ready when the single was released. Unless my information is faulty, 'Restless Feelin' is scheduled about the time Joey takes off for his tour of Japan in June."

"That's right. But it's not until the end of the month. Let's wait until the first Mirage video is finished," he decided, handing her back the contract.

Maren had the uneasy suspicion that he wasn't telling her all of the story. Why did he want to wait? Was it because of the impending sale? "Is there something you're not telling me?" she asked, accepting the contract and leaving it on his desk. He didn't comment on the fact that she didn't put it back into her briefcase.

"Such as?"

"Why you're hedging on the Righteous contract? That's not like you," she charged.

"I suppose it isn't," he agreed, "but I think it would be best for both parties if we don't get too involved with unfulfilled contracts until we've come to terms on the sale of Festival."

"You mean that you're going to keep the unsigned contracts dangling like the proverbial carrot until I sign on the dotted line?"

"That's not what I meant."

"But it's true," she pointed out, her cheeks coloring with unwanted anger. "Are you just stringing me along, Kyle?"

"Why can't you trust me?" he asked, his temper flaring in his cold eyes.

"Because trust is a two-way street, and I'm smart enough to notice when someone's deliberately baiting me."

"You've got it all wrong."

"Prove it, Kyle." Maren picked up the contract and waved it angrily in his face. *"If I'm wrong, sign the contract."* Her voice was shaking, and her eyes had darkened warningly.

"I don't have to prove anything to you, Maren," Kyle defended himself. His voice was low and menacing. "You know me well enough to realize that I'm as good as my word."

"Are you saying that I'm not?" she asked, wondering at all the hidden innuendos in his words.

"No, but I am asking you this much: If you were having any serious problems at Festival, you would tell me, wouldn't you?"

"Of course."

"Even if it threatened the sale?" he pressed.

"Kyle, what are you getting at? If there's something bothering you about my business, just spit it out."

"It's a purely hypothetical question," he lied, thinking of the Mitzi Danner video. He wasn't convinced that it had really been duplicated, but Ryan Woods had promised to bring it to him. Until he had his facts straight, he couldn't accuse her.

"Then you had better think about signing the Righteous contract. Joey is counting on both of us. I told him that I would talk to you, and if you agreed, we'd schedule his video into production."

"And if I said no?" Kyle asked, muscles rigid.

"I can't imagine why you would. But I told Joey that if I had problems getting the contract signed, I would call him and he could deal directly with you," Maren explained.

"Now *that's* a threat. I've been on the receiving end of Joey's hostility more than once."

"The choice is yours," Maren pointed out.

"Either I sign, or you sic Joey on me?"

"It's your decision."

Kyle smiled cynically. "I can handle Joey Righteous—I have before."

"Why do you insist on being so insufferably stubborn?" she asked in utter confusion. "Is this the kind of response I can expect from you if and when I sell the business to Sterling Records?" Her indigo eyes reflected her concern.

"I'm just being cautious right now," he reassured her. "We've had a few problems here, and I've got to get a handle on them before I take on any more." He took the contract from her hands and flipped it in the air. It fluttered downward to land in the middle of his chaotic desk. "It's after five," he noted, capturing her wrist with his hand. "Let's forget about business for the rest of the night."

Pulling her wrist gently forward, he enticed her to lean against him. "I can think of other things I'd rather concentrate on," he coaxed against her skin. His lips brushed lightly over hers, awakening her senses with their dewy promise. "Do you have any plans for tonight?" he asked, warm fingers lightly caressing her throat.

"I do now," she sighed, forgetting about Joey Righteous, unsigned contracts and Festival Productions, and letting her fingers run through his thick sable-colored hair.

He smiled cryptically, and his gray eyes sparkled. "Let's go upstairs," he suggested.

"Upstairs?"

"I have a place up there, a studio apartment of sorts, where I stay when I'm in town."

Maren tilted her head, lifted an eyebrow and viewed him through a thick fringe of dark lashes. "Are you attempting to seduce me, Mr. Sterling?" she teased.

"More than that," he promised with a rich laugh. "Oh, lady, what I intend to do to you." His smile was infectiously wicked as he swung his coat over his shoulder, picked up her briefcase in one hand and pulled on her wrist.

The apartment was located on the uppermost floor of the building. It was warmly decorated in tones of burgundy, navy and ecru with modern furniture clustered in small groupings near the windows overlooking the city.

"You call this a bachelor apartment?" Maren asked dubiously. It was true that all the living was concentrated in one large room, but it hardly qualified as the cramped quarters usually associated with a bachelor's apartment.

"I used the term loosely," he conceded.

"I guess. I think you could house three families in here."

He had released her hand, set down her briefcase and tossed his coat over the back of a plush chair. When he turned back to face her, his eyes drove deeply into hers, and she experienced a chill of excitement racing through her blood.

"Are you hungry?" he asked, taking both of her hands in his.

"Starved . . ."

"I ordered out . . . something very sophisticated and romantic," he whispered huskily.

A small smile, showing just the hint of a dimple and the flash of even white teeth spread across her pouty lips. "So you expected to entice me up here," she surmised.

"Hoped," he corrected. "I hoped to show you where I live when I'm in L.A." He crossed the room, walking past a heavy sectional sofa in muted shades of blue and gray. "Come here . . ."

She followed him to the tall windows on the far wall. From the apartment's vantage point high above the surrounding buildings, one had a panoramic view of the surrounding community of Hollywood. "I bet this is breathtaking at night," Maren commented, watching the flow of heavy traffic moving toward the freeways.

"If you stay long enough, you can see for yourself." He disappeared into an alcove, which Maren decided was the kitchen. Within a few minutes, he reentered the room and placed a large carton on the table.

"Pizza?" she asked as he opened the box.

"Warm pizza and cold beer," he stated.

"This is your idea of 'something very sophisticated and romantic'?" she inquired, laughter dancing in her soft blue eyes. "Why was I expecting Veal Oscar and chilled champagne?"

"I don't know," he replied, motioning for her to take a seat at the small table, "because I wasn't talking about the meal; I was referring to the company."

Maren's gaze locked with Kyle's, and she smiled under the warmth of his compliment. "If you're trying to charm me into signing the sales contract," she said, "you're certainly on the right track."

"This has nothing to do with your business or mine. This evening is just between you and me." He poured a glass of beer and handed it to her. "Is that all right with you?"

"Fine," she admitted, taking a sip of the cold liquid. "Just fine."

It was dusk when they had finished eating and had cleared the small table. The conversation had been light and carefree, and Maren had relaxed enough to kick off her shoes and feel the weave of the thick carpet through her hose.

Kyle opened one of the windows, and the sounds of the city reached upward to them. Muted voices, the rumble of car engines and an occasional shout or blast of music from a passing car filtered into the apartment.

Maren sat on the floor near the windows staring out at the looming night. She tucked her feet under her hips, encircled her knees with her arms and rested her chin on her kneecaps. "Do you enjoy living here?" she asked, as he sat next to her. "It's so different from the house in La Jolla."

He contemplated the curve of her jaw before replying. "It's been convenient." He reached forward and traced the soft column of her neck with his finger. The touch of his fingers against her throat made Maren's pulse begin to race. When she turned her head to look at him, she noticed that all traces of amusement had faded from his eyes. His voice became a throaty whisper, desperate with the heated yearnings of his body. "God, woman, you can't imagine what I've gone through these last two weeks, wanting you and not being able to touch you. It's nearly driven me mad."

All the lighthearted pretenses melted in the ever-lengthening shadows in the room. The light mood that had taken hold of Maren throughout the casual meal disappeared and was replaced by an aura of gravity. Kyle's eyes had darkened with restrained desire as he reached over and his forearms entrapped her in their intimate prison.

"Tell me you've wanted me," he commanded, holding her gaze with his smoldering eyes. "Tell me you've lain in bed alone and wished that I were there beside you, that I would appear and satisfy the ache within you."

His words enticed her heart to beat unsteadily. Her breath caught in her throat as she remembered the last lonely nights without him and the agonizing hours she had lain awake with only memories of his warm caress. "Oh, yes," she sighed, squeezing her eyes shut to emphasize her words. "I've wanted you, Kyle. . . . I've wanted you so hopelessly that there were times when I thought I couldn't stand being away from you a moment longer.''

Groaning in satisfaction, he let his hands move upward to cup her chin. ''You've got to be the most fascinating woman in the world,'' he proclaimed softly before pressing his anxious lips to hers. Tenderly, with as much restraint as his eager body could stand, he kissed her, and with an answering sigh, she parted her lips, quietly inviting him to explore and invade her, body and soul.

Their tongues met and entwined in an intimate dance of restless union that forced her blood to run in swirling rivulets of liquid fire. Her fingers caught in the heavy strands of his coarse hair as she pressed him closer to her. She felt his hand on her breast, kneading the aching mound through the soft fabric of the jersey dress. Her nipples were tight, her breasts swollen with need, ready for him and the wondrous feelings he could inspire. When he took his lips away from her mouth, she moaned in disappointment, but as his moist tongue lapped softly against her throat, Maren felt her body respond. The feminine ache within her burned as his tongue circled the hollow of her throat, leaving a wet impression on her skin and the soft neckline of her dress. Cool, moist fabric rubbed against her heated flesh, and a rosy blush of expectation colored her skin.

His lips moved to her shoulder and toyed with the buttons holding her dress together. Maren tilted her head to the side, letting her hair fall away from her neck and shoulders. His hands continued to hold the weight of her breasts, gently rubbing her taut nipples until they strained against the silky lace of her slip.

''Let me love you,'' he whispered hotly against her shoulder as he slowly unfastened one button.

''Dear God, Kyle, please,'' she murmured weakly.

Another button was released from its bond. His tongue moistened her skin, and she shivered in anxious response. Her throat was dry from the short raspy breaths coming from her lungs.

The final button slid through its hole, allowing the soft muscle of her shoulder to part the powder blue dress. Warm night air massaged her skin as the fabric gaped off her shoulder, exposing the elegant swell of her swollen breast. A tiny droplet of perspiration ran from her neck down the dusky path between her breasts, and Kyle captured it with his waiting tongue. He lowered the strap of her slip down her arm, baring her breast to his eyes. His groan was a savage admission of lustful surrender.

Lowering his head, he let his lips tenderly seize the bold nipple, while his tongue rimmed the dark point. Her cry of bittersweet agony ripped him to the bone, and she gripped his hair more tightly, desperately holding him more closely against her bosom. Hot breath fanned the wetted breast, and the ache within her grew to a white-hot intensity.

Drops of perspiration beaded his brow, and it took all his thin patience to withhold the act of love and prolong the agony. The desire in his loins throbbed for release, but he repressed the urge to tear off her dress and savagely lose himself within her. Instead he let his fingers slowly touch her calf and with feather-soft strokes move upward, sensuously feeling the tantalizing seduction of her nyloned leg beneath his fingertips.

Maren released a shuddering sigh when his mouth released her nipple and the night air embraced her naked breast. Her breathing became erratic; her breasts heaved with the strain of taking in air. She felt liquid warmth engulf her as his hand traveled in painstaking hesitation up the length of her leg.

The dress gathered and pulled as his fingers found her

inner thigh. Her small hands balled with frustrated longing as slowly—oh, lord, how slowly—he removed her undergarments before deftly tugging her dress over her head.

As she lay on the carpet in the near-darkness, Kyle's eyes roved restlessly over her body. She shuddered at their intimate touch. He was kneeling beside her, and he slowly began to unbutton his shirt. Maren watched in anticipation as the oxford fabric parted to display the finely sculpted muscles of his chest and abdomen.

When he slid the shirt down his arms, she reached up and let her fingers trace the supple curve of his biceps before haltingly touching his neck and lowering her hands to the flat rock-hard ridges of his chest. She noticed the way his muscles contracted as he shifted positions to remove his shirt and slacks.

Finally he was naked beside her, kneeling over her, his bold gray eyes holding her gaze with promises of mysterious longing. She ran her fingers up the outer side of his thigh, letting the soft hair on his leg bend upward as she reached for him.

He leaned closer and her heart pounded out an erratic cadence of passion as her arms encircled his waist. He twined his fingers through the tangled waves of her fiery hair as he settled against her. She could hear his heartbeat, watch the anxious desire in his eyes, feel the rock-hard contour of solid muscles as they slid over her own. His weight was a welcome burden.

Elbows propped beside her head, lips pressed hotly against hers, he moved slowly, parting her legs with his knee and teasing her by rubbing his body over hers in intimate persuasion. The pounding in her ears began to explode and she arched more closely to him, assuring him that what she desired most in the world was the feel of his passion erupting with hers.

Her eyes were glazed in surrender, and when Kyle

looked down upon her, seeing the way her damp hair framed her face, witnessing the ragged rise and fall of her breasts, feeling the heat of her body arching against his, he could no longer keep his primal urges at bay.

"I love you," he cried as he entered her, molding himself to her as man to woman. "I love you, Maren," he promised, straining against her flesh and filling her with all the love he could offer.

Chapter Nine

*M*aren slowly opened her eyes against an intrusive ray of sunlight piercing through the skylight. She stretched in leisure as she watched Kyle's sleeping form. His dark skin contrasted with the sky blue sheets, and his sun-streaked hair was tousled against the pillow. Smiling to herself, she reached forward and pushed the hair out of his eyes. Just as she did, his hand caught her wrist and his eyelids opened to reveal clear gray eyes.

"You weren't asleep, were you?" she asked with a knowing smile.

"I've been awake for nearly an hour." His eyes roved restlessly over her exposed shoulders.

"Why didn't you wake me?"

"Because I enjoyed watching you sleep." His eyes glittered seductively as he released her arm to drag the sheet slowly down her body. His eyes followed the bed sheets downward until the tops of her breasts were exposed. Light from the skylight warmed her naked skin, but she felt a sudden chill as his wet lips pressed against the swell of her breasts.

She moaned softly as a spreading liquid fire began to heat her blood. The sheet, now moist from the touch of his tongue, was pulled still lower, to drape across her abdomen and bare her dark nipples.

"Dear God, you're beautiful," Kyle groaned as he positioned himself over her. Gently his hand massaged one of her supple breasts, unhurriedly rubbing the soft mound until the nipple hardened in readiness.

Anxiously Maren arched against him, her body hungry for more of his enticing touch. He kissed her tenderly on the lips, teasing her until she twined her fingers in his hair and pressed her hot lips more urgently to his. His tongue rimmed the corners of her mouth, softly prodding her lips open. She felt the delicious warmth of his tongue touching the most intimate reaches of her mouth, and a small cry of desire formed in her throat.

His hands continued to knead her flesh, promising fulfillment as they touched and explored her body. Knowing fingers flattened against the small of her back, drawing her torso against his, letting her feel the urgency of his desire as he rubbed against her.

When his head descended to moisten a path down her neck, Maren felt her breath constrict. His lips pressed wet kisses against her collarbones, and she shuddered beneath his expert touch. I'm falling in love with him, she thought helplessly, and there's no way to prevent it.

Erotically he cupped a breast in the palm of his hand before easing his lips over the succulent nipple. She held on to his head, holding his body against hers, ignoring the doubts filling her mind and giving in to the pleasurable sensations welling within her. She felt the warmth of his tongue and the bittersweet pain of his teeth against her skin.

He kicked away the bothersome sheet separating their lower bodies and placed his legs between hers. The soft hairs on his thighs caressed her legs. When he lifted his head, his eyes had darkened to a smoldering hue of smoky gray and her wetted breast cooled in the early morning air.

"Darling Maren," Kyle murmured as he let his hands slide slowly down her rib cage, outlining each rib with his fingers. "How desperately I've wanted you." His admission came reluctantly, as if it were a sign of weakness.

"And I you," she replied, gazing dreamily into his eyes. She felt his muscles tighten, and he lowered his body over hers as he gently forced her knees apart.

A soft groan echoed deep in his throat when he at last gave in to the urges of his body and thrust himself into the invitation of her soft body. She sighed as they became one, and she held his body close to hers, content to feel the gentle rhythm of his love. He seemed to sense when her womanhood was fully aroused, and she felt his shuddering surrender at the moment of her fulfillment.

"Oh, Kyle," she moaned. "Please love me."

"I do," he promised. "Oh, lady, I do." His words were comforting and filled with conviction. Maren's eyes filled with unwanted tears and for one wondrous moment she let herself believe him.

"I want you to consider moving in with me in La Jolla." It was a simple statement and sincere. His heartbeat had quieted, and his dark gray eyes seemed to pierce Maren's soul.

Maren's voice caught in her throat, and she hesitated. The words of love he had whispered while making love to her had to be considered nothing more than vague endearments murmured in the heat of desire. They couldn't be construed as promises of a love everlasting. Maren knew that impassioned words of love deep in the night had a way of fading into forgotten vows with the coming of dawn.

"Did you hear me?" He pulled her more closely to him, molding her slim body to the contours of his. Maren's throat was rough with unwanted tears. She sighed deeply as she lay in the comfort and security of his arms.

"I heard you," she whispered, still facing away from him. I just don't know what to say . . ."

"Say yes," he persuaded gently as he pressed his lips against the back of her neck and breathed in the scent of her hair.

Her supple body became rigid in his arms. "Kyle . . . I know that I laid it on a little thick when we first met."

"What do you mean?"

She sunk her teeth into her lower lip as she gathered her thoughts. "You were coming on pretty strong, and I didn't really know how to handle it. All that talk about commitment, it doesn't matter, not now. At the time I was afraid of an affair."

"But now you're not? Is that what you're trying to say?"

"Now I'm not," she agreed softly.

Broad hands gently pushed on her shoulders until she was forced to face him. As she stared into his brooding eyes she thought she would like to drown in his gaze. Her love for him was so great that she could sacrifice her principles and live with him without marriage. She would never selfishly bind him to a marriage he didn't want.

As if reading her thoughts, he frowned and his dark brows drew downward in confusion while he brushed a stray lock of auburn hair out of her eyes. "And you'd be satisfied with an affair?'' Disbelieving gray eyes held her captive.

''Yes.'' Her voice trembled only slightly. ''Don't get me wrong, I still don't believe in casual sex . . .''

''I know that.''

''But I think . . . with us, it's more than that.''

''Of course it is. That's why I want you to live with me.'' His hands were resting on her bare shoulders and his thumbs slid temptingly against her soft skin. How easily he could coax her into doing anything for him.

Her fingers clutched the sheet as she shook her head. ''I can't do that.''

''Why not?'' He pushed himself up on one elbow to stare down at her.

She smiled despite the tears welling in her eyes. More than anything she wanted to live with Kyle and share his deepest secrets. She swallowed with difficulty. ''For one thing,'' she whispered hoarsely, ''I've got a lot of work to do . . .''

''Can't you do it as well in La Jolla?''

''Of course not! Kyle, be sensible! You know how tight my schedule is already; you're the one who put a crimp in it!''

''And you thought you had a little extra time to work on Joey Righteous' video.''

''That's hardly the same thing.''

''I know that, but can't you forget about work, just for a little while?'' he asked.

''Hard to do, considering that I'm in bed with the boss.''

''Don't think of me as the boss—just as your lover.''

She blushed at the thought. His hands took hold of her slender wrists and held them bound to her sides. Slowly he lowered his head and moistened the tip of one breast. The dark nipple hardened in response. ''Come with me,'' he suggested. When she laughed and tried to resist him, he only held her more tightly. "Come with me," he pleaded again.

"I'd like to, but it's impossible."

"Maren, please . . ." He released her arms to touch her tenderly on the chin. "Come down to La Jolla, just for the weekend. We'll talk about the future after that." He saw the protests forming in her eyes and fended them off with logic. "There's a lot of work you can do from the beach house. You can use the library. It has a desk and a phone . . ." He sensed that she was wavering. ". . . and a breathtaking view of the ocean."

"You're twisting my arm." She sighed longingly.

"Then say you'll come."

She considered his request and the earnest look of concern in his eyes. "Okay," she agreed, "but it can't be until tomorrow."

"That's fine with me." He kissed her on the cheek before rolling over to the edge of the bed.

"Kyle?" Her voice halted his movements.

"Why haven't you asked me about your offer on Festival?"

As he stood, he rotated to face her. She was huddled on her side of the bed, the sheet clutched tightly over her breasts and her eyes uplifted to penetrate his.

"I didn't think the timing was right."

"But I thought you wanted an answer."

"I do. I have an appointment scheduled later today with my attorney and Elise Conrad. Apparently she has some misgivings about the sales contract. Is that right?"

"There're a couple of things she wants cleared up."

"And if I satisfy her, will you be ready to sell?" he asked, regarding her carefully.

"I think so. Of course, I would have to talk to Elise first."

"Of course" was his clipped reply. He noticed the question forming in her eyes. Draped in the blue sheet, her tangled coppery hair framing her small face, she seemed more vulnerable than he had imagined.

"There's something I have to know," she said quietly.

He braced himself against the accusation he felt would surely come. "What?"

"You know that you're not obligated to me, don't you?" she asked.

"Obligation has nothing to do with the way I feel about you," he replied. He frowned darkly, his jaw jutting outward and his cold eyes drilling into hers in frustration. "I'm asking you to come live with me because I want to. Don't delude yourself into thinking it's out of any heroic sense of duty just because we slept together."

"Or because I haven't signed the contract of sale on Festival?" she prodded, witnessing the angry storm gathering in his eyes.

"You're incredible," he charged. "Sometimes that lingering sense of paranoia of yours surprises me, and that's hard to do. I'm used to dealing with all sorts of fears and phobias in this business, and I had the erroneous impression that you were a woman who really knew her own mind." He turned on his heel, angrily reached for his clothes and stalked furiously toward the bathroom. "I'm not about to dignify that question with an answer." With a final oath, he slammed the bathroom door and effectively cut off any further argument.

Maren pursed her lips together. "Coward," she whispered, pounding her fist into the pillow. Why did he get so furious? What was he hiding? She couldn't ignore the shadows of doubt that would cross his eyes. It was as if he distrusted her. Something wasn't right between them; Maren could feel it. There was something he wasn't telling her and it involved his purchase of her business.

Why did he have to be so damned cryptic and manipulative? Again Jan's warning echoed in her mind.

Maren's anger slowly simmered while she dressed. By the time Kyle emerged from the bathroom dressed only in black slacks, Maren managed a remorseful smile. His dark hair was dripping as evidence of a recent shower, and he seemed surprised to note that Maren was completely dressed and quietly sipping a cup of coffee. She sat in a chair by the windows near where they had made love the evening before. Observing him over the rim of her cup, her dark brows arched expectantly as he came over to her.

"You can be a real bastard when you set your mind to it," she charged with a sweet smile and a devilish glint in her eye.

"Only when provoked by the right woman."

Maren's lips pursed into a petulant pout. "I poured you a cup of coffee—it's in the kitchen."

He bent down and touched her shoulders with his fingertips. "You mean you're not going to get it and serve it to me?" he cajoled, his secretive smile pleading.

"Not on your life."

Kyle returned with the cup and sat in a chair facing hers. He slipped his arms through his shirt and left it gaping open as he sipped the hot black liquid. "Tell me," he suggested with a self-satisfied smile. "Are you always so even-tempered when you wake up?"

"Only when I'm provoked by the right man."

Kyle smiled. "Can I take you to breakfast?"

She shook her head and set her empty cup on the table. "Not today. Especially if I'm coming to La Jolla this weekend. I've got a million-and-one things to do." She checked her watch. "And I'm late as it is."

"Will you be at the meeting with Elise Conrad?"

"I plan to."

"Then we can have dinner afterward in La Jolla."

"Maybe," she replied.

"Other plans?" His eyes had darkened.

"I just don't know when I'll finish with everything I have to get done. If you remember, I've got to put 'Yesterday's Heart' into production immediately. Ted Bensen and I are going to run over the first scenes. They're a little tricky since the setting is the Depression. We have to be sure that the sites appear authentic and that there are no modern trappings to mar the effect."

"Then I'll call you at the office."

"Fine," she agreed, standing. "I'll try and wrap up everything by five, if I can, and I'll bring the paperwork to La Jolla."

She started toward the door, but his firm voice arrested her. "Maren?"

She turned inquisitively at the sound.

"Holly is living in La Jolla with me. I thought you'd want to know."

"Your daughter? But I thought Rose had custody . . ."

Kyle willed back the rage that overtook him every time he thought about his scheming ex-wife. "She does," he said. "At least, she has permanent custody for the time being."

"So Holly is visiting you?" Maren's thoughts were confused. Hadn't she read that Kyle's daughter was recuperating from a near-fatal auto accident?

Kyle tensed. Anger flashed in his gray eyes. He was careful with his words, but Maren could read the quiet wrath smoldering beneath the surface of his gaze. "Holly will be with me a few months—longer if I get my way." He set his cup on the table, and his shoulders slumped. "You must have read that Holly was nearly killed just before Christmas?"

Maren nodded silently, understanding for the first time the pain she had witnessed in Kyle's clear eyes. "It was a horrible accident," Kyle whispered. "For a while I wasn't certain whether Holly would pull through it." His voice had thickened, and he was forced to clear his throat. "Anyway, I just wanted you to know that she'll be at the house."

"And you still want me to come?"

"Of course."

"Don't you worry about setting the wrong kind of example by throwing our affair in her face?"

"Are you worried about what she thinks about you?"

"Yes. Aren't you?"

"No." He shook his head as if to relieve himself of a great sadness. "Holly and I don't communicate very well."

"This won't help . . ."

"I think it will. Holly needs to see that I can care for someone other than myself," he stated thoughtfully.

"And you're sure that I won't intrude?"

"Not a chance . . ."

Maren sighed in deliberation. Her love for Kyle overcame her fears. "Then I'll see you tonight."

A relieved grin broke across Kyle's rugged face. "I knew you'd see things my way," he said as he pulled a tie from the closet and knotted it around his neck before shrugging into his jacket.

"Your lack of confidence will lead to your undoing," Maren predicted, with just the trace of a smile.

"No, I don't think so," Kyle replied with a wink. He put his keys in his pocket. "I believe that my 'undoing,' as you so aptly phrased it, will come from a beautiful woman with a razor-sharp tongue."

Maren laughed, and the rich sound echoed against the

rafters of Kyle's apartment. He took her arm, opened the door and held her tightly to his side as they walked to the elevator.

The day was more hectic than Maren had predicted. Jan called in sick, forcing one of the production personnel to answer the telephones. Maren worked with Ted Bensen on the proposed sites for the location shots on "Yesterday's Heart." Of the three sites, only one was suitable for the Depression setting.

By the time Maren got back to the office, it was after three and her meeting with Elise Conrad and Kyle was scheduled for four. Fortunately Elise's office was nearby. Maren had just finished adjusting her lipstick and combing her hair, when the woman taking Jan's place stepped meekly into the office.

"Ms. McClure—I hate to bother you; I know that you're leaving; but this one guy keeps calling and insisting to talk to you." She handed Maren a stack of telephone messages. They were all from Brandon. "He's adamant about talking to you."

Maren disguised her dismay when she accepted the memos by smiling at the girl. "Thanks, Cary, I'll give him a call."

After the young girl had exited, Maren glanced regretfully at the clock before sliding into the desk chair and dialing the phone. It was several seconds before Brandon answered.

"Hello, Brandon. My secretary told me you wanted to get hold of me."

"Maren? What the devil took you so long?"

"I was out of the office," Maren replied, wondering why she bothered to explain herself to him. "What's up?"

"That's what I'd like to know," Brandon replied

somewhat angrily. Maren could picture the indignant arch of his brow. "The physical therapist seems to think he's done all he can for me."

"That's great," Maren replied with genuine enthusiasm.

"Oh, yeah, you think so. Now you won't have to fork out for the therapy."

"The money has nothing to do with it, Brandon. I was just relieved that you were back on your feet again."

"If you can call it that," he spat out.

Maren closed her eyes. The recovery she had been praying for obviously hadn't occurred. "Are you still having trouble?" she asked quietly.

"They told me I could never play tennis again."

"They've told you all along that might be a possibility," she reminded him softly.

"Tennis is more than just a game for me."

"I know that, Brandon."

"I was good. I was damn good! If it hadn't been for the accident . . . I'd probably have been number one last year."

The guilt within her twisted in her heart like a dull blade. "And the physical therapist says you can't play?"

"Not professionally."

"I assume the orthopedist concurs."

"Who knows? I never can get a straight answer out of that guy! He seems to think that it's all in my head. Easy for him to say."

"Have you talked to a psychiatrist?" Maren asked patiently, knowing the answer before Brandon replied.

"A shrink? Are you kidding? I don't need someone to psychoanalyze me, Maren; I need my legs back!"

"Wait a minute. The therapist says you can't play professionally. But you still can teach, right?"

"I don't know," he pouted. "I don't want to teach. I want to play—I have to."

"Maybe you will," Maren encouraged. "Look how far you've come. A year ago you thought you might never walk again."

"Well it doesn't help to have the therapist back out on me."

"Back out? What do you mean?"

"He seems to think that he can't do anything else for me. He wants to send me packing with a list of exercises."

Maren tried to remain patient. "It sounds to me as if you're making real progress. You knew that it would come to this."

"That's easy for you to say," he shot back hotly. "You've never had your career . . . your entire life, ripped away from you, have you?"

Maren's free hand clenched into a tight fist. "No, Brandon, I haven't. But I know that you have to work with the doctors and not against them in order to make the most out of the situation!"

"Yeah, well, tell that to them."

"What is it you want me to do?"

"Talk to the therapist, or get another. I'm on the verge of making it all work, I can feel it, but I've got to have help!"

"Why don't you talk to your doctors?"

"Because they won't listen to me! Damn it, Maren, is this too much to ask?"

Sighing, she replied. "No, it's not. I'm just not sure I'll have any influence."

"People with money always have influence!"

Maren bit back the hot retort forming on her tongue. She'd never let Brandon know how expensive his treatment was. Nor had she told him how tight her own pocketbook was. She had hoped that he might recover more quickly if he wasn't burdened by the knowledge that her financial condition was far from wealthy.

"I'll see what I can do," she agreed, glad that the trying conversation had come to an end.

"Good!" With this final remark, he hung up. Maren slammed the receiver into the cradle of the telephone.

Hot tears welled in her eyes as she thought about the hopelessness of her situation. "Damn it," she mumbled to herself as she pounded a small fist on the desktop. "Damn it, Brandon, why won't you help yourself?"

Looking up to the ceiling, as if in supplication, her shoulders slumped with the weight of her guilt. Whether or not Brandon fought for his independence wasn't the issue. It made no difference. It was her burden to help him, and she would shoulder it with all the strength she could find.

Plucking a tissue from a box on her desk, she dabbed at her eyes and vowed to herself to find some way to get Brandon back on his feet and able to earn his own way in the world. There had to be a way to slowly help him support himself.

Kyle's vicious accusations the first night she had been with him entered her mind. "You still love him," Kyle had accused, speaking of the unknown man who had wounded her.

"Not true," she whispered in the office alone. Her voice caught. "The only man I love is you," she said, wishing she were strong enough to confront Kyle with those same words.

By the time Maren had finished with the business in the office, she was already late for her appointment with Kyle. Ted Bensen had been bending her ear with production problems on the Mirage videos for nearly forty-five minutes before Maren could break away from him.

In the parking lot, before she could slip behind the wheel of her car, Joey Righteous had caught up with her, demanding information on his video for "Restless Feelin'." He was angry, but Maren was able to calm him down by taking him into her office and reassuring him that the video would be finished by the time he left on his tour.

Snarls in traffic were another delay. By the time she made it to Elise's office, Kyle, Ryan Woods and the attorney for Sterling Recording Company had gone.

"We hit a snag," Elise explained with a thoughtful frown. She was a woman of fifty-odd years with perfectly styled dark hair and snappy brown eyes.

"What kind of a snag?" Maren asked before dropping into one of the soft chairs surrounding Elise's desk.

Elise adjusted her reading glasses. "The price was reasonable; as a matter of fact, the entire offer on Festival seemed aboveboard."

"I don't understand." Maren stared at her attorney as Elise studied the legal document lying on the desk.

"It has to do with the employment agreement. I wanted Sterling to guarantee you three years of employment. *And* I wanted you to be able to purchase a large block of Sterling Recording Company shares with the money you'll receive for Festival."

"Kyle wouldn't go for it?" Maren guessed.

"He was advised against it, by that Woods character and Bob Simmons." Elise paused, seemingly intrigued with a particular clause in the contract. "Before I could convince them that we wouldn't budge on this issue, Sterling excused himself. Said he had to go back down to La Jolla." Elise shrugged her round shoulders. "So this

Ryan Woods told Sterling that under no circumstances was he to talk to you about the contract, not until he and I and Bob Simmons come to terms.''

"Bob Simmons is the recording company's attorney?''

"Right. He drew up the agreement.''

"So what should I do?''

"Nothing. Not until I sort this out with Simmons.'' She tapped her pencil on the desk. "And I'm going to give you the same advice. I know you might come in contact with Sterling because you do business with him. Whatever you do, don't discuss this contract. Just until I understand what Simmons and Woods want.''

"You act as if you don't trust them,'' Maren observed.

Elise shook her head and rubbed her jaw. "No—it's the other way round. They acted as if I intended to pull a fast one on Sterling Records. Can you imagine that?'' Elise's dark eyes took hold of Maren's.

"I don't know why,'' Maren stated honestly.

Elise waved off the serious mood. "Everyone's cautious these days, especially a person as famous as Kyle Sterling. He's a prime candidate for any number of lawsuits in his business. Someone complains about the copyright of a song—or a bootlegged copy of an album . . .'' Maren's heart seemed to stop beating, but Elise continued. ". . . or that Sterling Records stole another company's artist. Who knows? The point is, they have to be careful, and so do we. Until I get everything straightened out with Simmons, you should avoid talking about the offer—to anyone.''

"Do you think that Sterling Records will do everything we want?'' Maren asked cautiously.

Elise pursed her uncolored lips. "I don't know. From the way I read Kyle Sterling, he was more than willing to extend the employment agreement. It was the stock in

Sterling Recording Company that seemed to be the real bone of contention.'' Elise saw the concern in Maren's blue eyes. "Don't worry about it. Simmons promised to get back to me by Tuesday. This time next week we should have everything wrapped up, and if I get my way, you'll be a very wealthy woman!''

Chapter Ten

*E*lise's words rang in Maren's head as she drove southward, and she vowed to take the attorney's advice and avoid the subject of the sale of Festival with Kyle. Negotiations were too strained as it was, and there were always the lingering doubts he had concerning the pirated tapes. Though he hadn't mentioned the subject lately, it was always there, distancing Maren from him.

Maren returned to Kyle's manor by the sea with more than a trace of trepidation. Not only was the impending sale looming over her head, but there was also the meeting with Holly to consider. As Maren drove through the wrought-iron gates protecting the estate, she considered the delicate situation. The thought of confronting Kyle's daughter made Maren more nervous than she would like to admit, even to herself. What would the child think of Maren and her relationship with Kyle? Would Maren be able to handle the tense situation? Kyle had admitted that his relationship with his daughter was already strained. It was possible that Maren's unwelcome presence in the house would only add to the problem.

With a vow of determination, Maren got out of the car, reached for her briefcase and walked up the flagstones through the garden near the front door. Resolving to try her best to get along with Kyle's daughter, she reminded herself that Holly was still recuperating from the latest in a series of operations. She smiled as she pushed the doorbell. Chimes echoed throughout the house.

It was several minutes before the heavy front door was tugged open by a round Hispanic woman with a cautious smile and graying black hair neatly coiled atop her head.

"You're Maren," Lydia guessed before the visitor had a chance to introduce herself.

"Yes." Maren smiled with the ease and friendly manner she had acquired as head of a small production company. She was accustomed to meeting wary strangers. The stiff-spined housekeeper used her round body as a barrier to the entrance of Kyle's home. Obviously she was protective of Kyle and his estate. Piercing dark eyes roved over Maren distrustfully. "You must be Lydia," Maren surmised. Her clear blue gaze was steady and without pretense. "It's nice to meet you." Maren offered her hand to Lydia with a sincere smile. The Mexican woman took Maren's palm cautiously, but a slow grin spread over her round face.

Satisfied that the strange woman with the deep blue eyes was entirely different from Rose, Lydia moved slowly out of the doorway and ushered Maren inside the house. "Come in, come in," she invited with a merry grin and a twinkle in her black eyes. "Can I get you something to eat . . . or drink, perhaps?"

"I'm fine," Maren replied, but the kindly woman refused to be put off.

"Nonsense," Lydia persevered with a shake of her head. "How about a glass of iced tea? I have fresh lemon."

"You're twisting my arm," Maren said with a low laugh. She knew in an instant that she and Lydia would get along famously. The other hurdle to overcome was Kyle's daughter. Maren realized that winning Holly over wouldn't be so easy.

"Good." Lydia seemed pleased. "I was getting Holly a glass anyway. She's out on the deck, if you'd like to join her."

"Where's Kyle?"

"He had to go into town, but he promised to be back soon. He's been expecting you." Lydia turned toward the kitchen. "I'll bring the tea out to the deck," she called over her shoulder, and Maren was left with the distinct impression that the housekeeper *wanted* Maren to visit with Holly.

It's now or never, Maren decided as she crossed the familiar living room and opened the door leading to the covered deck.

Holly, wearing a lemon-colored T-shirt and cutoff jeans, was reclining on a chaise lounge. One leg was propped against the soft cushions of the lounging chair, and the girl was attempting to paint her toenails. Maren was surprised to note the healthy color of Holly's complexion and the girl's sure movements. Maren had guessed that Holly would be frail from her recent surgery, but it appeared that whether Holly would admit it or not, she was recuperating very well under her father's careful supervision.

At the sound of the door opening, Holly lifted her intense green eyes toward the intrusion. There was a light of expectation in her eager gaze, but when she saw Maren the gleam faded and genuine disappointment surfaced.

"Hello," Maren greeted warmly. She closed the door behind her and leaned against the railing. "I'm Maren McClure."

"I know who you are," Holly said rudely. "Dad told me you were coming." Holly's full lips drew into a pout as her insolent eyes moved away from Maren's face and back to an unpainted toenail.

Maren held her tongue at the girl's intentional rudeness. So this was how it was going to be. Unless Maren straightened a few things out with Kyle's daughter, the weekend would turn into a disaster. Holly's angry frown stated more clearly than words how deeply she resented Maren's company. It was going to be a long, hard uphill battle to win the child's confidence.

"Your father said that you only got out of the hospital recently. It's good to see you up and on your feet."

"Is it?" The teenager's tone indicated her total lack of enthusiasm. "I'll bet."

Maren's fingers tightened around the railing until the knuckles blanched and she could feel the warm wrought-iron press painfully into her palms. "Are you able to go to school yet, or do you have a private tutor?" Maren asked, eyeing the ignored stack of textbooks piled on the small table that also held a variety of shades of nail polish, cotton balls and nail files.

Holly sighed loudly and ignored the question. Maren tried again. "Do you always paint each nail a different color?"

With her brush poised carefully over her large toe, Holly lifted her eyes and impaled Maren with her frosty stare. "Look, lady," Holly said with a petulant frown, "you don't have to come out here and make chitchat with me. I really don't give a rip what you do with my dad, but you don't have to pretend that you're interested in me. It's no skin off my back."

"Are you always so defensive?" Maren asked, wondering if Holly was in her own manner trying to clear the air.

"Just tellin' it like it is." Once again she lowered her eyes to contemplate her toes.

Maren was thoughtful for a moment, not sure exactly how to handle the resentful child. She considered leaving well enough alone and going back into the house but thought better of it. No matter what Holly said, the girl was trying to get a reaction from Maren to understand where she stood with her father's latest girlfriend. Maren took one searching look at the calm sea as she gathered her poise to confront Kyle's willful child.

"It's not written in stone that you have to like me, you know," Maren said softly.

"What d'ya mean?" Holly asked, abandoning her task to give Maren her full attention. Though partially hidden, a slight trace of confusion knitted her brow.

"I mean that just because your father and I are seeing each other doesn't necessarily mean that you and I have to get along. If you would prefer, we could avoid each other."

"Oh, sure. Like right now, for instance."

"You mean that I'm intruding."

Holly paused, careful with the pretty woman whom she instinctively considered an adversary. This Maren was different from what Holly had expected. For one thing, she had guts, and Holly admired that. "Yeah, well, I guess so."

"Do you want me to leave you alone?"

"Why not?" Holly lashed out, her well-practiced mask beginning to slip. "I'm old enough to take care of myself."

"And smart enough to realize that you wouldn't want to," Maren ventured.

"As if you know anything about me," Holly baited, tossing her dark curls away from her face.

"I know enough about you to realize that you're not very comfortable living here with your dad. You don't really know what to expect from him and that scares you just a little."

Holly broke in. "I'm not *scared*."

Smiling quietly to herself, Maren was forced to agree. "Maybe that was a poor choice of words. What I meant to say was that I know you miss your mom. That's natural. A girl your age needs a mother whom she can talk to and confide in."

Holly's full lips pulled into a disgusted frown. "Next I suppose you're going to tell me that you can be that person."

"Of course not." Maren's clear eyes held the young girl's distrustful gaze. "No one can ever step into your mother's shoes, and I wouldn't want to try."

"Sure," Holly tossed out contemptuously, but Maren's words sounded sincere. No matter how corny she came off, the lady seemed to mean what she said.

"I was hoping we could be friends . . ."

Holly rolled her eyes skyward as if asking for divine intervention. "Fat chance," she whispered.

". . . but it's up to you. We can get along or not. The only thing I ask is a little polite civility from you, and I'll return the favor."

"God, don't you ever know when to lay off?" Holly asked angrily.

"I just wanted you to know that I'm not a threat to you."

"I *know* that already, so don't waste your breath."

A spark of indignation flashed in Maren's eyes, and Holly tossed her dark curls away from her small face.

"As I said before, the decision is yours . . ." Maren was about to continue, but the door from the kitchen opened and Lydia hurried out onto the deck with a tray of glasses filled with iced tea and sliced lemons.

"That looks wonderful," Maren said gratefully as she smiled at Lydia.

Lydia beamed under the praise and gave first Maren and then Holly a tall glass of the amber liquid. There was a third glass on the tray, but when Lydia didn't pick it up, Maren assumed it was meant for Kyle.

"Why don't you join us," Maren invited with a welcoming smile. "Holly and I were just having a get-acquainted chat." Holly's round eyes widened, as if she expected Maren to tell Lydia of the girl's rude behavior.

"I can't right now," Lydia apologized with sincere regret. "I've got a chicken in the oven that won't cook itself." She hesitated, casting a knowing look from Maren to Holly and back again. "Maybe later," she suggested hopefully.

"Whenever you can take a break," Maren said after taking a long swallow of the cool liquid. She held up her glass and smiled. "Thanks."

When Lydia disappeared into the kitchen, Holly turned her condemning eyes on Maren. "You've got Lydia eating out of the palm of your hand, too, don't you?" she charged.

"I wouldn't say that. We've just met. I was only being pleasant."

"Why? To get in good with Daddy?"

Maren pursed her lips, shook her head and closed her eyes. "No, of course not. Your dad seems to think a lot of Lydia. I can see why. She's a very generous person."

"You can tell all that from just meeting her?" Holly's smirk indicated her disbelief.

Maren raised a knowing brow. "Oh, yes, Holly. That and much more. When I meet a person, I generally can see right through her," she said pointedly. "You'd be surprised what some people try to hide—just because they don't feel comfortable about themselves."

"You're talkin' about me," Holly accused.

After taking a swallow of the tea, Maren sighed. "I'm talking about a lot of people, Holly." She took a long look at the sea before continuing. "I know that you resent me, and I understand that, really I do. You've been through quite a bit lately, and the last thing you needed right now was having to deal with your dad's latest girlfriend, right?"

Holly didn't answer, but a telltale blush crept slowly up her neck. In Maren's opinion, that was some small bit of progress.

"Look, I'll stay out of your way, if that's what you want. But I don't think that would be fair to me, your dad or yourself."

Gritting her teeth against the tears threatening her eyes, Holly lashed out. "I don't care what's fair to *you!*"

"Then think about your dad and yourself. Like it or not, you're stuck with each other for a while and the fewer waves you make, the smoother sailing it will be."

"Oh, yeah? Is that what you really think? Or is that just a way to keep me quiet? You'd do anything to get in good with Dad, wouldn't you?"

Maren shook her head. "No one's paying me to like you, or to even try and get along with you—it would just be easier that way. And for that matter, you may as well know that I do like you. I'm not really sure why," Maren admitted to the surprised child, "but I'd *like* to be your friend." A glimmer of triumph flickered in Holly's eyes but quickly faded when Maren added, "However, if it doesn't work out, it won't kill me." She picked up her empty glass and walked into the kitchen. "See ya later," Maren called in a cheery voice, leaving Holly to consider the unlikely woman to whom her father was attracted.

Maren would never have believed it, but the weekend that had started so badly with her confrontation with Holly did improve. When Kyle returned to the house, he was enthusiastic to see both Maren and his daughter. To her credit, Holly did seem to try and rise above the barriers she had erected between herself and Maren.

It was evident to Maren that the relationship between Kyle and his daughter was not as tense as Kyle had said. Maren noticed that a spark of expectation and love would light in Holly's eyes whenever Kyle would give the child his attention. There were arguments, of course, but the hostility that Holly had worn self-righteously on her slim shoulders seemed to have evaporated.

After dinner, Holly went upstairs to study, and Lydia refused Maren's offer of help with the dishes. "Come on," Kyle invited, "let's go for a walk on the beach." The look of longing in his clear gray eyes couldn't be denied.

Dusk was beginning to settle on the calm waters of the Pacific. Frothy waves broke against black rocks before running toward the beach. Purple shadows lengthened against the white sand and darkened the clear water.

The twilight was breathless. The usual breeze from the ocean had disappeared, but the smell of saltwater lingered in the quiet air.

"I'm glad you came," Kyle admitted, taking Maren's hand in his as they reached the bottom of the cliff. "I had a sneaking suspicion you might not show up."

"Why?"

He shrugged his shoulders and stared out to sea. "Maybe it's because you keep running away from me . . ." Serious doubts clouded his gaze. He watched the flight of a solitary gull as it circled above the waves, and then, as if dragging himself out of a distant pain, he looked down on her and smiled. "What do you think of Holly?"

Maren returned his grin, and a dimple enhanced the smooth contours of her face. Her dark brows arched at the question. "I think she's a handful."

"That's evasive."

"And the truth."

Kyle frowned as he pushed his hands, palms facing outward, into the back pockets of his gray corduroy slacks. "I suppose you're right," he conceded reluctantly. "She hasn't had much of a chance."

They started walking near the edge of the tide. "You blame yourself," Maren said quietly, guessing at the burden of guilt he silently bore.

"I'm her father."

"But she has a mother . . ."

At the mention of Rose, Kyle's head snapped upward. Anger, like a bolt of lightning, flashed in his eyes. "Not much of one," he said through clenched teeth, and then, as if to quell his storming rage, he shook his head and pushed his fingers through his thick hair. "I'm sorry," he whispered. "Rose and I haven't seen eye to eye, not since day one."

He sighed in exasperation. "My marriage was doomed from the start," he admitted, letting his thoughts revolve backward to a time in which reality consisted of twangy guitars, managers, and night after night in towns he'd never heard of. "When I met Rose, I was only mildly successful . . . still playing for peanuts. I'd had one song that had made a move up the charts, I think.

"Rose's career was just beginning to take off, and I was flattered that she would even notice me." He paused, as if looking for a reason for his actions. "I was young, and I didn't have my head screwed on right. Anyway, we got married, and the media loved it—not to mention the public-relations people." He frowned in disgust. "If I'm fair about it, I'd have to say that marrying Rose was the single most important thing I did to advance my career."

"You got married for your career?" Maren asked, masking the disbelief in her voice. Knowing Kyle as she did, Maren would never have thought he could do anything so callous.

"I didn't think of it that way, not at the time. I convinced myself that I really cared for her. She *acted* like she felt the same. As I said, it was mutually beneficial." He squinted into the gathering sunset, and his mouth turned down in disgust with himself.

Maren swallowed with difficulty. "You weren't in love?"

Kyle shook his head. "Who knows?" His jaw tensed. "I'd say not, wouldn't you?"

"I didn't know you then."

"You wouldn't have liked me if you had." His voice was flat and emotionless. "I don't think I liked myself, and after a few months, I didn't have any use for Rose. The feeling was mutual." He sighed contemptuously and stopped walking. "I suppose that was my fault, too."

"I don't understand," Maren replied, not knowing what to say.

He stretched out on the sand and studied the tide. Maren sat quietly next to him. "Neither do I," he admitted. "That whole period of my life doesn't make much sense." His gray eyes drilled into hers, and she noticed the pain of fifteen lonely years. "The marriage brought us national attention, and we did everything in our combined power to use it to our advantage. It worked. Suddenly the public couldn't get enough of our music. Record sales skyrocketed, and our egos didn't suffer much, either.''

Maren reached for a handful of sand and let the sparkling granules sift through her fingers. ''If you were having trouble, why didn't you slow down?''

''I don't know. Maybe the marriage wasn't that important. We were arguing all the time, and then Rose turned up pregnant.'' Kyle's eyes narrowed in disgusted agony at the memory. ''You should have seen her when she told me. She'd been to the doctor in the morning. When she got in to the studio where I was working, she threw some prescription at me and shouted out the news. 'Well, now you've done it. I'm knocked up. What're we going to do about it?' As if there were any question.'' He pounded his fist angrily into the sand.

Maren's eyes reflected her despair. Why would any woman react so negatively to having Kyle's child? To Maren, there could be nothing more precious than the thought of carrying Kyle Sterling's baby. Her stomach knotted at the picture Kyle was painting.

''I talked her out of the abortion, and I think Rose was relieved. When Holly was born, she even showed a little interest in the baby. I thought everything might work out, and I tried to convince her to give up singing to stay home with the child. That was my mistake. Rose threw a fit, and told me if it was so important, I could stay home and take care of the kid.''

''And you didn't like the idea?''

''I thought it was ridiculous—and now I wonder. Maybe I was wrong. I'm sure Holly would have been better off with me. I should have known that Rose wasn't cut out to be a full-time mother. She needed the night life, she loved the fame and she was addicted to the glitter.''

''And you weren't?'' Maren asked cautiously.

"I don't know." He grimaced as if studying a puzzle he couldn't begin to understand. "I guess I was too hard on Rose. I didn't want her to go back on tour because I couldn't stand the thought that Holly would be raised by a complete stranger. I thought that a child needed to be with her mother, no matter what. The trouble was that Rose was being pushed by her manager. He wanted her to work longer hours, take more tours, rush through another album."

Kyle stood and stretched his long frame as he squinted into the sunset, as if he were searching for the answers to his life. "Maybe things would have been different if Rose had allowed Lydia to look after Holly. Since Lydia had helped raise me, I knew that she would take good care of my child. Lydia had always loved Holly. But Rose would hear none of it. In Rose's estimation, Lydia wasn't good enough for Holly."

Maren stood next to him, and he let his fingers touch the soft strands of her hair. It shimmered in the dusk, framing her face in delicate coppery curls. Her brow was lined with anxiety as she listened to his story.

Kyle felt compelled to tell her about himself; he felt inexplicably drawn to her as he had never been drawn to a woman. The complexities of his life didn't interfere; nor did he care for the moment about Festival Productions, pirated videos or sales agreements. All he wanted was for Maren McClure to understand and trust him. And he needed to trust her, though he knew it would be a mistake. Her incredible blue eyes sought his, encouraging him to continue.

"I guess the fights increased after Lydia left. Rose and I had nothing left in the marriage except our child. We stuck it out because of Holly." His voice had taken on a new dimension, and his quiet rage was replaced by scorn. "A couple of years later—Holly was about three at the time—I caught Rose with a member of the band, a kid about eighteen. Their affair had already been going on for a few months, and I had suspected as much, but it still came as a shock to me.

"Rose indignantly demanded a divorce, and I agreed. The only thing I wanted was custody of Holly. Rose flipped. I don't really understand why; maybe Rose's motherly concern was deeper than I suspected. Anyway, Rose refused to give up Holly. We argued, and she promised that if I fought her, she would give me a vicious custody battle that would throw us and our child onto the front page of every scandal sheet in the country."

"So you gave in," Maren guessed in a hushed voice. Tears burned at the back of her eyes and threatened to spill. The agony on Kyle's rugged features was deep and tortured. How long had he borne the scars of a past he couldn't change? The emotions he expressed reached out to Maren, and she wanted to soothe him, comfort him, hold him to her breast and whisper words of solace to him long into the night.

"I hate to think of it as giving in," he replied. "I did what I thought was best for Holly, and I've regretted it ever since." His voice quieted. "You might have noticed that Holly and I don't get along very well."

"I don't think it's as bad as you make it."

"Only because we've made tremendous strides in the last couple of weeks."

"Because she's been living with you?" Maren asked.

"Or because Rose rejected her!"

Maren's heart stopped. "What do you mean?"

"I mean that now, right after the kid's latest surgery, Rose decided to leave her high and dry!" The anger burning in his eyes sparked.

"If you don't want to talk about it . . ."

"But I do!" He clutched her shoulder in a death grip.

"I've been trying to tell you about Holly for a long time."
Seeing the startled look in her eyes, he released her arm.
"Oh, hell! What do you care?"

"I do care, Kyle," she reassured him, touching the tips
of her fingers to his chin. Her voice was low and husky.
"I think I care too much . . ." Her blue eyes caressed his.
"I want to know everything about you," she admitted.

Kyle rubbed his temple. The quiet of the night was
disturbed by a rush of wind off the sea. Its breath, now
cool with the night, ruffled Kyle's dark hair. "You know
about the car accident?"

"I read about it."

"Then you know that Rose was at the wheel when the
car skidded into oncoming traffic?" His voice was deadly.

"Yes," Maren whispered. According to the newspaper
article, Rose had been speeding in the rain. The oil-
slickened streets had become dangerous for ordinary
traffic. When Rose applied her brakes at a tight corner, the
Jaguar had slid and slammed into a car heading in the
opposite direction. At the time of the article, no one
expected Holly Sterling to survive.

"Rose's carelessness nearly killed my daughter!"
Kyle's teeth clenched, and his hands balled with his barely
controlled rage. His eyes had turned vengefully dark.

"But I thought that Holly recovered."

"She has—but not thanks to Rose." His voice was flat
and self-condemning. "Or maybe that's my fault, as well.
Even after her first stay in the hospital, she wasn't
completely well. Her most recent surgery was to correct a
problem with scar tissue in her uterus."

"But she's all right now?" Maren asked hopefully,
thinking of Holly's future.

"We're not sure. Right now, everything looks fine, but
if Holly starts having problems again, she might be forced
to have a partial hysterectomy."

Maren swallowed back the lump forming in her throat. The thought of a fifteen-year-old girl suddenly facing a future without the ability to bear children was devastating. Shadows of pain darkened Kyle's eyes. "And you blame yourself," she thought aloud.

"Holly's my child, Maren. I should never have let Rose get custody."

"Oh, Kyle—"

"I should have protected her!"

"You couldn't have known . . ."

"But I did know, damn it! I knew Rose wasn't fit to care for her, but I let it happen. I didn't fight hard enough for my child. You said it yourself, I gave in, and I never intend to give in again. I'll never let Holly suffer at the hands of her mother anymore. I let Rose and her threats about causing a scandal intimidate me. I should have let the gossip columnists write whatever they damn well pleased and fought for my kid!"

"We've all made mistakes," she offered.

"Maybe so. But that was the last one I'll make concerning Rose."

Maren let the silence speak for itself. Kyle needed time to let go of his anger. No words from an outsider could still the storm of emotions raging within him. She watched him noiselessly and waited until she noticed the tight muscles in his jaw softening.

"Now that Holly is living with you," she said, touching him on the forearm, "maybe things will be better."

"This is only a temporary arrangement," Kyle replied. "Rose was offered the lead in a movie about a country-western singer. It's being shot on location in Texas, and that's why Holly's here. Even though Holly had barely recovered from her last surgery, Rose took off for Texas the moment she was offered the part." He let his forehead drop into his hand and rubbed his brow. "I've asked my attorneys to start proceedings for me to gain permanent custody of Holly.''

"Does Rose know that?"

"Not really, but she must suspect . . . she knows how I feel about that kid."

Maren was hesitant. "And what about Holly. What does she want?"

"I don't know."

"Have you asked her?"

"Not yet. I thought I'd wait until my attorney tells me how good my chances are of getting custody." He placed a comforting arm over her shoulders and tried to relieve some of the genuine concern in her eyes. "Don't worry—somehow I'll make it work," he promised, kissing the top of her head. "I believe that if you want something badly enough, you can get it."

They walked back toward the steps. Above them, high on the cliff face stood the proud hacienda. Warm lights illuminated the windows and invited them back inside.

Chapter Eleven

Only a few interior lights welcomed Maren into the dim rooms of the hacienda. Once in the hallway, Kyle wrapped his arms possessively around her waist and pulled her tightly against his lean frame. "Stay with me tonight," he suggested huskily. "I want to make love to you until dawn and wake with you still in my arms." His lips brushed her eyelids, and her blood began to race in her veins.

"But what about Holly . . . and Lydia?"

"Holly's already asleep, and Lydia's gone for the night. It's only you and me."

"Kyle—"

"Stay with me."

It was impossible to deny what she, too, needed so desperately. "How could I possibly refuse?"

"Would you want to?"

Seductive indigo eyes held him transfixed. "Never," she whispered. His mouth captured hers hungrily, and his palms pressed urgently against her back, kneading the soft muscles until she moaned in expectation. The light fabric of her cotton blouse was a frail barrier to the warmth of his touch.

As if on cue, he lifted her from her feet. One arm supported her back, while the other captured the bend of her knees as he carried her upstairs. She twined her arms about his neck, content to bury her head in his shoulder and hold him dearly. He smelled so tantalizingly masculine. The scent of him mingled with the tangy odor of the sea, awakening feminine urges deep within her.

He didn't hesitate, but carried her into the master suite. Softly kicking the door shut, he strode across the room and through another door to deposit Maren in a sunken tub made of gray marble and rimmed in blue tile. When she began to feebly protest, he shook his head and smiled, conveying to her how desperately he wanted to please her. After deftly unbuttoning her blouse, he slid it off her shoulders. Slowly he unfastened her bra and placed the flimsy garment atop the shed blouse.

Her nipples, ripe with desire, hardened under his watchful stare, and she had to suck in her breath when his fingers touched her abdomen and lightly brushed against the waistband of her jeans. Slowly, sensually, he slid the zipper down before lowering the pants over her hips and down the length of her legs. Her skin heated when his fingertips brushed against her, and she moaned in contentment when, at last, he removed all of her clothing. She lay naked in the tub, peering into his eyes as his gaze roved restlessly over the soft contours of her body.

He turned on the faucet, and the tub began to fill. The touch of his eyes was far hotter than the water in the tub. Without looking away from her elegant form, Kyle reached for the sponge and submerged it in the water. Maren shivered as the water crept slowly up her skin.

Gradually he squeezed the sponge over her breasts before lathering them with soap. His hands slid invitingly against her skin, teasing her nipples until the breasts became swollen with desire. Maren shifted in the water and closed her eyes with a soft sigh. She felt her breasts becoming engorged and the nipples becoming taut under the wet caress of his hands. A warm tide swirled in her bloodstream, starting in the deepest part of her and rushing upward through her body in ever-increasing fervor. She moaned his name.

Kyle slowly washed her hair and her back, letting his fingers graze the soft flesh of her buttocks. Her eyes were only half open, the indigo irises observing him through the veil of her thick black lashes. Her auburn hair clung to her face in wet ringlets, making her appear innocently seductive. Her rosy skin gleamed from the water. Long slender legs, high firm breasts and a face that was as vulnerable as it was strong enticed him.

She smiled lazily upward, and her blue eyes twinkled playfully.

"You're a witch," he muttered, as he leaned over the tub and his lips found hers.

"And you love it," she murmured, returning his heated embrace.

He stripped off his clothes and tossed them aside before wrapping his arms around her waist and dragging her from the bath. Water spilled over the sides of the tub as he pulled her upward and pressed her warm body against his.

His tongue probed her mouth, and he groaned with the savage need ripping through his loins. Gently he carried her to the bed and using the weight of his body, forced her against the cool coverlet. Her body moved against his fluidly. The dewy water acted as if it were oil, allowing his muscles to glide over hers. He couldn't wait. Capturing her eager lips with his, he ran his anxious fingers down the slippery hill of her breasts, past her abdomen, to gently part her legs.

He shifted until he was positioned over her, where he could stare into the blue intensity of her eyes in the moonlight. Moving his aroused body suggestively over hers, he touched her as intimately as had the bathwater.

Maren groaned in frustration, and her fingers dug into the lean muscles of his back. The bittersweet torture was driving her mad with desire. Her heart thudded painfully in her chest, and her breathing had become erratic. She sighed into his open mouth and thrilled when his tongue touched the soft recesses behind her teeth, plundering the sweetness therein. His fingers were as warm as the water had been, teasing her, toying with her, until at last his body covered hers and she felt the whirlpool within her turn molten.

As he came to her he whispered her name in the darkness. She joined him recklessly, allowing herself the luxury of his physical love. She needed to be touched by him, wanted all of him—for as long as possible. The love within her grew as he murmured her name.

"Love me," she pleaded, praying that his desire for her was more than physical. But her cries were lost in the night as he blended into her, shuddering as his need was fulfilled. She tasted the salt on his skin as her teeth sank into the hard muscles of his shoulder.

When their heartbeats had quieted, and their breathing had slowed, Kyle propped himself on one elbow to gaze down on her. "What happened to you, Maren?" he asked softly. Noticing the confusion in her eyes, he repeated, "Your marriage—the man who hurt you. What happened?"

Her chest became constricted. She didn't like to think about Brandon. Especially not now, not after making love to Kyle.

"It was a long time ago," she said, turning away from him.

His hand cupped her chin and forced her head back in his direction. Concern shadowed his eyes. "Tell me about it."

"There's not much to tell." When he didn't press her, she closed her eyes for a moment and sighed. "It's a part of my life that I'd rather not dwell on," she admitted.

"Because you're still in love with him?"

"I don't think I ever did love him."

"I find that hard to believe," he said, a steely edge to his words.

"Why?"

"Look at you," he replied gruffly. "Every time we get near the subject of your marriage, you clam up." She shook her head as if to deny his accusations, but he wouldn't let it rest. He seemed obsessed with it. "I don't understand what's going on, Maren. For the most part, you seem like a pretty together lady—in your business, dealing with Holly, anything, but the minute the conversation gets too close to that marriage of yours, you put up these false walls to protect yourself."

Maren started to protest, but Kyle placed a silencing finger to her lips. "There's no use denying it, Maren; something in that marriage of yours isn't quite what you'd like me to believe."

Angrily he sat up and then stalked across the room, grabbing a thick robe from his closet and throwing it over his shoulders. As if in explanation he said, "I think more clearly when I'm not touching you." He sat on the corner of the bed and eyed her. "Damn it woman, I don't understand you, not at all.'' Raking his fingers through his dark hair in impatience, he stared at her. His eyes were dark and condemning, his lips compressed into a determined line. ''What are you doing here—playing me for a fool?''

Rage sparked in her blue eyes. ''Of course not.''

''Then explain yourself. Doesn't sleeping with me mean anything to you?''

''It means a lot to me,'' she whispered.

''But not enough to give me the truth?''

''I've never lied to you, Kyle,'' she whispered defiantly.

''Then why don't you tell me what it is you want from me.''

She took in a deep breath before sitting up and holding the sheet over her breasts. If only she could tell him how much she loved him . . .''I don't want any more than you're willing to give,'' she said evenly, ignoring the pain twisting in her heart and pushing back the threat of burning tears. ''But what about you? What do you want from me? My body? My undying affection? *Or my production company?*''

''I'm not going to be deterred by your accusations. I just want to know about that ex-husband of yours.''

''Why?''

''Because I think there's something you're not telling me, and I don't have the time to waste on another man's woman.''

She felt her hand snap backward, but before she could slap him, Kyle's hand took hold of her wrist. ''Another man's woman?'' she repeated incredulously. She let her eyelids fall shut and smiled grimly to herself. ''Is that what you think?''

Releasing her arm, he shook his head. ''Quite honestly,

Maren, I don't know what to think." His hand dropped slowly to his side. "You turn my head around . . ."

"And you don't like it," she finished for him with a catch in her voice.

"I don't understand it. And what's more," he continued, his temper flaring in his steely gaze, "I won't be played for a fool."

She tilted her head defiantly upward. "You don't understand me at all."

"Because you won't let me."

Tossing back the covers, she reached for Kyle's shirt and slipped into it, then walked out of the room and onto the deck facing the sea. Kyle's deck lay above the deck off the living room, and the view of the dark Pacific was just as breathtaking. Maren hoped she would absorb some of the tranquility of the calm sea.

Taking deep breaths of the sea air, she attempted to clear her head and let her indignation dissipate. Why did it matter what Kyle thought of her? How had she let herself become so hopelessly in love with him when she was still irrevocably bound to Brandon? Dear God, how had she let her entire life be turned inside out by Kyle Sterling? She pounded her small fist on the railing and shook her head in desperation. A few weeks ago her most urgent problem had been a few unsigned contracts from Sterling Recording Company. Tonight the problems with the contracts seemed light-years distant. Even her concerns over the sale of Festival had vanished with the night.

Leaning against the railing, she stared down at the blackened sea. The night wind blew across the tranquil waters of the Pacific and touched her face with its cool breath before catching in the coppery strands of her hair and lifting them away from her face. Maren didn't notice. Her thoughts were too turbulent; her emotions too raw.

Powerful floodlights secured to the cliffs cast their ghostly illumination on the water, exposing the waves as they crested over the craggy rocks near the shoreline and ran in frothy rivulets to the shadowed sand.

The bedroom door opened and closed. Bracing herself against the railing, Maren continued to stare at the sea. She felt the rugged strength of Kyle's arms encircle her abdomen. His warm breath whispered familiarly against her ear. "You know that you mean much more to me than just the beautiful owner of a company I'm hoping to acquire." Maren's throat became dry, and her fingers tensed over the railing. Her heart fluttered as he kissed her softly on her neck and her cool skin quivered at his tender touch. Everything seemed so right with him. "From the first time I saw you, sipping champagne at Mitzi Danner's party, I knew that you were incredibly alluring. I was intrigued." The admission was whispered quietly, as if he were talking to himself.

"So intrigued that it took you nearly a year to find me?" she threw back callously. His words were burning a hole in her heart.

"I didn't want a woman complicating my life—because of Holly."

"So you ignored me?"

"You left the party early. I did look for you," Kyle replied. Maren remembered his aloof stance at the party that night. She envisioned his quiet, understated manner, his brooding gray eyes and his rakish smile. She had been as wary of him as he had been of her.

"That was nearly a year ago," she whispered, her long fingers clenching. "Don't expect me to believe that I captivated you then. Too much time has passed, and you've been in my office since . . ."

"As I said, I didn't need or want a woman complicating

my life . . ." His voice was as persuasive as the clear
California night. Maren had to fight the urge to turn
around and let her arms twine around his neck. She
wanted to cling to him and never let go, but she couldn't.
Not yet. There was still Brandon to consider. She closed
her eyes to erase the memory of him.

"And you do now—want a woman to complicate your
life?"

"Not just any woman," he replied into her hair.
"Maren, I want you." Maren felt the lump in her throat
begin to swell uncomfortably. He sounded sincere. She
pressed her eyelids more tightly together but couldn't stem
the tears from pooling in her eyes.

Her voice trembled. "So what do you want to know
about Brandon?" she asked softly.

She felt his arms release her before forcing her to turn
and face him in the shadowy night. His gray eyes drove
into hers, as if searching her soul. "I need to know what
he means to you."

"Nothing," she responded with a sigh. "I thought I
loved him once . . ."

Kyle's jaw hardened and his eyes turned dangerously
cold. "But now you're not sure?"

Maren was forced to smile despite the tears in her eyes.
"I grew up believing that love was eternal," she explained. "Either I was incredibly naive or I wasn't in
love."

"You can't make the distinction?"

"Not easily."

His eyes narrowed in the darkness. "Why do I still get
the impression from you that you can't let go of him . . .
not entirely at least?"

"Because I can't," she admitted, her unwavering blue
gaze filled with honesty and pain. She saw the anger

surfacing in his stormy gray eyes, and she touched the tips of her fingers gently against his shoulders. He flinched under her touch. "Let me explain," she insisted.

"Please do." His voice was flat. All emotion was hidden.

"Brandon and I were married when I was still in college. I was young, and I thought I was in love. I managed to finish my senior year, but Brandon was too restless. He dropped out of school to become a professional tennis player . . ."

Kyle inclined his head. Vaguely he remembered a flash in the pan by the name of Brandon McClure. The man had had an incredible serve, which was accompanied by an equally explosive temper. In Kyle's opinion, Brandon McClure never had a chance. He was his own worst enemy. Tennis was a game of complete concentration and skillful manipulation. With only a couple of obvious exceptions, few hotheads made it into the top ranks of the pros.

"What happened?" Kyle demanded.

"To make a long story short, it wasn't long before I realized that he was having an affair. The woman was someone I knew and worked with." She paused. "There were other women. He admitted as much."

"So you divorced him?" Kyle's voice was low. The question seemed dangerous.

Maren took in a deep, ragged breath and tore her gaze away from Kyle's angry gray eyes. The pain of the divorce still bothered her. She looked toward the dark sky, and moonlight brushed a silvery sheen into her dark hair. "No. We separated for about six months, I guess. It was my fault. I opposed the idea of divorce and let it drag out. Even when we finally agreed to actually go through with the proceedings, I didn't feel comfortable about it . . . as if in some way, *I* had failed."

"And you never got over that feeling?" Kyle guessed.

Maren shook her head from side to side and pinched her lips together to hold back the sobs of regret that were forming in her throat. "No," she whispered. "A while back . . . it had been several years since the divorce was final, Brandon called and suggested that we spend the weekend together skiing in Heavenly Valley." Her hand slapped the railing as the memories that she tried vainly to forget came back to her.

"I realized it would probably be a mistake. He was talking about reconciliation, and I knew at the time that too many years had passed. But I decided to go because . . ."

"You still loved him," Kyle accused.

"*No!*" She pursed her lips together in determination. "It wasn't love that made me consider starting over with him; it was pride: stubborn, foolish pride, because I'd failed! Nothing as heroic as love was involved.

"I wasn't with him more than half an hour when the first argument started. I determined then and there that it would never work out, and I was relieved. But I decided to spend the rest of the afternoon skiing because Brandon had already bought the lift tickets."

As she gazed into the distant night Maren tried to construct her thoughts so Kyle could understand the helplessness of her situation with Brandon—why she couldn't let go of him. "Brandon started skiing down the most difficult run, racing down the slopes as fast as he could. I could tell that he was tired, but he wouldn't give up. I think he was trying to work off some of the anger . . ."

"What anger?"

"His anger at me."

"For refusing to go back to him?"

She shrugged her slim shoulders. "I don't know. But

he was angry with me. Anyway, he wouldn't listen to reason when I tried to stop him. He pushed me aside and told me that he could do anything he damn well pleased. Rather than cause a scene, I gave up and let him go.''

"And he fell," Kyle said, remembering the accident. Maren's story reminded him of an article he'd seen in the sports page of the *Times* a couple of years ago. At the time, he hadn't made the connection between Brandon McClure, the bad-tempered tennis pro and Maren McClure, owner of Festival Productions. But why would he? They were divorced at the time and the article had made no mention of Brandon's ex-wife.

"Right," Maren agreed, her small shoulders slumping beneath the soft fabric of Kyle's oversize shirt. The horrifying memory of the accident flashed vividly before her eyes.

Kyle's voice seemed far away. "From what I understand, he'll never play tennis again—not professionally." At least that was the speculation at the time. Since the first report, Kyle had read nothing about Brandon McClure.

"It's worse than that. He may not be able to play at all, or walk without the aid of a brace." She felt suddenly tired, drained of her strength.

"Maren?" The coldness in his voice forced Maren to rotate and look at him. "Do you feel responsible for what happened to him?" Undercurrents of tension charged the cool night air.

"Partially," she conceded.

"That's ludicrous!"

"I've told myself the same thing a hundred times over, but I just can't seem to convince myself."

Leaning against one of the posts supporting the roof, Kyle studied her. He folded his arms over his chest and his square jaw jutted into the darkness. Deep lines of concern webbed from the corners of his eyes. "So how does this affect you now? It was all in the past: unless there's something you haven't told me.''

Kyle stared at her, noting every reaction on her elegantly sculpted face. He sensed that McClure still had a hold on her and it involved more than guilt. Gritting his teeth together to cut off the possessive feelings entrapping him, he waited.

''It isn't just in the past,'' she admitted, rotating to face him. She noticed the tense angle of his jaw, the flexed muscles straining in his chest and the glint of steel in his eyes. ''Brandon always had a way of living beyond his means . . .''

''I can believe that,'' he cut in.

Ignoring the sarcasm in Kyle's voice, Maren continued: ''Even the money he won on the tour couldn't begin to support his life-style. At the time of the accident, Brandon was in debt and had let his major medical insurance policy lapse. Only a small policy was left to pay a portion of the hospital bills.''

''So you've been supporting him,'' Kyle concluded, his lips thinning in controlled rage. No wonder the profits from Festival Productions had been bled from the company. Maren had been using that money to support Brandon McClure. Kyle's thoughts turned dark. *''Do you still live with him?''*

''Of course not,'' she replied, surprised by his accusation. ''I told you that part of it is over!'' She saw his muscles relax slightly. ''Brandon's in a rehabilitation center working with a physical therapist.''

''I assume he doesn't have a job and you're footing the bill.''

''He's only been walking with the brace for a few months,'' Maren snapped, wondering why she felt so suddenly defensive of a man who had done nothing but hurt her. She let out her emotions in an angry sigh. ''I think he'll be able to work again soon. Until he does, I have to help him.''

''Why?''

''Because he doesn't have any other family,'' she replied. ''Haven't you been listening to me? It's my fault he went skiing that weekend. If it hadn't been for me, he'd probably still be playing tennis, for God's sake!''

She was shaking with the intensity of her emotions. She felt chilled to the bone. Kyle opened his robe and folded her against him, letting his arms and the soft folds of cloth protect her from the night air.

Softly he kissed the top of her head. She let her arms tighten around his naked torso and leaned her head on his chest. ''I think your husband's career was over before it began,'' Kyle stated reassuringly. ''I read about him; he couldn't control his hostility. It worked against him rather than to his advantage.''

''Your opinion.''

''The truth.''

The protests forming in her throat died. For years she had been deluding herself that Brandon would have made it on his own. The gravity of Kyle's face and his firm words helped convince her that Brandon would take advantage of her as long as she gave him the opportunity. She had only to remember Brandon's last near-frantic call.

''For the time being,'' she said, ''Brandon is my responsibility.''

''Until when? Until he decides he can make it on his own? Or *you* get tired of carrying the burden? *When?*''

''It will work out,'' she said vaguely.

''When Brandon McClure decides that he's tired of sponging off his ex-wife.''

She was tired and her voice was bitter. ''I don't see that it's any concern of yours what happens to Brandon. It won't affect my decision to sell Festival Productions one way or the other, and that's why I'm here, remember?''

"Is it?" he asked in a throaty whisper. With one long finger he traced the length of her bare arm and a shiver of anticipation darted down her spine.

His embrace became more possessive, and his eyes drilled into the mystery of hers. "Tell me again," he persuaded, "why you're here."

With a surrendering sigh, she leaned heavily against him. "I'm here because I want to be," she admitted, listening to the steady cadence of his heart. This is where I belong, she thought, alone with Kyle in the night, letting him hold me.

"Come on," he whispered. "Let's go to bed."

His arms supported her as they walked through the door and back into the warmth of the rambling hacienda.

Chapter Twelve

"I want you to marry me."

Kyle's voice was the first sound she heard as she awoke. Maren opened her eyes and stared into the dark gaze of the man she loved. She smiled and stretched.

"I thought we weren't going to discuss marriage."

"Only because you're so damned independent." Kyle sat up in the bed and ran his hand over the stubble of his beard.

"Should I consider that a compliment?" she teased.

"Damn it, Maren, I'm serious. I want you to marry me and live with Holly and me here in La Jolla." His tanned brow was creased and his coffee-colored hair, streaked from the sun, was rumpled. He clasped his hands behind his head and stared up at the ceiling. "I've been thinking about this all night; it's the only answer."

"And what about my work?"

"We could handle it here."

"I don't think—"

"Sure, we'll have to be in L.A. once or twice a week to supervise what's going on, but there's no reason you can't work out your ideas and those sketches here."

"There's a lot more to it than that," she stated, trying to quiet her racing heart. Kyle had asked her to marry him! It was what she wanted most, and yet it couldn't be. Not now. "I'm involved with the actual shooting of the sequences and some of the editing, not to mention hiring the actors, renting the soundstages . . ."

"But don't you have people who can supervise that sort of thing?"

"To some extent . . ."

"And once you've sold the company, things will be that much easier," he suggested.

His words had the effect of salt on an open wound. She stiffened in the bed. "Elise advised me against talking with you or anyone from Sterling Records about the offer, until we can come to some sort of an agreement."

He looked at her as if she were out of her mind. "And just how are we supposed to do that if we don't discuss the offer?"

"Elise thought she could straighten things out with Bob Simmons."

"And then he'll want to discuss it with me, in private. It doesn't make a hell of a lot of sense, Maren. We can wrap this thing up this morning." He turned to face her. "I thought you were the kind of woman who made her own decisions."

"I am."

"Then why the hell do you have to rely on Ms. Conrad?"

"Because she's my attorney!"

"Do you really think I would try to pull a fast one on you?" His silvery eyes impaled her. "Don't you trust me?"

"Kyle, this has nothing to do with trust . . . it's business!"

She rolled over and started to get up, but he caught her wrist, forcing her back on the bed. "This is not business . . . not anymore . . . this is *us*."

"You're clouding the issue."

"And you're avoiding it!"

She jerked her hand free of his grasp and got out of bed. "Maybe you're right," she allowed, struggling into his bathrobe and seating herself in a chair across the room. She stared at him with intense indigo eyes as she brushed her hair away from her face with her fingers and crossed her shapely legs. "You want to talk business? What about right now?"

"Fine with me." He rolled off the bed and pulled on a pair of khaki-colored jeans.

"Why don't you start by telling me exactly what you have in mind for Festival, if I decide to sell?"

"It's in the offer . . ."

"Refresh my memory."

"Only the ownership will change. You can still run the operation any way you wish, with the exception that Festival will be in the same building as the record company and you'll spend most of your time working from the library here."

She arched her eyebrows elegantly. If only she could believe that his proposal of marriage had nothing to do with his desire for the company. He'd married once to promote his career. Would he marry again to bolster the income of Sterling Records? Dear Lord, she hoped not!

"I'll pay you a fair price for your company," Kyle said,

breaking into her thoughts. "Even Elise has agreed about that."

Maren nodded, tapping the tips of her fingernails on the arm of the chair.

"I've been honest with you, Maren. I need your talent as well as your company. Elise mentioned that you wanted a three-year employment agreement. It's yours. As far as I'm concerned, you're the talent behind Festival Productions. Without you, Festival is just another production company, and they're a dime a dozen." He sat on the edge of the bed, his eyes holding her unwavering blue gaze. Resting his forearms on his thighs, he stared at her. "We can work together," he said softly, "after we're married."

She tried to speak but couldn't find her voice. She had to shift her gaze away from his penetrating stare. "You tried that once before," she reminded him. "It didn't work with Rose."

"Rose has nothing to do with this!" Every muscle in his body became rigid. "Haven't you been listening to what I just said?"

"I'm trying, Kyle," she replied, her voice wavering and tears filling her eyes. "Dear God, I'm trying."

"Then hear what I'm saying. I want you to be my wife, and it has nothing to do with also wanting the production company." His dark gaze grew deadly, and the lean muscles in his forearms flexed. "I made a mistake with Rose, and I'll be damned if I ever make that same mistake again. I want you to live with me because I don't want to live without you. I *love* you, Maren."

The tears pooling in her eyes began to run down her cheeks. How long she had waited to hear those words, and how desperately she wanted to believe them. He stood and unhurriedly walked across the room. "Can't you see how much you mean to me?'' Lowering himself to one knee he touched her shoulders. As she stared into his brooding eyes she thought she would like to drown in his gaze. Her love for him was overpowering, and she could never find it in her heart to tie him down with a marriage he didn't want.

"Maren, please marry me," he said. His fingers slid under the folds of the robe and his thumbs moved seductively over her soft skin. How easily he could coax her.

"I don't want to rush into anything," she replied quietly, hoping to stop the tears streaming down her face. "This is the eighties. We don't have to get married."

"Unless we want to."

"It's not that I don't want to marry you," she reassured him, softly touching his chin. "I just need a little time to think it over."

His smile was wistful. "All right," he agreed reluctantly. "Now let's go downstairs, and you can tell me how far you've come on the Mirage videos."

"We're going to work at this hour of the morning? It's Saturday."

"I've got to convince you that you can live here and still do your work," Kyle reminded her. "And I've only got a couple of days to prove it."

Wiping away her tears, she laughed. "Give me a couple of minutes to shower and change, fix me a huge breakfast and *then* I'll get to work."

"Lady," he responded with a widening grin. "You've got yourself a deal!"

Saturday and Sunday passed too quickly, and Maren realized that she was beginning to feel a part of Kyle and his intimate family. Holly's hostilities slowly evaporated, and Lydia seemed elated that Maren was in the house.

During the day Kyle took Holly and Maren sailing, and in the evenings they walked along the beach.

The meals were a time of laughter and warmth, especially when Lydia was able to stay and sample her own talents. Everything the elderly woman prepared was superb, and Lydia positively beamed when Maren insisted on helping her in the kitchen in order to discover the secrets of Lydia's culinary skills.

If Holly disapproved of her father's relationship with Maren, she managed to hide it. Several times the young girl caught Kyle holding Maren in a loving embrace, but Holly only smiled at the intimate couple.

The only black spot on the remainder of the weekend occurred just before Maren left. She was packing her clothes into her suitcase when Kyle came into the bedroom. "I hate to see you leave," he stated, watching Maren's movements as she leaned over the bed and folded a blouse into her bag.

"Oh, but I must," she quipped, looking behind her and sliding a suggestive glance in his direction. "That president of Sterling Records becomes positively unglued if I'm late with anything."

He caught the look of provocation in her eyes and noticed the way her jeans hugged her hips. "You're going to have to marry me sooner or later," he responded, mentally calculating how long it would take to strip off her jeans.

"Why's that?" She locked the suitcase and turned to face him, balancing herself on the edge of the bed. "And don't give me that lame excuse of making an honest woman of me."

He lifted his palms in mock surrender. "I wouldn't dream of it."

"Well then?"

"I think it would be best for all of us."

The laughter in her eyes faded. "I don't think Holly would appreciate me stepping into her mother's shoes."

Kyle strode across the room, pushed the suitcase off the bed and sat next to Maren. His gray eyes held hers in a smoky embrace. "Holly adores you . . ."

"She *tolerates* me." Maren let out an uncomfortable sigh. "I'll admit, that's progress and a lot more than I expected, but a far cry from adoration."

Attempting to rise, Maren felt strong hands grab her arm and pull her forcefully onto the bed. She fell onto the comforter and felt the persuasive strength of Kyle's body stretched near hers. Her auburn hair fell away from her face in tangled disarray, and her clear indigo eyes searched his. Her skin was flushed, and Kyle knew she was the most intrinsically beautiful woman he had ever met. This one woman had changed his entire outlook on life.

"Why won't you consider my proposal?" he demanded, his hands tightening behind her back. She felt each of his lean muscles pressed supplely against hers. His warm breath fanned her face, and though she tried to ignore it, her heart began to thud irregularly.

With all the determination she could gather, she replied. "I think it's time for total honesty, Kyle."

"I'd agree."

One of her delicate dark brows cocked. "Would do?"

He smiled and gave her a short shake. "Out with it, woman. What's on your mind?"

"There's more to it than worrying about becoming a stepmother to Holly," she admitted.

"I figured as much."

"How much of this . . . proposal has to do with the buy-out of Festival?" She felt his arms tighten rigidly around her.

"None."

"Then why do I get the feeling that you're holding something back from me . . . that something about Festival Productions is bothering you? If it's not the sale, then what?" Confusion clouded her gaze, and Kyle was forced to unburden himself.

"Of course I want you to sell Festival to me, and I expect that you will, once we change the terms of the offer to satisfy Elise." He released her slowly and propped his head on one elbow so he could study the slightest reaction on her face. "Ryan Woods thinks that he's found a pirated copy of Mitzi Danner's latest release."

Maren's eyes widened. "The video of 'Going for Broke'?"

"Right."

"That's impossible," she stated, her mind whirling. That tape was barely back from editing.

"Not according to Woods." Was it his imagination, or did a tremor of fear darken her eyes?

"We haven't even sent the finished product over to Sterling Records yet."

"I know."

Anger replaced disbelief. "So you assume that someone at Festival is ripping you off?"

"I don't know. I haven't seen the tape myself, but Ryan Woods seems pretty sure of himself, and he knows his business."

"There must be some mistake . . ."

"I don't think so." Kyle's voice was as calm as the steely look in his eye. "But I'm waiting to see the evidence myself . . ."

"*Evidence?*" Maren cried. "Good Lord, Kyle, you make it sound as if I'm some kind of criminal!" She pulled herself off the bed and stood up before glaring down at him. "Why didn't you tell me?"

"I wanted to be sure." Dragging himself to his feet, he towered over her, accepting the anger in her gaze.

"Are you?"

"No, not yet."

She ran trembling fingers through her hair. "But you expect to discover something," Maren guessed.

"I don't know. I'm not certain that someone from Festival's involved. The only thing we can do is wait until Ryan somehow finds a way to get a copy of that tape."

"Dear God . . ."

"Okay, so I told you my secret," he stated, drawing her attention back to his hard face. "What about yours?"

"I don't have any . . ."

"I'm talking about Brandon."

Every muscle in Maren's body froze. She hadn't expected her ex-husband to be included in the conversation. Lifting her eyes to meet his condemning gaze squarely, she managed to hide the fact that her stomach was doing somersaults. "What about Brandon?" he charged. "How long do you intend to support him?"

"Until he can get a job on his own."

Sparks of anger lit his cold gaze. "If he wanted to be employed, I'm sure he could be." Kyle's lips drew into a frown of disgust. "What I'm *not* sure of is how badly you want to be free of him."

Maren's rage matched that of her attacker. "That's a low blow, Kyle. You know that I'm only helping Brandon until he can get back on his feet again."

"No matter how long it takes?" Kyle charged.

"Until *I* know for certain that he could hold a job if he wanted to."

Maren grabbed her suitcase and strode angrily out of the room and down the stairs. She could hear Kyle's footsteps behind her, but she refused to turn and face his angry stare. Attempting to appear as calm as she could under the circumstances, she pushed open the kitchen door, hoping to track down Lydia and Holly so she could say good-bye.

Both Lydia and Holly were seated at the kitchen counter. A textbook was lying open-faced in front of them as they sipped lemonade and chuckled merrily to themselves. Holly began to murmur a simple phrase of butchered Spanish, and Lydia laughed so hard she had to wipe the corner of her eye with her apron.

"*Dios,* girl," Lydia smiled. "Have you ever thought about studying French instead?"

Holly giggled and closed the book. "How do you say 'I've had enough'?"

"What's going on in here?" Maren asked with an interested smile.

"Lydia's teaching me Spanish," Holly replied, sliding her instructor a mischievous glance.

"Not me," Lydia denounced fondly. "You're a lost cause."

Pretending to be miffed, Holly mumbled. "Oh, yeah, just wait. When I ace the test, guess who'll want all the credit?"

"And I'll deserve it," Lydia added with a warm smile for the girl. Maren laughed, but felt a growing sadness when she realized how attached she'd become to Kyle and his small family. She heard him enter the room on her heels, and she knew that if she didn't make her farewells hastily, she might not find the heart to leave.

"I just came to say good-bye," she announced regretfully.

Holly's smile faded. "Will you be coming back soon?" the girl asked, hoping to appear uninterested. Lydia's worried gaze studied Maren, communicating the elderly woman's concern for Kyle's daughter.

"I don't know," Maren admitted honestly. The argument with Kyle was still burning in her heart. She glanced at him and penetrated his brooding stare. He cared for her. She could see it as clearly as if it were written on his face. Maren smiled and touched Holly lightly on the arm. "Of course I'll be back, I'm just not exactly sure when. . . . I've got a job, you know."

"Yeah, just like Mom," Holly replied thoughtlessly.

The comment settled like lead in the room. An awkward silence followed, and Kyle's eyes, dark as night, watched Maren intently.

Lydia nervously twirled the pencil she had been using while helping Holly study. She cleared her throat before speaking. "Are you sure you can't stay for dinner? . . . There's plenty of food." Lydia's dark eyes were hopeful.

"I'm sure there is," Maren agreed. "And really I'd love to, but I just can't. Not tonight."

Kyle's silence charged Maren with the lie, but she ignored him and didn't bother to protest when he took her suitcase from her hand and held the door open for her. "This is your decision, you know. You could stay if you wanted."

"I think we both need a little time to sort things out," she objected. Her cool gaze held his firmly. "If you're right about the problem at Festival, I'm going to find it."

A look of concern crossed his face. He looked at her profile, pondering the gentle contours and the intelligent depths of her eyes. A soft sea breeze ruffled her hair, and he wished to God he could find a way to make her stay with him. In frustration he rubbed the back of his neck.

"Don't go jumping off the deep end on me," he warned. "Not until we're sure about this thing. It might get sticky." Together they walked outside toward Maren's car.

"Are you trying to say 'dangerous'?" she accused flatly.

"I just want to know that you'll be careful. I wouldn't have brought any of this up to you, but you insisted."

"Now you sound like a private eye on one of those ridiculous detective shows. You're the one who started this," she reminded him.

"Not me; one of your employees."

"You *think*."

He opened the car door for her and placed the suitcase on the backseat. She slid into position behind the steering wheel, pausing as she poised her keys at the ignition. The car door shut, and she had to squint against the blinding glare of the sun through the open car window. "I wish you'd reconsider," he suggested in a rough voice filled with intimate memories.

"You know that's impossible." She started the car, but before she could put it into gear, his fingers had captured the sun-gilded strands of her reddish hair, forcing her to look up again. In silent promise, he kissed her upturned lips.

"I'll miss you," he vowed, wondering at the dull ache pounding between his temples as he watched Maren wheel the sports car down the long driveway. Pushing his palms into the back pockets of his jeans, he wondered if there would ever be a day when she would trust him enough to stay with him.

Kyle had been as good as his word. Elise had called the following week and been happy to report that the offer was completely satisfactory. As a show of good faith, Kyle had offered Maren a bonus program that would allow her to use the money to purchase shares of Sterling Recording Company stock. The attorneys for Sterling were rewriting the offer, and it would be ready to be signed by the end of the month.

Maren was so swamped with work that she didn't have a chance to breathe. Everything that could go wrong with the Mirage video did. There had been lighting problems in the sound stage, some of the costumes had been lost for nearly two days before being found hidden in a trunk near the location site and a small accident with fireworks exploding at the wrong time had shorted out the amplifiers. Fortunately no one had been hurt.

"I tell ya," Ted Bensen had stated at a meeting earlier in the week. "It's almost as if this Mirage sequence is jinxed. If I didn't know better, I'd swear we were being sabotaged!"

Maren had dismissed his complaints as a way for Ted to vent his frustrations. She couldn't blame him for being concerned: The problems were unlikely, but not inexplicable. Maren remembered the first video she had done for Mirage. Compared with it, the problems with "Yesterday's Heart" seemed insignificant.

What bothered her more than the puzzling events happening to the Mirage video was Jan. The secretary's attitude had become frigid, and try as she might, Maren wasn't able to communicate with her. Jan's work hadn't suffered, but her remarks to Maren about the impending sale of Festival were severe.

"Why do you think we've had all these problems with the latest Mirage Video?" Jan had asked with a knowing glint in her brown eyes. "Why now? I'll bet Kyle Sterling is behind all this. He's trying to find a way to force you to sell!"

"That's ludicrous," Maren had replied indignantly. "He knows I intend to go through with the deal."

"Sure," Jan had responded with a frown. "But you haven't done it yet, have you? I think Sterling is just hedging his bets!"

Maren had pushed aside Jan's pointed comments and attributed them to overwork and a lousy situation with Jake. No doubt the secretary was feeling very insecure, and the fact that Festival was going to be sold didn't help the situation.

The first break in Maren's seven-day work weeks came nearly three weeks from the time she had left La Jolla. Fortunately, despite the unlikely delays, Maren had been able to accomplish more than she had hoped in the twenty-odd days and had even started work on Joey Righteous' video, once Kyle had signed the contract. She had seen Kyle fleetingly during the long three weeks. He had called several times and had been able to come to L.A. to watch the location taping of "Yesterday's Heart." But their time together had been short, and all too quickly he had returned to La Jolla, leaving her alone and taking with him the signed agreement of sale for Festival Productions. It had been a difficult decision for Maren, and more than once she had experienced the uncanny feeling that she had made an irreversible mistake in agreeing to sell the one thing she had worked so hard to create. In handing Kyle the signed document, Maren had given Kyle the opportunity to free himself of any commitment to her.

With her work load slightly less burdensome, Maren decided to take Kyle up on his open invitation. She deserved a small vacation.

It was evening by the time she had packed. She decided to take the scenic route along the coast back to La Jolla. That way she wouldn't have to concentrate on the snarls of traffic that backed up the freeways, and she would be able to consider all that had happened to her in the last few weeks.

The drive was pleasant and carefree. Wind from the Pacific Ocean blew through the torrey pines that clung tenaciously to the parched bluffs overlooking the sea north of La Jolla. Maren let out a contented sigh as she drove southward and noticed that the final rays of a dying sun turned the blue waters of the Pacific various shades of brilliant gold.

In the short time she had been with Kyle, Maren hadn't felt that the problems between them had been resolved. Perhaps her agreement to sell Festival Productions would change all that. She certainly hoped so. Elise Conrad, Maren's attorney, had assured Maren that Kyle's offer to buy out Festival was not only legal, but also more than equitable. In Elise's estimation, Maren would never get a better offer. She advised her client to sell and escape from the rigorous daily routine of running the business. Reluctantly Maren had agreed. The one shining spot in the entire transaction was that Maren would finally be able to pay off Jacob Green and get out from under his slippery thumb.

Before leaving for La Jolla, Maren had called Brandon. It was a stilted conversation, and though he did admit that he felt better physically, he wasn't able to accept the idea of working at a desk job for the rest of his life. He'd consulted several career analysts, but none of the employment they had suggested appealed to him. After the action and glamor of the tennis circuit, a dull job of pushing papers just didn't cut it.

Brandon had indicated that his physical therapy sessions were nearly finished and that he hoped Maren would consider letting him reside in the condominium they had shared when they were married. Though it was her part of the divorce settlement and she now rented it to an elderly couple, Brandon reasoned that she could drum up some excuse to evict them. After all, what was he to do? He couldn't very well support himself, at least not yet.

Maren had hung up the phone with trembling hands. A wave of nausea rushed up her throat as she realized that Kyle had been right. Brandon had been using her, playing upon her sympathies and guilt all along. Her ex-husband was avoiding taking any responsibility for his own life. When she considered all the guilt she had borne over Brandon's unfortunate accident, a new feeling of self-awareness took hold of her: His accident wasn't her fault. Maren didn't *owe* Brandon anything.

And so, soon she would be working for Kyle, she mused to herself as she passed through the familiar gates guarding his estate. She found the thought pleasant, if a little unnerving. The largest step of all had already been taken. Filming was complete on the first Mirage video, and editing would be finished within a couple of weeks. A celebration was planned for the first showing of the tape.

Maren turned off the car motor, and a pleased smile spread over her face. The only thing she hadn't been able to accomplish in the last few weeks concerned Mitzi Danner's videotape of "Going for Broke." Maren had come across no evidence to indicate that Mitzi's tape had been duplicated. She was still bothered by Kyle's accusations, but had come to the conclusion that Ryan Woods, whoever in the world he was, had made a mistake—an incredibly big mistake.

Maren walked briskly to the front door with newly felt confidence. Perhaps things were going to get better. Before she could knock on the door it was pulled open and Lydia greeted her with worried eyes.

"Thank God you're here," she murmured, hastily making the sign of the cross over her breasts.

"What's wrong?" Maren's heart leapt to her throat. The anxiety in Lydia's dark eyes and the pained expression on her face made Maren's pulse race.

"Come in, come in," Lydia insisted, moving out of the doorway. She rambled for a minute in rapid Spanish before realizing that Maren couldn't understand a word she was saying. *"Dios,"* she whispered. "It's Holly."

Maren's eyes widened in horror. She grabbed Lydia's arm as she imagined a gamut of horrible accidents occurring. Her heart felt as if it had stopped beating. "What's wrong? Has something happened?"

Lydia nodded gravely. "That woman called!" she spat out.

"What woman—who called? Is Holly hurt?"

Lydia attempted to allay Maren's worst fears. "She bleeds, but it's from the heart," the elderly woman whispered. "That mother of hers . . ." Once again communication was broken by Lydia's rapid stream of Spanish.

"Hold on, Lydia. Calm down and explain to me what happened—*in English.* Where's Holly now?"

"She's down at the beach . . . I think. . . . She wouldn't talk to me. . . ."

"What about Kyle?"

"He's with her."

Maren's worries subsided slightly. Slowly she let out a gust of air. "Maybe I shouldn't intrude."

"It wouldn't be intruding. Holly needs you . . ."

"She's got her father."

"She needs a woman who cares for her," Lydia stated emphatically.

"Like you."

"Dios, no!" Lydia replied, shaking her graying head. "I am like the grandmother . . . with you it's different."

She took Maren's arm and hustled her toward the back door. "You go. Maybe you can talk some sense into her."

More to placate Lydia than anything else, Maren decided to track down Holly and Kyle. If there had been some family disturbance with Rose, Maren doubted that she could help and secretly thought it better for father and daughter to work it out alone. However, she slowly descended the weathered steps and squinted into the dusky twilight. Several hundred yards northward she spotted Kyle and Holly sitting on the beach. Maren took her time approaching them.

"Lydia insisted that I come looking for you," she stated when she was still several feet away from the two huddled figures. Kyle looked up, and the lines on his face indicated the strain he had been enduring. Holly refused to raise her eyes, but Maren noticed the wet tracks from recent tears on her cheeks. Maren's heart ached for the sad girl with the trembling lower lip. "If I'm intruding . . ."

"I'm glad you're here," Kyle interrupted, but Holly refused to comment. "Maybe you can explain a few things to Holly," he suggested, his gray eyes pleading.

Maren took a tentative seat near the girl. "Maybe I can. I was a fifteen-year-old girl myself once," she allowed, rubbing the toe of her tennis shoe into the sand.

"Did your mom work?" Holly charged, her frail voice catching on a sob.

"Yes, she did," Maren admitted. "She was a school-teacher. Taught English at the high school I attended. It was a terrible burden. I *never* got away with anything."

Holly lifted a suspicious eye, as if to see if Maren were bluffing. The sincere look on Maren's studious face convinced her that Maren was for real. "Did she ever miss your birthday?" Holly asked in a voice so low it was lost in the surf.

Maren frowned as she thought. She studied the disappearing horizon before turning to Holly. "I don't remember. I doubt it. She was pretty big on birthdays, Christmas, and all the other holidays. I think I'd remember if any of them were skipped."

"Yeah, I thought so," Holly sniffed, stiffening her spine. Kyle placed a comforting arm over his daughter and pulled her against his side. The look he cast Maren was filled with the pain he was bearing for his child.

"Is that what happened?" Maren asked softly. "Did your mom forget your birthday?"

Holly had trouble trusting her voice. When she replied, it quavered. "Oh, she remembered all right. It's just that she thinks she has to stay in Texas longer than she planned and . . . well . . . she won't be able to see me on my birthday. I'm going to be sixteen . . . and . . . she promised me a big party." The tears Holly had been fighting slid silently down her cheeks. "She doesn't love me," the girl said flatly.

"Oh, I doubt that," Maren responded, with a gentle smile. Slowly she reached out and touched Holly's curly hair. Kyle's eyes reflected his surprise. "I'm sure your mother loves you very much," Maren maintained as Holly broke into sobs. "Some people have difficulty expressing their love . . ."

"She's sending me a birthday present," Holly interrupted angrily. "But she can't seem to find the time to come home!"

Maren hesitated, finding it hard to defend Rose. "Look, Holly, I know that sometimes it's hard to understand your mother. But you have to think about it from her perspective. Her career is very important to her . . ."

"More important than I am!"

"I don't think so." Kyle eyed Maren suspiciously, but Maren continued. "She probably knows that you're safe and well-cared-for here with your father, and right now she can't afford to let her career slide. Soon you'll be grown and out of the house, and what will Rose have other than her career?''

Holly let out a ragged sigh, and her teeth sank into her lower lip. ''You act as if you understand her—why would you?''

''I'm only trying to give her the benefit of the doubt . . . and, if it's a party you want, I know one where you'll be an honored guest . . .'' Maren's eyes held Kyle's confused gaze. The angle of his chin warned her that she had better know what she was doing.

''What party?'' Holly asked, distracted at least partially from her own misery.

''Well, it might not be as grand as a sixteenth-birthday party, but I'm planning a celebration next week because I've just finished a very important piece of business.'' Kyle's eyebrows lifted in interest. ''And the best part is that I think all of the members of Mirage will be there.''

''Really?'' Holly sniffed back her tears.

''Really. What do you say?''

Kyle looked as if he were about to interfere, but the determination in Maren's gaze deterred him.

''Oh, Maren,'' Holly sighed, temporarily forgetting her woes. ''Is it all right if I bring a friend?''

''Of course.''

In a gesture overflowing with gratitude, Holly wrapped her small arms around Maren's shoulders and smiled. ''Thank you,'' she whispered. ''I . . . I'm sorry I gave you such a bad time the last time you were here.''

''It's all right . . .''

Abruptly Holly stood. ''I'm going to call Sara right now. She'll be out of her mind!'' With that she cast one last smile at her father, turned and raced back toward the house.

A cryptic smile spread over Kyle's thin lips. "It seems that you've just won another victory," he decided as he watched his daughter disappear up the stairs along the cliff face. "Holly thinks you're wonderful."

"Of course she does," Maren said with a slow-spreading grin. "I just offered her the chance of a lifetime: to meet J. D. Price, teenage heartthrob and hunk *extraordinaire*." Her laughter warmed the night.

"So you think you bribed her?"

Maren shook her head. "Bribe has such a distasteful connotation. I prefer to think that I charmed her."

"Just like her old man?"

Maren smiled wickedly. "Well, maybe not in the same manner." She sobered as a thought struck her. "Holly went to the doctor last week, didn't she?" Kyle nodded. "Well, what's the prognosis?"

Kyle closed his eyes. "Dr. Seivers seems to think that she's fine. Her uterus seems to have healed properly and though there's a slight chance that more problems could arise, he's not worried."

"Thank God," Maren whispered in relief.

"You really care for her, don't you?"

"Yes," Maren admitted with a shy smile. "I was only kidding before. She's the one who's charmed me."

Kyle's arm reached out in the darkness, Moonglow caught in her eyes and he pushed on her wrist, causing her to lose her balance. She fell back on the white sand, her hair framing her face in tangled waves of auburn silk. Leaning over her, Kyle studied the finely sculpted shape of her oval face and the mystery in her blue eyes.

"I've missed you," he admitted in a voice as rough as the sea. Leaning forward, his lips brushed softly against her throat. At the tenderness in the gesture, she gasped. Her love for this man seemed to overflow into the night.

Watching him through a dark fringe of lashes, she was

forced to concede the truth. "And I've missed you . . . hopelessly." She lifted her head and captured his lips with hers, feverishly showing how desperate her longing had become.

"How long can you stay with me?" he asked, dark gray eyes holding hers fast.

"As long as you want me to . . ." she sighed.

"Forever?"

One word hung in the air between them, drowning out the sound of the relentless tide.

"Oh, Kyle," she answered, yearning with all her heart to accept his proposal and share her life with him. There was nothing she wanted more in this life than to share his darkest secrets, love his only child and sleep with his arms wrapped securely around her breasts each night.

"I'm serious, Maren. You know that. Please marry me."

How could she refuse that which she most wanted? On this lonely star-studded night, lying on the silver sand, his body pressed urgently against hers, she could find no objections to his request. "Of course I'll marry you, Kyle," she sighed, giving in to her most intimate desires. "I'd love to." She closed her eyes and felt the warmth of his lips molding impatiently to hers.

"Dear God, Maren," he said, lifting his head to contemplate the enigma in her eyes. "You don't know how long I've waited to hear those words."

She wrapped her arms around his neck, and he kissed her once again. A warmth, starting in the deepest region of her soul, began to spread slowly through her body. How many nights had she lain awake aching for this man? Now at last, he was hers.

Chapter Thirteen

The week passed by in a flourish and rush of activity. Maren spent every waking moment at the office, and she was so absorbed in the final editing of the Mirage video and planning for the celebration that was to take place that she had little time to notice anything else. It was Friday afternoon before she could catch her breath, and the party was scheduled for the next day.

At four o'clock Jan came into the office carrying cold drinks from a nearby fast-food stand. "You're an angel," Maren said gratefully as she accepted the opaque paper cup and took a long drink.

"You've called me a lot of things," Jan remarked with a sad smile. "But that's the first time you referred to me as an angel."

"An oversight on my part," Maren thought aloud. "But it doesn't matter. When all the dust has settled on the buy-out, you should be getting a raise."

Jan's smile quivered. "How did you arrange that?"

"I'm in tight with the boss." Maren laughed, giving Jan a broad wink and playful smile. She felt lighthearted and incredibly happy. There was a disturbed light in Jan's large brown eyes, and Maren imagined that things weren't going well for Jan. The secretary seemed nervous—as if she wanted to get something off her chest.

"So tell me," Maren prodded gently. "How're things with you and the baby?"

Jan perked up at the mention of her pregnancy. "As well as can be expected, I guess. I did have a little trouble last week, but it wasn't anything serious."

Maren's smile faded. "What kind of trouble?"

Jan waved off the concern in her employer's gaze. "Nothing really. Last Wednesday morning I bled—just a little."

"Why didn't you stay home?" Maren asked, astounded. "You could have had the day off—or the rest of the week, for that matter."

Jan shook her head and bit her lower lip. "I had too much work to do . . ."

"Cary could have handled your work. Look, I don't want you jeopardizing your health or the baby's . . ."

"It's no big deal . . . I saw the doctor, and he seems to think everything will be fine if I just take it easy . . ."

"Are you?" Maren demanded, trying not to sound overly concerned. Jan's worries about her pregnancy explained the secretary's nervousness and anxiety. Jan was worried sick about losing the baby. It didn't seem fair. First Jan had trouble with Jake . . . now this.

Tears clouded Jan's gaze, and she tried vainly to hide them by wiping her eyes with the back of her hand. "I wish you wouldn't worry so much about me, Maren." She bit at her lower lip. "There's something you should know."

"What's that?" Maren asked quietly.

"Oh, God, Maren, I wish—" The telephone rang before Jan could finish her thought. Jan started to get up to answer it, but Maren waved the secretary back into her chair.

"I'll get it," Maren said with a heartfelt smile. Jan looked tired and distraught. At least Maren understood her worries. Setting her soft drink aside, Maren picked up the receiver. "Festival Productions, Maren McClure speaking."

"What happened—did you get a demotion?" Brandon's voice charged with a nervous laugh.

"Not exactly." Maren's tone was frigid, and Jan knew immediately that her boss was involved in a private conversation. Ignoring Maren's gestures for her to remain in the room, Jan hoisted herself out of the chair and waved at Maren, before silently mouthing her good-bye.

"I'll see you tomorrow," Jan whispered as she left the room, smiled at Maren and shut the door thoughtfully behind her.

"I hadn't heard from you in a while and I thought I'd call to check up on you," Brandon stated with a nervous laugh. "What's new?"

Maren's spine stiffened. "I was going to call you, as a matter of fact," she replied.

"Oh?" Brandon's voice was interested but wary. He could sense a difference in his ex-wife.

"I wanted you to know that I'm planning to get married this summer."

There was a surprised gasp on the other end of the phone. "Anyone I know?" he asked, with just a hint of sarcasm.

"Kyle Sterling." Why was she so reluctant to give Brandon that bit of information?

"*The* Kyle Sterling? Jesus Christ, Maren!"

Maren broke the uneasy silence that had settled over the stilted conversation. "So, I've been giving some thought to you."

"Nice of ya," he retorted angrily.

"I've decided to give you ownership of the condominium, Brandon. Since I don't use it, I don't really need it, and the couple who rent it are planning to move at the end of their lease, which is in about six weeks. I've already had the papers drawn up. You can pick them up from Elise Conrad, at her office." Once again there was weighty silence as Brandon considered Maren's offer. She silently prayed that he would accept the condominium they had shared when they were married. It held too many memories of the wasted marriage, and Maren never had the heart to live in it. As it was, she had rented it and used the income to pay for Brandon's medical needs. She would only be too glad for him to accept that piece of real estate, which still reminded her of the painful divorce.

"Is this the kiss-off?" Brandon asked.

"I think it's time we went our separate ways."

"Easy for you to say. You're marrying into big bucks, so you don't want to bother with a cripple!"

"Brandon, you're not a cripple. I've talked with your doctors and your physical therapists. They all seem to think that you're fine. And your career counselor says he can put you into a job as soon as you're willing. I think . . ." she paused, wondering just how to handle him, and then decided that honesty was what he needed. ". . . I think it's time you decided what you want to do with your life."

"And what would you say if I told you I wanted you?" he asked softly.

"I'd say that you're wrong. We tried, Brandon. It didn't work. *You're* the one who decided that." When he didn't immediately respond, she concluded: "It's up to you whether you want the condo or not. Just give Elise a call. Good-bye." With finality, she replaced the receiver. "Thank God it's over," she murmured as she pulled herself upright and hurried out of her office to look for Jan. Maren had been left with the uncanny feeling that Jan had had something she wanted to discuss with her before the conversation was cut off by Brandon's untimely telephone call.

When Maren entered the reception area, she realized that Jan must have left for the weekend. The clutter on Jan's desk had been cleared and there was no sign of the blond secretary. Whatever it was that Jan had wanted to say would just have to keep.

Within a few minutes Ted, from production, stopped in with the finished product of the Mirage video.

"Better late than never," Maren quipped as she accepted the cassette. "How does it look?"

"See for yourself," Ted suggested with a smile and a weary raking of his fingers through thinning blond hair. There was a satisfied look in his eyes.

"That good, is it?" Maren asked as she placed the cassette into the recorder and watched as J. D. Price and the rest of Mirage sang and acted out the lyrics of "Yesterday's Heart." A pleased grin stole over Maren's lips. "It's a winner," she thought aloud.

"You bet it is," Ted agreed.

"Now we'll really have something to celebrate tomorrow," she replied, rewinding the tape and watching the video a second time.

"It should be a big day," Ted surmised, lighting a cigarette.

"It will be interesting to see Mirage's reaction to this tape," she said, mentally noting that Kyle's reaction would be just as worthwhile.

"I think J.D. will be pleased."

"Let's hope so," Maren murmured as she took the cassette from the recorder and locked the black cartridge in the file cabinet. "We'll find out tomorrow night, won't we?"

"We'll knock 'em dead," Ted predicted as he turned to go. "And let me tell you, it's been a long time coming. After that unscheduled blowup with the fireworks, I was ready to throw in the towel."

"Good thing you didn't."

"I guess so. See ya tomorrow." He ambled out of the office leaving Maren to turn out the lights and lock the door.

Saturday dawned perfect for sailing. The party, which was primarily to celebrate the buy-out of Festival Productions by Sterling Records, was to be held on Kyle's yacht, at his insistence. After an afternoon of sailing around Santa Catalina Island, the yacht would return to her private berth near Long Beach. At that time, Maren planned to unveil the Mirage tape, hoping that everyone involved with the making of the video would get to see it.

Invited guests streamed onto the yacht under the brilliant southern California sun. Some of the guests were dressed casually in beach wear, while others stepped onto the deck in glamorous gowns and dripping in jewels. When the eclectic group seemed complete, the gleaming white vessel set sail for the short trip.

Maren was in a festive mood. She was dressed casually and felt as carefree as the wind. Mingling with the guests, she accepted congratulations on the sale of the production company. And for the first time in several years, she felt unburdened with thoughts of her ex-husband. She was free to love again, and she was hopelessly in love with Kyle.

Sunbathers crowded the polished wood deck, while other guests clustered in the main salon, drinking cham-

pagne and sampling a lavish display of hors d'oeuvres.
Liveried waiters were prompt to refill a glass or offer the
trays of appetizers. Champagne flowed from a fountain
near an extraordinary seafood buffet.

"You really know how to throw a party," Maren teased
when Kyle made his way over to her. A flash of white
teeth warmed his tanned face.

"Thank you." He placed a possessive arm around her
waist and leaned over the railing to watch the prow of the
yacht knife through the clear blue-green water.

"Who're you trying to impress?" Maren asked, her
eyes twinkling mischievously.

"Just one lady," he admitted with a devilish grin.

"You didn't have to host a party to impress me," she
sighed. The wind caught in her hair and pulled it free of
her chignon. Salt sea spray caressed her face. "I was
already interested."

He leaned with his back to the railing, and his gray eyes
roved over the crowd milling on the deck. His smile
broadened as his eyes rested on his daughter. She and her
friend were sunning themselves while sitting in lounge
chairs. "I've got some good news," Kyle announced,
letting his eyes linger on Holly.

"Oh?"

"Well, actually, it's good news for me, but it might be
a difficult adjustment for Holly." His lips drew into a
contemplative frown. "Rose called this morning."

At the mention of Kyle's ex-wife, Maren's stomach
knotted. "She wanted to talk to Holly?"

"That's the surprising part. She didn't want to speak to
Holly at all. As a matter of fact, she didn't want Holly to
know about the conversation until she'd worked out a deal
with me."

Maren was instantly on guard. "What kind of a deal?"
she asked anxiously.

The waiter interrupted Kyle's response by offering slightly unsteady glasses of champagne from a silver tray. Kyle accepted one for himself and handed another to Maren. When the slim steward disappeared into the crowd, Kyle continued. "It seems that Rose has finally seen the light."

Maren took a drink of her champagne. "What do you mean?"

"Rose has taken up with some singer in the movie. He's not playing the lead, but that's beside the point."

"What is the point?" Maren asked, raising her brows in anticipation.

"Rose assured me that the new man in her life is not just a casual fling. But there is a problem. She wants to cut a record with him, and she's going to move in with him. He lives somewhere near Dallas and the last thing he wants is Holly."

Maren raised her eyes to meet Kyle's angry gaze. "So Rose is going to give you custody of Holly after all—just because this guy doesn't like kids." Maren couldn't hide her surprise. Her heart bled for Holly.

"That's about the size of it," Kyle admitted grimly.

Maren disguised her disgust. "Good. Holly deserves to be with you."

"With *us*," Kyle amended. "She'll be with us."

"And I'm thrilled about it," Maren said honestly, with tears shining in her eyes. "I can't think of anything that would make me happier than living with you and your daughter."

Relief flooded Kyle's ruggedly handsome features. "You're a very special woman, Maren McClure," he stated, taking her into his arms and kissing her softly on the lips. "Do you think that I could persuade you to drive to Las Vegas with me tonight so that we can quit talking about getting married and just do it?"

"What about Holly?"

"She's staying the weekend with Sara. We'd be alone until Monday."

"It sounds like heaven," Maren murmured, closing her eyes. She didn't realize how tired she was. The last six weeks had been frantic and she couldn't think of anything more perfect than spending a quiet weekend alone with Kyle.

"Consider it," Kyle suggested, just as Grace, his secretary, approached them and offered her congratulations. The plump woman seemed genuinely pleased. "This one," she pointed accusingly at Kyle, "needs a woman looking after him."

Maren laughed aloud. "I'd say you've done a pretty good job of that."

"At the office, yes. But he needs more than that. Good luck to the both of you," Grace said with a satisfied smile as she turned back toward the refreshment table.

"You've been spreading rumors about us," Maren accused with a merry laugh. "And I love you for it."

"Guilty as charged," Kyle replied, finishing his glass of champagne. "But the only people I told our little secret to were Grace, Lydia and Holly."

"So she did know about it! That little stinker. When Holly boarded the yacht, I thought she looked like the cat who ate the canary, feathers and all!" Maren looked deeply into Kyle's amused gray eyes. "So tell me, how did your daughter take the news?"

"Very well. As a matter of fact, I think that she and Lydia had a little wager about it."

Maren's dark brows arched elegantly. "Is that so. Did Lydia give up on Spanish and start teaching Holly the techniques of gambling?"

"Why don't you ask Holly," Kyle said with a laugh. The sound of his laughter was rich and managed to touch the darkest corners of Maren's heart. When he tightened his arms around her waist, Maren imagined she could die in the warmth of his gentle embrace. How was it possible to love one man so desperately?

Holly strode up to Maren and her father. "So when are you going to make the official announcement?" she asked.

"Any day now," Kyle replied.

"I'm so happy for you," Holly said, looking at Maren. "This old guy needs someone to keep him in line."

"Old?" Kyle repeated with a vexed look crossing his face.

Holly ignored his mock anger. She threw her small arms around Maren's neck and hugged her. "It's wonderful," the girl whispered to Maren, and Maren had difficulty holding back her tears. She felt as if her heart would burst with happiness.

The white vessel rounded Santa Catalina Island just as the sun sank into the horizon. By the time the yacht was docked back at Long Beach, it was dark and all of the guests had wandered into the main salon. The room was thick with cigarette smoke as everyone waited to witness the first showing of "Yesterday's Heart." A crowd huddled around the screen in a tight semicircle. All five members of Mirage had their eyes riveted on the screen.

Maren slipped the tape into the recorder. In a flood of sound and visual effects, the throbbing music of Mirage dominated the room and the screen offered an image of a spurned lover singing angry lyrics while walking down an empty street during the Depression. The editing was perfect, and J.D.'s charisma blended with the pouty disdain in Janie Krypton's intriguing eyes.

When the tape had ended, there were roars of approval from the crowd: "Let's see it again!" "That was great!" "What an inspired idea!" All of the comments were enthusiastic, and Maren felt as if a great weight had been lifted from her shoulders. The room was filled with smiles and the popping of champagne bottles being uncorked until Holly Sterling turned her confused eyes on her father.

"What's the big deal?" she asked, aware that members of Mirage were eyeing her warily.

"What do you mean?"

"I've already seen that video," Holly stated weakly.

Kyle's smile fell from his face. The clatter of voices hushed. "I don't understand."

"I saw that video yesterday at Jill's house," she said, her round eyes searching for Maren.

"Are you sure?" Kyle asked as the cold hand of suspicion climbed up his spine.

"Daddy, I told you. I saw 'Yesterday's Heart'!" Holly repeated.

"What's going on here?" J. D. Price thundered. "You told me you wouldn't release the video until I approved!"

"And I meant it," Kyle said evenly.

Price stopped dead in his tracks, his thick brown brows pulled into an angry frown. "What are you trying to tell me, Sterling. If you haven't released it, how did she see the video?" Price's brilliant blue eyes sparked with vengeful fire. "What the hell are you saying—that the tape's been *pirated?*"

"I don't know," Kyle replied, his gray eyes searching the crowd for Maren.

"I'll sue!" Price roared. "Goddamn you, Sterling, I'll sue you for every cent you've got!"

Maren's knees sagged and she had to lean against the wall for support. What was happening? Dear God, had Kyle been right all along? Was someone really stealing her tapes and duplicating them for the black market?

Angry members of Mirage separated Kyle from Maren, but when his wrathful gray eyes found hers, she felt as if a dull knife had been thrust into her heart and slowly turned, to let her bleed slowly in an agonizing death. Without completely understanding her motives, Maren ran from the room and out onto the deck. She took deep gulps of sea air before she managed to get a hold of herself. A nauseous feeling rose in her throat and her hands were shaking, but she was able to make it down the walkway to the dock. She raced to her car and roared out of the parking lot.

She couldn't remember the drive to the office. She had driven mechanically, her head pounding with questions she couldn't answer. *Who* would steal the tapes? *Why? How?* Her hands were still shaking when she unlocked the door of Festival Productions, raced up the stairs and switched on the lights. All she could think about was the unspoken accusation in Kyle's dark eyes as he had stared at her across the crowded salon. *It was as if he thought she were the culprit.*

Tears began to stream down her face as she realized that everything was lost to her. Her business was sold and the love she had basked in was gone. A raw ache took hold of her, tearing her apart from the inside out. Opening the file drawer, she counted the copies of "Yesterday's Heart." None of the cassettes was missing. Slowly she placed each cassette in the recorder, watching to see that it hadn't been mismarked. Everything seemed in order. "Get a hold of yourself," she whispered.

She huddled on a corner of the couch, wrapping her arms around her legs and resting her forehead on her knees. "There has to be an answer," she told herself. Something didn't add up. Ted had just finished editing the Mirage tape yesterday and yet, Holly insisted that she had seen that very tape the same day. How could it happen? Carefully examining the past two weeks, Maren slowly found a possible answer. It occurred to her that on

Wednesday, Ted had mentioned that he had an edited version of the Mirage tape but wasn't happy with it. The tape was too rough and needed the final editing for polish. He had left the tape in the offices overnight and reworked it later in the week. The editing changes had been minor and only a professional would have noticed the slight variations in the scene sequences. That rough version *had* to be the copy Holly had viewed.

But who? Who would do this to her?

Lost in her confused thoughts, Maren didn't hear the intruder until the sound of heavy steps racing up the stairs caught her attention. Maren lifted her head, and her heart leapt to her throat as she rose to face whoever was entering her domain. The tears she attempted to keep at bay fell from her eyes as she recognized Kyle. She wanted to run to him, to let her head fall against his chest, but the wariness in his eyes forced her to remain still.

"I figured you'd come here," he stated. A pain, as raw and naked as the night itself, lingered in the silvery depths of his gaze.

"I had no idea . . . ." she whispered, but the hard jut of his jaw cut off the rest of her plea.

"Let's go," he ordered, the strain around his eyes overshadowing his rough command. "One of your employees . . . I think her name is Jan, is in the hospital."

"But she was on the yacht," Maren objected, concern for her friend evidenced in her words.

"I know." Kyle's voice was gentler. "She collapsed on the floor just after you left the salon."

"Dear God," Maren cried. "The baby."

Most of the drive was spent in silence. Maren was numb from the agonizing events of the evening. When Kyle finally parked his car in the hospital parking lot, Maren spoke.

"Do you know . . . did she lose the baby?" she asked.

"I didn't know there was a baby involved," Kyle replied. He placed a comforting arm on her shoulder. "But she was hemorrhaging pretty badly."

Maren closed her eyes and took in a long breath. "Let's go."

Kyle's grip on her arm tightened. "The reporters have already gotten wind of all this," he warned.

"Great," Maren replied. "Wouldn't you know?"

There was pandemonium at the hospital, and when Kyle and Maren entered the lobby, several reporters shoved microphones in Kyle's face. The questions all had to do with the rumored pirating of several Sterling releases, to which Kyle replied a stern "No comment." Flashbulbs popped until a security guard for the hospital hustled the reporters out of the building and Maren and Kyle were led to a waiting room.

"Where's Holly?" Maren asked, concerned for Kyle's child. How was the young girl reacting to all the commotion over the tape?

"She's at Sara's house. Lydia is going to pick her up in the morning."

Maren's pained blue eyes searched his. "God, Kyle, I'm so sorry about all of this . . ."

"It's all right," he whispered, clutching her hand. "You didn't know." His gaze was filled with the conviction of the trust he felt for her.

"You're incredible," she whispered. "How did you know that I wasn't involved?"

"Oh, Maren," he sighed. "Don't you realize how much I love you, how much I trust you? I've known all along that you couldn't be a part of this." Relief took hold of Maren.

"Are you Maren McClure?" a young intern asked Maren as he strode purposefully into the waiting room.

"Yes."

He looked at the chart he was carrying. "Jan Sommers wants to see you." The young man observed Maren through thick glasses. "I advised her against seeing anyone, but she's absolutely insistent about talking to you." His myopic gaze was severe. "Please make it brief."

Maren asked the question uppermost in her mind. "What about the baby?"

The doctor shook his head and frowned. "We couldn't save it," he said wearily. "As for Ms. Sommers, I've given her a sedative that will begin to put her to sleep very shortly."

"I won't stay long," Maren whispered, understanding the intern's concern.

Kyle took Maren's arm and led her to Jan's room. The lump forming in Maren's throat refused to dissolve as she saw Jan's thin form lying on the hospital bed. "Hello, Jan," she whispered, reaching for her friend's hand.

Jan turned her head to face Maren. Black smudges darkened the skin around her eyes. "Maren," she whispered, her eyes filling with lonely tears. "I lost the baby."

"I know," Maren replied in a throaty whisper.

"I wanted that baby," Jan said, taking her eyes away from Maren's comforting gaze. "I really wanted him."

The words of reassurance stuck in Maren's throat. "You should rest," Maren stated. "I'll stay with you."

"You shouldn't," Jan sobbed.

"Of course I should; you're my friend . . ." Jan held up her palm to cut off the rest of Maren's explanation.

"No . . . no, I'm not. Just listen to me a minute. There's something I want to tell you, something I've tried, but couldn't." Maren's eyes widened with the realization of what was to come. She had to fight to keep the nausea at bay. "I was the one who took the tapes," Jan admitted with a ragged sigh.

"I don't think you should be talking about this right now," Maren interjected, looking down at the wan form on the bed. "You're tired."

Jan impaled Maren with her tortured gaze. "No, Maren; this is something I've got to say. Right now, while I have the courage. I took those tapes. Last month it was 'Going for Broke' and last Wednesday I stole 'Yesterday's Heart'."

"But, Jan, *why?*" Maren asked, shocked and un-accepting of Jan's tearful admission.

"For Jake."

"Oh, Jan, no."

"Look, Maren, you know that I would never have done anything of the sort. It was Jake's idea and I refused. Even though I was pregnant with his child, I wouldn't stoop to theft. Then . . . well, then he threatened me. He said that if I didn't help him he would beat me."

"Why didn't you go to the police?" Maren gasped.

"I started to . . . after one of our fights, but he caught up with me and I ended up with bruised ribs. I . . . I almost lost the baby." Jan wept bitterly at the memory. "I didn't want to lose my child and I was stupid. It was wrong and I should never have done it and I don't expect you to forgive me. I just want to make a full confession and implicate Jake. It doesn't matter if he tries to hurt me now . . . there's no baby to protect."

Maren fought the sobs threatening to erupt from her throat. Her fingers wrapped over Jan's thin hand. "There's nothing to forgive, Jan." The secretary's eyes blurred and she turned her head aside. "I'll call Elise Conrad in the morning, Jan. Maybe she can help you out of this."

"I really don't care, Maren; I just want to see Jake get his," Jan sighed as her lids became heavy.

"Do you know where we can get hold of him?" Kyle asked, against Maren's better judgment.

"I think you can find him at our old apartment. I moved out yesterday and he's already got another girlfriend. I guess he's been seeing her for the past couple of months. Maybe it was because I was pregnant . . . who knows? I'm . . . I'm very tired."

"Are you all right?" Kyle asked Maren, who was visibly pale.

"Fine," Maren lied. "I just had no idea . . . poor Jan."

Kyle called the police while Maren had a cup of coffee in the lounge. When she was certain that Jan would be all right, Maren let Kyle take her home.

Within a few hours the police called Kyle's apartment and informed him that they had arrested Jacob Green, who, upon hearing the evidence against him, confessed to stealing the tapes. He also admitted that he had coerced Jan into helping him by threatening her with physical and mental abuse.

After resting fitfully in Kyle's embrace, Maren finally fell asleep in his arms just before dawn. She didn't wake when he left the apartment, and it was not until several hours later that his loud reentry finally roused her.

"What time is it?" she asked groggily, noticing the sun streaming in the windows of Kyle's apartment.

"Late." He watched her as she stretched on the bed. There was still a trace of sleep in her eyes, and it made her seem incredibly soft and vulnerable.

"Where have you been?" she asked, pulling herself to a sitting position against the pillows. The sheet draped away from her body, showing off the lacy slip she had used as a nightgown. The sculpted ivory lace only partially hid the seductive curve of her breasts.

"I've been busy, dear lady, and I've accomplished a lot," he said with a smile as he eased himself onto the bed next to her.

"Tell me all about it."

"Gladly," he said, gently nuzzling her neck.

"First of all, I think your friend Jan is off the hook. Green's confession to coercion, coupled with the fact that Jan implicated him, should be enough to save her—or at the very least put her on probation. I'll see to it that she gets a good lawyer," Kyle said thoughtfully.

"That's wonderful."

"Also, Green admitted to trying to sabotage the Mirage video. He was the one who engineered the explosion; he stole the costumes."

"And the lighting problem?" Maren asked.

"He didn't admit to that. It was probably just coincidence."

"It doesn't matter," Maren said. "The important thing is Jan." Maren looked up at him with eyes filled with love. "You're incredible," she whispered. "What about Mirage?"

"Ryan Woods managed to calm down J. D. Price. We offered Mirage a more lucrative contract and it seems that J. D. has reconsidered. He's not going to sue after all."

"You *have* been busy, haven't you?"

"Well, we're going to have to see how it all turns out. There's going to be a lot of adverse publicity."

"Until Jacob Green is exposed to the press."

"That might take a few days," Kyle observed. "Oh, there is something else I wanted to discuss."

"What more?" Maren inquired.

"It's good news," he said silkily as his lips brushed against the top of her shoulder and pushed the strap of her slip down her arm.

"Sounds interesting," she responded, imitating his seductive tone.

"Lydia has promised to watch Holly for the entire week—while you and I spend our time honeymooning on the yacht . . ."

A provocative grin spread over Maren's lips, and a wicked twinkle lit her indigo eyes. "Honeymoon?"

"That's right. You and I are going to be married as soon as possible—you've been putting me off too long."

"You won't hear any arguments from me."

His lips gently touched hers. "Then we'll be married this afternoon."

"I can't wait."

The pressure on her mouth increased, and she tasted the sweet promise of his words. Surrendering to the happiness welling within her, Maren wrapped her arms possessively around Kyle's neck. "I love you, Maren," he groaned, holding her close. "And I'm going to make sure that I never lose you."

"Promise?" she asked, looking into his clear gray eyes.

"Forever."

Genuine Silhouette
sterling silver bookmark
for only $15.95!

What a beautiful way to hold your place in your current romance! This genuine sterling silver bookmark, with the distinctive Silhouette symbol in elegant black, measures 1½″ long and 1″ wide. It makes a beautiful gift for yourself, and for every romantic you know! And, at only $15.95 each, including all postage and handling charges, you'll want to order several now, while supplies last.

Send your name and address with check or money order for $15.95 per bookmark ordered to
Simon & Schuster Enterprises
120 Brighton Rd., P.O. Box 5020
Clifton, N.J. 07012
Attn: Bookmark

Bookmarks can be ordered pre-paid only. No charges will be accepted. Please allow 4-6 weeks for delivery.

N.Y. State Residents
Please Add Sales Tax

Enjoy romance and passion, larger-than-life...

Now, thrill to 4 Silhouette Intimate Moments novels (a $9.00 value)— ABSOLUTELY FREE!

If you want more passionate sensual romance, then Silhouette Intimate Moments novels are for you!

In every 256-page book, you'll find romance that's electrifying...involving... and intense. And now, these larger-than-life romances can come into your home every month!

4 FREE books as your introduction.

Act now and we'll send you four thrilling Silhouette Intimate Moments novels. They're our gift to introduce you to our convenient home subscription service. Every month, we'll send you four new Silhouette Intimate Moments books. Look them over for 15 days. If you keep them, pay just $9.00 for all four. Or return them at no charge.

We'll mail your books to you *as soon as they are published.* Plus, with every shipment, you'll receive the Silhouette Books Newsletter absolutely free. *And Silhouette Intimate Moments is delivered free.*

Mail the coupon today and start receiving Silhouette Intimate Moments. Romance novels for women...not girls.

Silhouette Intimate Moments

Silhouette Intimate Moments™
120 Brighton Road, P.O. Box 5020, Clifton, NJ 07015

☐ YES! Please send me FREE and without obligation, 4 exciting Silhouette Intimate Moments romance novels. Unless you hear from me after I receive my 4 FREE books, please send 4 new Silhouette Intimate Moments novels to preview each month. I understand that you will bill me $2.25 each for a total of $9.00—with no additional shipping, handling or other charges. There is no minimum number of books to buy and I may cancel anytime I wish. The first 4 books are mine to keep, even if I never take a single additional book.

☐ Mrs. ☐ Miss ☐ Ms. ☐ Mr.   **BMDL24**

Name   (please print)

Address   Apt. #

City   State   Zip

(   )

Area Code   Telephone Number

Signature (if under 18, parent or guardian must sign)

This offer, limited to one per household, expires June 30, 1985. Terms and prices subject to change. Your enrollment is subject to acceptance by Simon & Schuster Enterprises.

Silhouette Intimate Moments is a service mark and trademark of Simon & Schuster, Inc.

If you've enjoyed this book, mail this coupon and get 4 thrilling

Silhouette Desire®
novels FREE (a $7.80 value)

If you've enjoyed this Silhouette Desire novel, you'll love the 4 <u>FREE</u> books waiting for you! They're yours as our gift to introduce you to our home subscription service.

**Get Silhouette Desire novels
before they're available anywhere else.**

Through our home subscription service, you can get Silhouette Desire romance novels regularly—delivered right to your door! Your books will be *shipped to you two months before they're available anywhere else*—so you'll never miss a new title. Each month we'll send you 6 new books to look over for 15 days, without obligation. If not delighted, simply return them and owe nothing. Or keep them and pay only $1.95 each. There's no charge for postage or handling. And there's no obligation to buy anything at any time. You'll also receive a subscription to the Silhouette Books Newsletter *absolutely free!*

So don't wait. To receive your four FREE books, fill out and mail the coupon below *today!*

SILHOUETTE DESIRE and colophon are registered trademarks and a service mark of Simon & Schuster, Inc.

Silhouette Desire,® 120 Brighton Road, P.O. Box 5020, Clifton, NJ 07015

Yes, please send me FREE and without obligation, 4 exciting Silhouette Desire books. Unless you hear from me after I receive them, send me 6 new Silhouette Desire books to preview each month before they're available anywhere else. I understand that you will bill me just $1.95 each for a total of $11.70—with no additional shipping, handling or other hidden charges. **There is no minimum number of books that I must buy, and I can cancel anytime I wish.** The first 4 books are mine to keep, even if I never take a single additional book.

☐ Mrs. ☐ Miss ☐ Ms. ☐ Mr.

BDDLR4

Name _____ *(please print)*

Address _____ Apt. #

City _____ State _____ Zip _____
( )
Area Code   Telephone Number

Signature (If under 18, parent or guardian must sign.)

This offer, limited to one per household, expires June 30, 1985. Prices and terms subject to change. Your enrollment subject to acceptance by Simon & Schuster Enterprises

READERS' COMMENTS ON SILHOUETTE ROMANCES:

"I would like to congratulate you on the most wonderful books I've had the pleasure of reading. They are a tremendous joy to those of us who have yet to meet the man of our dreams. From reading your books I quite truly believe that he will some-day appear before me like a prince!"

—L.L.*, Hollandale, MS

"Your books are great, wholesome fiction, always with an upbeat, happy ending. Thank you."

—M.D., Massena, NY

"My boyfriend always teases me about Silhouette Books. He asks me, how's my love life and natu-rally I say terrific, but I tell him that there is always room for a little more romance from Sil-houette."

—F.N., Ontario, Canada

"I would like to sincerely express my gratitude to you and your staff for bringing the pleasure of your publications to my attention. Your books are well written, mature and very contemporary."

—D.D., Staten Island, NY

*names available on request